THE ELSEWHERE

for anyone who is or has ever been a child ™

Dear Hal
Your response was so powerful
and so respected, it really
helped me keep going when
my fear threatened to overwhelm me —
or frustration ———

by Lorna D. Saunders

Love
You

your good
friend

1?/10/0?

First Edition
Printed in the USA, October 2002

ISBN: 1-887016-01-5
Library of Congress Control #95-094030

Edited by William K. Saunders
Cover art and illustrations by lj freeheart
Image rescue by Sharon Spurgin

This is a work of fiction. All characters and events portrayed in this book are products of the author's imagination.

ISBN 1-887016-01-5

52695

9 781887 016018

Kralor Press
P.O. Box 1867
Magdalena, NM 87825
505-854-3800
kralorpress@gilanet.com

To my husband, Kraig,
for thirty eight years of the kind of love
and companionship that made this book possible

A Special Appreciation

I couldn't have done it without you:

My gifted, astute and perservering editor, Kraig Saunders

My magical illustrator, lj freeheart

My talented and dedicated image rescuer, Sharon Spurgin

And my family of friends: Ann J. Salinger, Vivian Russell, Hal Alpiar, JoAnn Appling, John Lee, Nancy Tanner, Kuan Tikkun, Beverly Mingola, Charlie & Kolleen Sunde, Diane Ayer.

...who helped me stay with it, especially when the fun part of writing the book was over and the humbling process of editing it began.

And thank you, Jordan, for posing and Christi who "spoke in the pure language of the cosmos," urging her 'Grami' to finish the cover.

Last But Not Least

Thanks to the family of my imagination who showed
up in an unending stream, just to be in this book.
I was surprised, delighted and sometimes overwhelmed.
I had no idea...

For information on reproductions of the cover and illustrations please contact us at:

Kralor Press

P.O. Box 1867
Magdalena, NM 87825

505-854-3800
kralorpress@gilanet.com

Part One

The Elsewhere

I will go
where you don't know.
I will be
where you can't see.
I will play
so far away
no one will find
what's on my mind.
The Elsewhere.

I will be
behind a tree
and in the sky
or in your eye,
in the ground
and all around,
in the air
and everywhere.
The Elsewhere.

I will own
what can't be known.
I will build
what I have willed.
I will see
what cannot be.
I will feel
what's really real.
The Elsewhere.

Sometimes I hear
voices quite near.
Sometimes I see,
looking at me,
those who first came
and gave it its name.
The Elsewhere.

They whisper and tease
and do what they please
but I will eat fire
and live on a wire
and balance the moon
on the end of a spoon.

I will be free
and all that is me
and no one will know
where I go.

The Elsewhere.

Chapter One

The Books With The Golden Edges

Laura was a little girl with long red hair. She had a mother and a father but no sisters or brothers.

Her father was older than her mother. Once he'd owned a large hotel in the country, where he'd met her mother who worked there one summer, but he lost the hotel in a fire.

Sometimes there was a sadness in her father's eyes, especially when he was tired from a long day at the tailor shop where he now worked six days a week. Laura loved her father very much. His sadness made her want to comfort him. Each night when he came home from work and settled into his favorite chair she would climb in his lap and kiss him on his nose. This always made him smile, and when he smiled the sadness went away.

Her mother had no time to comfort anyone. She was always cleaning or about to clean, a process that seemed to have no end. What was cleaned today, had to be cleaned tomorrow and the next day and the next. Each morning, as soon as Laura's father left for work, the ritual would begin.

Working vigorously, her mother would strip yesterday's fresh sheets from the beds, spray the mattresses with nasty-smelling disinfectant that made Laura sick, drag the mattresses to the windows and drape them over the windowsills to "air." Then her mother would attack the floors, removing all the newspapers she'd laid over them the day before to keep them from getting dirty. She would take the floor rag from its nail beside all the other rags, each with its own purpose, each on its own nail. She would get down on her knees and scrub the spotless floors until they were more spotless. Then, after waxing them, she would put down fresh newspapers to keep them clean for the next day's scrubbing.

Sometimes during the long days she spent alone with her mother, Laura would be so full of things she wanted to say, she would follow her mother around while she cleaned, being careful to step only on the newspapers. Sometimes Laura would sing a song she'd learned. Her mother would tell her she had no music in her voice. If Laura recited a poem she'd made up her mother would criticize her because her poem didn't rhyme.

At times her need to share her feelings and dreams, or even to be noticed, was so intense Laura would try to help her mother clean, hoping she would stop for a moment and listen. In her urgency Laura sometimes picked the wrong rag to clean with. Her mother would snatch it from her impatiently, once leaving a jagged line of blood on Laura's hand with her sharp fingernail. Eventually Laura stopped trying.

When her father came home at night all the things locked up inside her came rushing out. Her father treated them like gifts to be treasured. And he always brought her a present, even though her mother scolded him for "spoiling" Laura. Ordinarily, her father gave in to her mother but about presents for Laura he was firm.

Her favorite present was four thick books with golden edges and a satin ribbon to mark your place. She and her father read them together. He told her the books were a secret door to magic worlds, worlds they could always share. They told about everything that ever happened or could happen, and she and her father would read them together till the end of time.

Sometimes after dinner her father would invite her mother to join them, offering to help with the dishes. But her mother didn't trust anyone else with the dishes. Each time she refused to join them Laura saw a hurt look in her father's eyes but once she was settled in his lap and they opened one of the books with the golden edges his hurt look would go away.

The books had colorful pictures of enchanting worlds where people led exciting lives, worlds of glowing camp-fires and crystal palaces, of stars and moons and singing mountains. The people in the pictures were very real to Laura, even though some of them were birds or plants or elephants or kings. She felt as if she'd met them in person and talked to them. Sometimes she would turn the soft white pages and make up stories about them, stories she gave her father as presents. He would listen attentively, his eyes filled with love.

Sometimes when her father read to her his voice would trail off as if he were listening to a distant music. He would get a faraway look. The rhythm of his breathing would change. He would tell her that if she listened care-fully she too could hear the music. It came from some-where beyond the books with the golden edges, out near the edge of time.

Sometimes they would turn to a favorite illustration and make up a story together, creating a world together

— *their* story, *their* world. For *them*, the books with the golden edges would truly never end.

* * * *

One very cold night in the darkest time of winter there was a loud knock at the door. Laura awoke in alarm. She felt something terrible had happened; she felt cold all the way through. She heard a man's voice and then her mother cry out. When the door closed Laura rushed to the window which was covered with frost. She rubbed some of it away so she could see who the man was. He was a policeman. He glanced back at the house, got into his car and drove away. The oddness of his visit in the middle of the night and her mother's strange cry filled Laura with dread.

She climbed back into her safe, familiar bed, taking with her a very special present her father had recently given her, a large Pinocchio puppet. He had told her it was a magic playmate to keep her company when he wasn't with her.

In a little while her mother came into the room without turning on the light. She stood over Laura's bed. Laura hugged Pinocchio, pretending to be asleep. Her mother tried to pry the puppet from her arms. "Pinocchio is lonely," Laura cried out, clutching the puppet. "He needs me. Ask Daddy!"

"Daddy is gone," her mother said in a dead voice, sending chills through Laura.

"Please," Laura pleaded, terrified. "Pinocchio is afraid! He has to sleep with me!"

"He's only a puppet. He has no feelings," her mother said coldly. "Go to sleep. I have no time for your nonsense."

"Puppets do so have feelings," Laura sobbed. "Daddy told me so!"

Her mother tore the puppet from her arms. "Your father is dead," she said with terrifying finality and rushed from the room, dropping Pinocchio near the door.

Laura lay in bed trembling, cold all around her and inside her. She didn't know what 'dead' meant but she knew the world had been emptied of warmth. She was alone in a terrible coldness. She wanted to be held, for the cold to go away.

She tip-toed to the door of her room and opened it. Seeing her mother on her knees in the semi-darkness, scrubbing and scrubbing the same spot on the spotless floor, something in Laura froze. Her tears contracted into an icy lump inside her.

She picked up Pinocchio from where her mother had dropped him and took him back to bed with her. Hugging him tight, she felt the icy lump inside her begin to melt a little. His wooden body seemed to grow soft in her arms like a person's body. "Oh, Pinocchio, Pinocchio!" If only he could really be alive like her father had promised.

"Of course I'm alive," Pinocchio said brightly.

"Oh!" Laura said, startled.

"I'm your magic playmate."

"That's what Daddy said!" Her father had been right!

"Of course he was."

"Oh, Pinocchio, can you help me find him?"

"I can try."

"We can go out to the edge of time," she said eagerly, "like in the books with the golden edges. Maybe we will find him there."

"We can try," Pinocchio said cheerfully. "We can surely try."

From that night on, when the world was fast asleep, Laura would get out of bed, put on her favorite white organdy dress, the one her father made for her, wake Pinocchio with a hug and climb on his comfortable back, and together they would fly off in search of her father.

Chapter Two

Voyager

They were a colorful pair whooshing through the blackness of space, Pinocchio with his rainbow colored suit, pointy yellow hat and ruby-red nose, Laura with her long red hair flying, her white dress fluffed out like a cloud. They traveled so close to the stars she could almost touch them. She imagined the ice-crisp feel of them and how her fingers would tingle.

Out in the comforting silence of space she could feel her heart beat in time with the big heart of the universe.

* * * *

From a distance all planets looked pretty much the same but as they got closer Laura discovered that different planets were different colors. Laura loved colors — she could even taste them and hear them like music. You could tell a lot about a planet's personality by its color.

Once they stopped on a small gray planet where they met some people who were as gray as their planet. When Laura asked them what their planet was called they didn't even look up from what they were doing. Their planet, they told her grudgingly, was called Work and they were Workers, and now would she go away and stop interrupting them. They were very rude. Laura wondered why they minded being interrupted; after all, they didn't seem to enjoy what they were doing. There was no laughter, no talk above a whisper, no music, hardly any light. They just kept doing the same things over and over, like her mother when she cleaned the floor.

She and Pinocchio were about to leave when Laura felt a vibration under her feet. When she asked the Workers about it they told her she was imagining things and they were too busy to bother with imaginary things or people who imagined them, and they weren't going to answer any more questions.

This only made her more curious. She knew the vibration was real. It took some doing, but she convinced the always cautious Pinocchio that they should follow it and see where it led.

They wandered through gray gloom until they reached a spot where the vibration was very strong. If it hadn't been for a skinny crack of light they might not have noticed they were standing on a manhole cover. Laura persuaded Pinocchio to help her move it. Tugging it aside, they jumped back, startled by an explosion of light and noise. A nearby gray Worker screeched in terror and scurried away, never having seen such light nor heard such noise. The air became thick and dark around them. Even the planet got darker, as if to conceal Laura's discovery.

Delighted to find something lively going on beneath the drab surface, Laura was eager to see what was down there. Followed by the reluctant Pinocchio, she descended, intrigued to find the deeper they went the louder the music and the brighter the light. The deeper they went the more Pinocchio wanted to return to the surface, whereas the deeper they went the deeper Laura wanted to go.

When they got to the heart of the gray planet they found a wonderful party going on. Crowds of happy people in funny hats and bright costumes were blowing noisemakers. Some were dancing on their toes or singing into microphones; some were riding roller skating elephants; others were blowing trumpets or juggling colored balls or playing harps while standing on their heads. A troupe of clowns was parading around on brightly colored stilts. People with flowing, fluorescent hair were talking to some computers. The computers were talking back, making fun of what they were being asked to print out. The hosts were television sets with legs, displaying food on their screens and showing people around.

Laura marveled that all this could exist at the heart of planet Work, glad to discover work didn't have to be all dull and gray.

* * * *

They made so many trips and visited so many places Pinocchio began to complain. He wanted to pick a place and stay there but Laura wanted to keep going. She was collecting stories to tell her father when she found him again. Besides, it was fun to go to different places and see new things.

Pinocchio didn't care about new things. He preferred familiar comforts and sweets. He really loved sweets. Once Laura had awakened in the night to find him eating candy with the wrappers still on. In the morning her mother had scolded her for eating the candy. Laura explained it was Pinocchio but her mother didn't believe her.

On one of their trips Pinocchio was overjoyed to find a candy-striped planet called Oasis. Some kind person had set it spinning in the universe so travelers could refresh themselves. Oasis served heaping ice cream sundaes with lots of nuts and cherries and whipped cream in brightly colored bowls that kept things nice and cold. There were frothy sodas and shakes in every flavor served in sparkling glasses. Signs encouraged everyone to eat their fill.

Sometimes Pinocchio overdid and got sick, but that never discouraged him from wanting to return. Eventually, a visit to Oasis became one of the few ways Laura could persuade him to continue their adventures.

It was very important to Laura to visit worlds beyond worlds, worlds she and her father used to talk about. She felt closer to him when she was out among the stars.

* * * *

She and Pinocchio both loved a planet called Contentment, home to the CatPeople. It was creamy white, soft and inviting. Each place on the planet independently decided what time it was and what kind of weather it wanted. At any given moment there was some place on Contentment where the sun shown or a storm blew or the night was cold and quiet.

The CatPeople had fur coats that suited all climates. However, as good hosts they provided for the comfort of visitors, stocking caves all over Contentment with clothing for every size, shape and dimension. Some of the clothes were so strange Laura found it hard to imagine what people who could wear them would look like.

Of all the CatPeople, Laura loved Loki the most. He was fluffy white with kind green eyes and bits of silver sprinkled across his brow. Known as the Mediator, he was greatly respected even among people as fiercely independent as the CatPeople. His calming presence had stopped many a cat fight.

Whenever she and Pinocchio visited Contentment Laura could count on Loki to listen wisely to her hopes and dreams. He would lie down beside her, next to the fire, his eyes half closed, purring. She would stroke his soft white fur and whisper secrets into his pink ears. If she felt sad or wistful, he would sense it and climb into her lap, his whiteness becoming one with the whiteness of her dress. He would lick her nose and make her giggle. After a peaceful while he would purr them both to sleep.

Loki was kind to everyone, even the pesky kittens everyone else scolded and shooed away. He let them jump on him and play with his tail. It was delightful to see him stroll through a grove of blue trees with his tail held high and a tumble of frolicking kittens following behind.

Lying by the fire, his tummy full of cake, Pinocchio was very relaxed, having found on Contentment the haven he'd always wanted. This made it harder for Laura to persuade him to continue their explorations. He had been her dear companion since the night her father died. It made her sad and a little scared to think of going on without him.

She too felt peaceful and safe on Contentment. But she knew she would never find her father there. And beyond that, still far away in the mysterious distance, there were other things she wanted, things for which she had no name. Just thinking about it stirred something scarey but sweet inside her.

* * * *

One night Laura noticed a particularly lovely, dark green planet. When she asked Pinocchio to take her there he absolutely refused. He told her the planet was called Enigma and long ago something terrible had happened there. It was haunted by ghosts who kidnapped visitors and spirited them away to who knew where.

Laura was not convinced. Pinocchio always believed the worst about places he'd never been. With its luscious, subtle shades of green and its minty aroma scenting the air, Enigma seemed very inviting. After much cajoling she got Pinocchio to take her close enough to hear the shuffling and whispering of the ghosts. To her they didn't seem threatening, but Pinocchio refused to set foot on the planet.

As they came away Laura looked back at Enigma longingly, unprepared for Pinocchio's sudden stop. Maybe he'd changed his mind! No, he was pointing at something white and big as a planet, swimming toward them through the dark ocean of space.

Laura was intrigued. She didn't know planets could swim; she thought they stayed more-or-less in orbit. Though once you thought about it, swimming planets seemed like a good idea. They could visit each other and get acquainted, maybe swim to other galaxies together.

As the white planet got closer Laura saw it was not really a planet, at least not like any she had ever seen. It was a white whale big as a planet. As it got closer it got smaller, which was not the way things usually were.

The whale had the bluest eyes and the longest lashes and the pinkest smile and the neatest white beard and a bouquet of flowers sprouting from the top of its head.

"Hi Laura. Hi Pinocchio," said the whale, turning over on its back and doing a few graceful backstrokes in space.

"How do you know our names?" asked Laura.

"Someone must have described you."

"Who?" Laura asked eagerly. Maybe it had been her father.

"Just someone," teased the whale.

"But who?" Laura demanded to know.

"Someone who wants me to find you, I guess."

"Why won't you tell me?" Laura asked impatiently.

"When you're ready to know, you'll already know," the whale bantered, backflipping off into the distance, getting bigger as it went, then getting smaller as it came back again.

Despite her impatience Laura was fascinated. "How do you get bigger and smaller?"

"Sometimes I need to be big and sometimes I need to be small," said the whale twirling on its tail.

"Could I do it too?"

"You are getting bigger; you're growing up, aren't you?"

Laura could see the whale wasn't going to tell its secrets. "Why do you look like a planet?" she asked, changing the subject.

"Do I?" The whale playfully flicked its tail, sending a scattering of small stars sailing out of sight.

"No, you look like a whale, sort of."

"I am a whale. Sort of."

"Are you a girl whale or a boy whale?"

"Which do you think?"

"You must be a girl," Laura decided. "You have such long lashes and very pink lips and flowers on your head."

"What about the beard?" teased the whale.

"It looks stuck on."

The whale laughed heartily, shaking loose a shower of stardust. "Listen, kid, you and me, we're supposed to do some traveling together."

"Oh," said Laura, trying not to show her interest. "What makes you say that?"

"Just a hunch."

"Would you take me where I wanted to go?" she asked, glancing over at Pinocchio.

"Most of the time."

"Where would we go the rest of the time?"

"Where I want to go."

"What about Pinocchio? Can he come too?"

"I don't think he wants to."

"How do you know?"

"Oh, I just know."

"Maybe you're wrong." But Laura knew the whale was right.

"Maybe. But I'm not."

"You're so stubborn."

"I like you too, kid," said the whale, making spirals with its tail. "So, how about it?"

"Pinocchio, would you like to come?"

"If you want me to," he said loyally.

"You want to go back to Contentment," Laura said wistfully.

"I hate to let you down."

"You've found what you want."

"Are we still friends?" Pinocchio asked, a catch in his voice.

"Of course," Laura assured him, giving him a hug. "But I have to find my father."

"I know." He glanced over at the whale. "Do you think you can trust it?" he whispered.

"I think so. The whale is very stubborn," she said loud enough for it to hear, "but I think it's okay."

Pinocchio was silent for a moment. "I'm sure going to miss you."

"Oh, Pinocchio, me too," said Laura, trying not to cry. "I'll come visit you. Don't stop too long on Oasis and get sick."

Pinocchio laughed. "I'll be good," he promised. Taking off, he blew her a kiss, and rocketed away for Contentment like a bright rainbow. Laura watched till he was out of sight.

"See," said the whale, "I knew he wouldn't come."

"Oh, shut up."

"It's okay," the whale said understandingly. "Hop on."

Climbing onto the whale's back, Laura steadied herself as it slowly turned its great bulk toward the unknown.

"I'll be your new best friend," promised the whale.

"We'll see." But secretly Laura was pleased.

Chapter Three

Expanding Her Horizons

Mr. and Mrs. Loveseat were watching the fights on TV. Everywhere you looked there was a mess — empty soda cans, candy wrappers, used paper plates, half-filled food containers with green fuzz growing in them, even a giant popcorn machine that no one bothered to turn off; it just kept coughing up popcorn like exploding stars. Aeons and aeons of Mr. and Mrs. Loveseat's leftovers floated in space around them. Over time, the area had become the Universal Dump. Bits and pieces of everything that ever existed wound up here. The stench was awful.

"Why is everything so messy?" asked Laura.

"It's the Great Chaos," explained the whale. "Everything that ever was or will be is here. Kind of like a stew with everything dumped in."

"It's smelly."

"Don't let the witches hear you."

Off in the distance Laura saw a mysterious glow
where shadowy figures flitted to and fro.

The Witches are brewing,
the Witches are stewing,
out at the edge of Time.

No one knows what they grow,
no one knows what they know,
out at the edge of Time.

The secrets they keep
go very deep,
out at the edge of Time.

There they are basting,
there they are tasting,
out at the edge of Time.

Witches are few
who know how to brew
dark stew in the Pot of Time.

All of Life's creatures are waiting,
all of Life's creatures are stating,
there's more at the end of Time.

But Witches don't tell;
they keep secrets well,
out at the edge of Time.

Everything grows
and anything goes,
out at the edge of Time.

Slime and rice,
fruit and mice
rush to the edge of Time.

All things begin
and all things win,
out at the edge of Time.

Nothing departs
and nothing starts,
out at the edge of Time.

Some of us play
and some of us stay,
out at the edge of Time.

All of us go
but none of us know
what's at the edge of Time

"The witches are in charge of cooking all this stuff," explained the whale.

"Like food? In a pot?" Laura was astounded.

"A huge cauldron."

"Yuck. I think I'll watch TV with Mr. and Mrs. Loveseat."

"I didn't hear them invite you," teased the whale.

"If you're going to sit in the middle of nowhere with no walls and the only TV, people are bound to drop in."

"You have a point," said the whale, laughing.

Laura marched over to the popcorn machine, catching some popped kernels as they shot out. "Hi," she said to the Loveseats. "My name is Laura. Can I watch TV with you?"

They didn't look up. They were too preoccupied with

the fight between the Sun and the Moon who were slug-
ging it out for control of Time.

It was the same old thing for as long as anyone could
remember. Twice a day the Sun and the Moon climbed
into the ring. The Sun was very flashy in gold trunks and
he had a powerful punch. But the Moon was slick and he
had most of the Stars on his side.

At twilight, the Moon, in silver trunks, a cluster of
Stars adding weight to his punch, would knock out the
Sun and it would be night. Then the Moon would throw a
victory party. He and the Stars would stay up all night
celebrating till they were woozy. When the Sun awoke,
gold trunks flashing, he would surprise the sleepy Moon
and Stars, sending them flying with one powerful punch.
Then it would be day.

Mr. and Mrs. Loveseat were betting on different sides,
which kept the fight interesting for them. The rest of the
universe had long since stopped taking sides.

Laura looked around for a seat but there was only Mr.
and Mrs. Loveseat. It didn't seem right to sit on them.
"Maybe we should go somewhere else."

"How about the Big Beach?"

"Is it smelly like this?"

The whale laughed. "No."

"Let's go now."

"Don't you want to stick around for some of the
witches' stew?" the whale asked playfully.

"Oh, whale."

"Okay, hop aboard," said the whale, boosting her up.

As they moved gracefully through space Laura found the whale's gentle rocking motion very soothing.

"You're awfully quiet," said the whale.

"I'm just thinking."

"What about?"

"If we're best friends I should know your name. Whale could be any whale, but you're my special whale."

"Am I really your special whale?" the whale asked, flicking its tail.

Laura felt suddenly shy.

"If you don't feel like talking we could try something different," suggested the whale. "Sometimes best friends can hear each other's thoughts. Would you like to try?"

"Okay."

"Concentrate real hard and pretend you can hear my name. Just let your thoughts float and see if you can hear it."

The soft, silent winds of space and the whale's gentle rocking motion were very relaxing. Laura let her thoughts gradually drift, drift, drift... She gave a start. "Amanda!"

"Are you sure?" the whale teased.

"Oh, Amanda," Laura laughed. She didn't mind being teased if they were really best friends.

* * * *

It was a holiday weekend at the Big Beach and the line in front of the Money Booth wound clear around the asteroid. Amanda groaned. "I forgot, it's Imagination Weekend. Everyone in the universe has an account here."

"Do I have an account?" asked Laura.

"Of course, silly. Everyone does."

The one-armed Money Giver was prepared for the holiday crowds and concluded transactions rapidly. Before long it was their turn. They stepped into the booth and closed the curtain behind them.

"Watch what I do," said Amanda, pressing four stars in a hop-skip pattern. A window opened in the sky and a giant hand reached down, releasing a shower of transparent discs.

"Oh," said Laura. "It's the prettiest money I've ever seen."

"It's Thought Money," Amanda explained. "It's transparent and weightless so it can become however much you need."

"Could I send some to my mother? She's always worrying about money."

"Thought Money is only good at amusement parks."

"Oh," Laura said, disappointed. "My mother doesn't like amusement parks; she says they're a waste of time."

"Gee, that's too bad. A lot of people feel that way. Things like amusement parks, Thought Money and Imagination Weekend just seem silly to them."

"I guess some people don't like to have fun," Laura said pensively.

"That's right."

"Amanda," Laura said, brightening. "My father loves
amusement parks. He took me lots of times. Maybe that's
where we'll find him."

* * * *

By the time they got to the Big Beach it was packed.
Pumpkins with short legs sunned themselves next to
snakes with no legs. Frogfolk hopped back and forth with
goodies for their tadpoles. A long-haired willow and a
handsome blue spruce stood rooted to the spot, their
branches entwined. Some teddy bears tried to calm four
angry black bears who thought they'd been insulted by
some pandas. Four pale green lima beans with spindly
arms and legs were having an animated conversation with
several golden raisins. Flocks of colorful bird-beings frolicked overhead along with a covey of apparitions. An
arrogant bunch of goodie-two-shoes, thinking they were
better than anyone else because they had servants instead of arms, sauntered along the water's edge on their
exceptionally long legs, their foot-long noses stuck a mile
in the air. They were preceded by their servants, slouch-
ing, slippery slugs, who cleared a path for them. The only
people taller than the two-shoes were the mega-folk who
were so tall no one had ever seen what they looked like
above their kneecaps. The fascinating variety of
PeopleKind explained the strange clothes Laura had seen
in the caves of Contentment.

She particularly liked the Enchanted Poets. You
couldn't actually see them with your eyes as much as
sense them in the space between things where they
danced instead of walking and sang instead of talking.
Their singing was so beautiful Laura wanted to listen
forever.

"Let's go eat," Amanda said impatiently.

"Oh, Amanda, listen."

"I'm hungry."

"But I might never hear them again."

"Not a chance," grumbled Amanda. "If you can hear them, you're stuck with them forever."

"Don't you like to hear them?" Laura asked, puzzled by the way Amanda was acting.

"They're pests! They make you see things that aren't there, feel things you can't feel," Amanda complained. "All they do is talk and talk, sing and sing. They make everything sound so wonderful you start expecting things to be that way."

"But maybe things can be that way."

"Let's go eat."

* * * *

The hot dogs were the best Laura had ever tasted. She had three. Amanda ate five hundred. The bill was enormous but one disc of Thought Money took care of it.

They strolled along the boardwalk eating ice cream cones, watching the happy crowds, catching snatches of conversations.

"Amanda, how come we all understand each other when everybody's so different?"

"We're not as different as you think," said Amanda. "Remember the witches' song about *slime and rice, fruit and mice?* We're all made from the same stuff cooked up in the same old pot."

"I guess," Laura said uncertainly.

"Let's go on the roller coaster," Amanda suggested.

"I'd rather go on the merry-go-round."

"Again?" said Amanda. "We've been on the merry-go-round three times. We haven't been on the roller coaster once."

"I don't like roller coasters."

"Have you ever been on one?"

"I'll get sick."

"How do you know you'll get sick?"

"I just know."

"But it's lots of fun," Amanda insisted. "Once you've tried it you won't be afraid anymore. Look at the people waiting to get on. Do they look afraid?"

"Maybe you should go with them."

"Don't be such a scaredy-cat."

"I'm not a scaredy-cat." Laura said miserably.

"Look, I'm your best friend," said Amanda, giving her a hug. "Would I ask you to do something that wasn't okay?"

* * * *

The bright red ribbon of cars ascended higher and higher. Over the roar of her fear Laura heard the others shouting: "HIGHER! HIGHER!" She closed her eyes, not daring to look.

"HIGHER! HIGHER!" they shouted as they passed through the clouds. "HIGHER! HIGHER!" they wailed in the wind. "HIGHER! HIGHER!" She clamped her jaw shut to keep from screaming. "HIGHER!" they shrieked.

She braced herself for the Big Drop. The wind whipped wildly around her. She felt a rush of fear, of exhilaration, the taste of salt tears, felt herself letting go, letting the wind take her until she was the wind, free, free!

Down she fluttered, down like a leaf ...down...down... The bright red ribbon of cars came gently to a stop.

"See," said Amanda. "I told you it was fun."

"Oh," sighed Laura, still riding the wind. It was much better than fun.

* * * *

After the fireworks, people collected their things and started to leave. Laura stood on the boardwalk anxiously watching the passing faces.

Amanda could tell something was wrong. "I'm sorry I called you scaredy-cat."

Laura started to cry.

"What's the matter? What's wrong?"

"I hoped maybe we'd find my father here."

So, that was it. "Just because he wasn't here doesn't mean we can't find him."

"Yes, that's right," Laura said hopefully.

"You're probably supposed to have more adventures. So you'll have more stories to tell him."

Laura looked at her friend gratefully. Just then she heard the delicate, high, sweet singing of the Enchanted Poets.

> *All things dear*
> *are always near.*
> *All things dear*
> *are waiting there,*
> *over the edge of Time.*

"Come on, let's go," Amanda said cheerfully.

"Where?"

"Home."

"I don't ever want to go home," Laura said, alarmed.

"I mean my home."

"Oh," Laura said, relieved.

"You'll love it."

"They won't mind if you bring home a stranger?"

"You're not a stranger. You're my best friend," said Amanda, giving her a hug. "I'll even let you swim in my secret swimming hole."

"I can't swim," Laura said shyly.

"My cousin Dora is a great teacher. She can turn cats into catfish. You'll be a mermaid in no time."

Chapter Four

Encounter On The Beach

Laura sat on the smooth white sand at the edge of the Great Sea watching Amanda and her cousins, the dolphins, play in the waves.

Cousin Dora had been very patient teaching Laura to swim. At first Laura kept her arms and legs stiff which made her sink, but with Dora's help, she overcame her fear of the water, just as she'd overcome her fear of the roller coaster. Once she learned to relax and trust the waves to carry her she became quite a good swimmer for someone without fins. Though she couldn't dive as deep or stay down as long as Amanda and her cousins, she could go deep enough for it to be dark as night, and she began to realize what was on the land was also in the sea and in the sky. Starfish were akin to stars, catfish to cats, seaweed to grass and mermaids were just like her, only with fins.

Amanda's family did all they could to make Laura feel welcome. They fussed over her meals — even serving

things they didn't like but which they knew she preferred. They took her on magical weekends to beautiful
hidden grottos. They went on picnics to the great reef
just over the horizon. They introduced her to every seal,
porpoise and fish in the neighborhood, all part of their
extended family, a family so extended some of the con-
nections were hard for even them to follow.

Though they tried to include her in everything sometimes their chatter about faraway friends and shared
experiences made Laura feel lonely, reminding her how
much she missed reading the books with the golden
edges with her father and listening to the music from
their magic place. No matter how much she loved
Amanda, she knew there were some things they could
never share.

* * * *

Amanda called out to tell her she and her cousins
were going sounding. Laura knew this meant they would
be going very deep and would be gone for quite a while.

Alone on the vast expanse of smooth, white sand, she
lay back and looked up at the cloudless sky, letting her
thoughts drift lazily away, letting herself float free in a
universe of sky without land or horizon — sky dreaming
— not caring which way was up or down.

After a while she sat up. Everything looked strange.
The light had changed. Looking down the beach she saw
a thin gray figure in the distance. Something about him
made her heart beat faster. As he walked slowly toward
her he occasionally bent down to pick up something from
the sand, putting it in a sack he carried over his shoulder. What was he collecting?

"*Memories,*" whispered a voice.

He seemed not to notice her. As he got closer she saw he was very frail. He was dressed all in gray, his wide brimmed hat casting his face in shadow. She wanted to go to him, to see his face, but something held her back.

Stopping, he pulled a shining stick from his sack and wrote something in the sand. He turned toward her. She held her breath, expecting to see his face, but before she could, he vanished. "No!" she cried.

The empty beach stretched into the distance.

She ran to where he had been. Before the sea rushed in and swept it away she saw what he had written. *LAURA.*

The man in gray had been her father!

* * * *

That night when they were alone Laura told Amanda what had happened. "Why couldn't I see his face? Why didn't he speak to me?"

"Maybe he was a hologram."

"A who?"

"It's like a telegram, only with pictures."

"He looked so real," Laura said wistfully. "Who could have sent the hologram?"

"Maybe someone wants you to know that your father is watching over you," Amanda said sympathetically, turning off the light.

Lying in bed awake, Laura wished she could have kissed him. Even if he was just a hologram. "Amanda, are you asleep?"

"Almost."

"Maybe whoever sent you to find me sent the hologram."

"Could be."

"Well, who sent you?"

"I don't know. Sometimes you just get the impulse to do something. You know how it is."

"Maybe my father sent you."

"Whoever it was, they knew your name."

"Pinocchio's too. It must have been my father."

"Makes sense to me," yawned Amanda.

"How can we find him?"

"We'll figure out something. Now, let's get some sleep."

"Maybe the witches would know."

"They certainly act like they know things," Amanda grumbled. "Now, go to sleep."

"Somebody must know."

"We'll find out tomorrow."

"Amanda, this is important!"

"Okay, okay." Amanda turned on the light and sat up.

"Let me think about this... Hmm, it just might work."

"What? What?"

"The Enchanted Poets always talk about making things wonderful. Maybe they can help."

"Oh, yes!" Laura said excitedly, "let's send them a hologram."

"Better make that a telegram. They like words, especially ones that rhyme."

It had to rhyme.

> *Poets dear*
> *have you been clear*
> *out to the edge of Time?*
>
> *Will I find*
> *my father there*
> *out at the edge of Time?*

"It doesn't all rhyme," Laura said apologetically, remembering her mother's criticism.

"Kid, it's terrific. I'm impressed."

"It's fun. I could do this all night."

"Yeah, I bet," laughed Amanda. "Now go ahead. Finish it."

"Okay, how about...

> *Poets dear*
> *have you been clear*
> *out to the edge of Time?*

*Will I find
my father there,
out at the edge of Time?*

*Do you know
how I can go
out to the edge of Time?*

Signed, Laura.

"Great. Except for one thing."

"What?"

"Shouldn't it say how can WE go?"

"You mean you'd go too? I wasn't sure..."

"Like Pinocchio, you mean," Amanda said under-standingly. "Listen, kid, not knowing where you were or what you were up to would drive me nuts."

"Then I guess you'll just have to come with me," Laura said happily.

Chapter Five

Tale Of The Little Princess

The Great Poet himself invited Laura and Amanda to his Serene High Studio, the rarest of honors. He sent his golden coach for them. It was covered with precious stones and pulled by four white horses with gossamer wings.

Perched atop the highest pinnacle of the Singing Mountains, the Great Poet's studio had a cosmic view which helped him with his work. Made of iridescent crystal with the subtlest hint of almost-color spun into it, and having real gold trim outlining its fluid shapes, it was known as the building without bones.

Laura was dazzled.

Even Amanda was impressed, though she tried not to show it. "I thought poets starved in garrets," she joked.

"Not necessarily," said a gentle voice that seemed to

come from everywhere at once.

"Oops." Amanda was embarrassed.

Laura giggled.

A tall man with lustrous white hair and smiling, age-less eyes appeared. His slender frame was clothed in robes of softest white interwoven with threads of the iridescent almost-color. Carrying himself with an easy dignity, he seemed to glide across the marble floor, his golden sandals not quite touching down.

Laura felt an impulse to climb in his lap.

"Please do," said the Great Poet, settling himself on a billowy cloud pillow.

"You can hear what I'm thinking," Laura said, delighted.

"You can hear our thoughts too, for you are one of us," explained the Great Poet, helping her up into his lap. "We are pleased with your poem, child." He reached into a pocket of the cloud pillow. "We have a present for you." It was a golden notebook.

"Oh!" Laura exclaimed. It was real gold with a silver zipper. Her name was embossed on it in stars. "Thank you!"

"It is your magic notebook. Only you may write in it."

Amanda was pleased for Laura, but for her part, being around Enchanted Poets made her uncomfortable. I guess I'm not like them, she thought.

"Ah, but you are close, my dear Amanda," said the Great Poet. "It is only a matter of willingness."

"Willingness?" Amanda was puzzled.

"Willingness to cherish what can only be imagined but never confirmed."

"Oh."

Remembering the purpose of her visit, Laura wondered if the Great Poet could help her find her father.

"I believe I can bring you closer to him."

"Maybe I can find him if I go out to the edge of time. Is that very far?"

"Yes. But not too far."

"We used to listen to music that came from somewhere beyond the books with the golden edges. Daddy said if I ever couldn't find him the music would help me. But I can't hear it anymore."

"The music is still there, child. Now, let me tell you a story."

THE LITTLE PRINCESS

Once upon a time, in a very happy kingdom next to the Dark Zone, there lived a beautiful Little Princess with long red hair. Her father, the Good King, loved her more than all his treasure, more than life itself. She was his beloved and only child. Through her, he felt the continued happiness of the kingdom was assured.

The Good King was much loved and trusted by his subjects. Each Sunday they would be welcomed in the great hall of the palace where they sought his advice. This was known as the Time of Advising and was a tradition treasured by the people and their King.

The Good King always made certain the Little Princess was by his side on this day, on her small throne next to his grand one. He wanted her to learn how to rule with wisdom and kindness and he wanted his people to value her as he did. There would come a time when he would have to depart for the realm from which no one returns and she would become Queen.

The Little Princess was enchanting in her cloud-white dress. On her long red hair she wore a crown of stars. It was a small crown but perfect, and the stars on it were real.

Her father wore his Crown of Wisdom, a golden halo, tilted at a most attractive angle. He explained to the Little Princess that he did so because wearing his halo perfectly centered might make his subjects feel their King was too perfect and therefore unapproachable. He wanted them to be at ease in his presence.

The Little Princess loved her father and knew he was very wise so she followed his example and set her own small crown of stars at the same attractive angle which brought a smile of approval from her father. Though he never commanded her to do things his way, he always let her know when he approved of her decisions.

The Good King did not wish to have his subjects worship him or bow to him. He wanted them to love him as they would a wise and loving father. At the Time of Advising comfortable chairs were arranged before his throne and his subjects were invited to seat themselves for refreshments and consultation.

After each question the King would turn to the Little Princess and she would whisper her answer into his ear. When he thought her answer a wise one he would allow her to offer it. When he felt it was not wise or the best answer, he would give his own. After his subjects left the great hall he would ask his daughter if she understood why his answer was better. In this way, the Little Princess learned more and more about being a good ruler.

Sometimes when the Time of Advising was over, the Little Princess and her father would tour their joyful domain. Its beauty and peace always made her happy. The people of their kingdom had everything they needed for contentment because their King was generous and loved his people, sharing not only his fortune but his happiness in them, in his daughter and in the goodness of life. Just as he taught the Little Princess, by example, he set an example for his people, teaching them to be kind to each other and share their good fortune. Under his reign jealousy and greed vanished from his kingdom. The people were happy in their labor and bountifully rewarded.

The King took great pride in the beauty and wisdom of the Little Princess. Together they would travel to other kingdoms so they too would come to know and love the Little Princess. Alliances would be important when she became Queen.

Only the Dark Zone was forbidden to her. Her curiosity about it was very great. "It is the place where all good things are lost," warned her father. Since he never forbade her anything without good reason the Little Princess never went near the Dark Zone, but the thought of it lay uneasily in her mind.

Though the kingdom was next to the Dark Zone it was protected from the evil spirits who dwelled there by the great Power of Good the King possessed. The fortunate kingdom flourished in peace and plenty until one terrible day when the Good King, weary from a pilgrimage to the farthest reach of his kingdom, fell into a deep sleep and was set upon by an army of evil gremlins who rushed out of the Dark Zone and took him away to their evil domain.

An impenetrable darkness fell over the land. Flowers withered on their stems; fields of growing things died; there were no more births, no food, no light, no joy anywhere in the kingdom. A pall of sorrow covered all.

Without the Power of Good to repel them, evil armies plundered the land and enslaved people, committing acts of terror, turning neighbor against neighbor, friend against friend, loved one against loved one. Everywhere the evil armies went they sowed wickedness, panic and despair, casting the Spell of Forgetfulness over the kingdom and erasing the memory of the Good King and their former happiness from the minds of most people.

But the Little Princess did not forget. Nothing could make her forget the deep love she had for her father. She could neither eat nor sleep. She felt she was drowning in an ocean of tears. Without her father the palace was empty and cold. Driven by despair, the Little Princess fled the palace and wandered the kingdom alone, weeping for her father and the unhappiness of their people.

She wandered aimlessly for many weeks, neither seeing nor caring where she went until one day the clear song of a bird penetrated her grief. Looking up, she saw the loveliest bird she had ever seen

> I'm a golden bird
> in a silver tree.
> Look at me.
> Look at me,
> Lovely to see.
> I'm so glad to be
> a golden bird
> in a silver tree.

Charmed by the beautiful bird and its cheerful song, the Little Princess felt her gloom lifting.

I'm a golden bird
in a silver tree.
Listen to me.
Listen to me,
Singing happily.
I'm so glad to be
a golden bird
in a silver tree.

The little bird reminded her of all the goodness, beauty and joy her father had shared with her and their people. She realized he would want her to overcome her grief and find some way to restore happiness to the kingdom he loved so much.

She sought the help of wise men and fools, wizards and witches, seers and saints. Not one could tell her how to save the kingdom and bring her father back. At last she came upon a grizzled old hermit seated by a campfire near the edge of the Dark Zone.

"Princess," he called out to her," I may be able to help you. Come sit by me and look into the Fire Of Knowledge." The Little Princess looked into the fire but saw only darkness. "Look deeper," the hermit urged her. She began to sense movement somewhere in the darkness as evil gremlins skittered through slime doing their dastardly deeds. Looking deeper, she saw the slime was crawling with mindless, slithery things with violent red eyes and flaming poisonous tongues. The sight of them made the Little Princess weak with fear but she knew her only hope of rescuing her father lay in facing the evil demons.

"I must warn you, Princess," said the hermit, "the Dark Zone casts an evil spell, transforming all who dwell there. Should you find your father you may not know him."

"I will know him with my heart."

"Should you know him you may be unable to bring him back."

"I will find a way."

"Should you bring him back he may not be as he once was."

"I will love him as he is."

"You are brave, Little Princess, and good, like your father. He would be proud. But there is great danger in the Dark Zone," warned the hermit. "No one can guide you through it, not even your father. You must face the Dark Zone alone."

The Little Princess would not be dissuaded. Nothing in the Dark Zone could be as devastating as grief or as debilitating as fear. The door to the Dark Zone closed soundlessly behind her.

* * * *

At the loss of the Little Princess the kingdom sank deeper into despair. Those not under the Spell of Forgetfulness strove to keep hope alive. They stationed a swift messenger at the door to the Dark Zone, his trumpet ready to blare, his strong legs ready to carry him to the palace with the news, should the Good King or his daughter appear. But after a time even the faithful began to despair.

The hermit sat by his fire, peering into its heart, searching for the Little Princess. At last he saw her, frozen with fear, surrounded by slimy hissing demons who taunted and threatened her.

Trapped in their den of darkness, the Little Princess

struggled against the invisible bonds of fear, her mind dashing to and fro, trying to escape the terrifying demons, the only light coming from the evil red glow of their hate-filled eyes. Panic mounting, she returned their hate with her hate, their rage with her rage, feeling herself changing into something vile and venomous as the demons themselves.

Horrified, she realized her transformation was destroying all the beauty and joy her father had instilled in her. They would soon be lost in this foul cavern of fear, this evil place where all good things are lost, leaving only ugliness and evil to reign.

The horror of this became greater than her fear, dissolving the bonds that held her. The evil demons recoiled. Fear was their only weapon. Freed of fear, the Little Princess felt the Power of Good leap back to life in her, blazing like a flame, scorching all demons before it.

She plunged triumphantly into the core of darkness where her father was held, her bright Power flooding the darkness with light.

* * * *

It was Sunday morning, traditionally the Time of Advising. The empty thrones of the Good King and the Little Princess were shrouded in the dust of sorrow. Seeking comfort, those few who still had hope gathered in the great hall of the palace. But there was nothing to comfort them, not even an echo of the Good King's laugh.

Suddenly, the horn of the messenger sounded. A babble of excited voices could be heard, getting louder and louder. A crowd approached the palace. Those inside the great hall rushed out onto the balcony as darkness lifted from the land. A jubilant throng poured through the palace gates, bearing on their shoulders the beautiful young Prin-

cess, more radiant than she had ever been. Perched on her brilliant, flying hair, and tilted at a most attractive angle, was the golden halo of her father. She had brought the Good King home.

* * * *

Laura knew the ending was happy but somehow it made her feel sad.

"Sometimes," explained the Great Poet, "if you are brave you can turn sadness into happiness." Setting her down from his lap, he stood up, seeming to become slightly transparent.

"The Little Princess was very brave," Laura said thoughtfully. "Even when it was very dangerous."

"For there to be bravery there must be danger," said the Great Poet, becoming even more transparent. "The important thing is the Little Princess never gave up her belief in the beautiful things her father had taught her. Eventually, this brought her great happiness."

"Will I ever find my father?"

The Great Poet smiled. "Yes, Little Princess, I believe you will. The night your father died you chose the right path, going bravely through a door he left open for you."

"But,"

"Trust," said the Great Poet, his words coming from afar. "Trust yourself and your companions, and the goodness of the universe."

Chapter Six

The Desert Rats

After leaving the Great Poet Laura felt more confident, ready for something new, but she couldn't think what.

"Give yourself time," said Amanda. "You'll think of something."

Laura took out her magic notebook but after a few minutes she set it aside. Restless, she picked up the Criminal Gazette from Amanda's father's chair and began to read. It was nothing like the books with the golden edges. There were so many interesting new words and phrases. "Amanda, what's the Club Galaxy?"

"The Club Galaxy," Amanda said, surprised, "where'd you hear about that?"

"In this magazine."

"Oh, that, well, it's a place where people go to play games and have a good time."

"Could we go there?"

"I don't know, " Amanda said carefully. "It's kind of different from what you're used to."

"I want to go someplace different."

"We'll see."

"What does it mean, off the beaten path?" Laura asked, not noticing as the phrase slipped out of the newspaper and into her magic notebook, leaving a blank space behind.

"It means far away."

"How far?"

"It's stuck off in a real remote part of the universe."

"Why did they put it so far away?"

"The Holier-Than-Thous raised such a fuss the owners had to put it way out there."

"Who are the Holier-Than-Thous?"

"Oh, a bunch of busy-bodies who don't want anyone to have any fun."

"They don't?" Laura found it hard to understand. "Have you ever been there?"

"Quite a few times," Amanda chuckled. "Forcing the Club to be so far away makes it more like forbidden fruit." Laura's notebook made a slurping sound. "The joint is always jumping."

Laura giggled, imagining a building jumping up and down on pogo-stick legs. "Does it really have showgirls covered in diamonds?"

"Rhinestones, more likely."

"It says diamonds." Laura looked for the page to show Amanda, but there was only blank space where the words had been.

"Trust me, rhinestones."

"The Club Galaxy sounds wonderful."

"It is," said Amanda, "all those bright lights and glitter.

"Are sugar daddies some kind of candy?"

"Alright already." Amanda said, laughing. "We're going. But first we'd better do a little shopping."

* * * *

Located in a duty-free zone, Hot Goods Haven supplied the illicit to the elite. Laura and Amanda were assigned a Shopper's Helper to carry their purchases and make sure they were paid for. With some of the clientele one could never be too careful.

Shopper's Helper in tow, they made their way to the Extra Stupendous Costume Department. Laura was dazzled by the bins of glitter. "Oooo!" she squealed, plunging her hands into bin after bin, pulling out fistfuls of fake jewels, sequins, rhinestone-encrusted feathers. "These are wonderful! They make noise in my eyes!"

Joining in the fun, Amanda flipped sequins and jewels in the air with her tail, showering them both with glitter. They left Hot Goods Haven so loaded with flash they could barely walk.

* * * *

A RocketBus normally seated two hundred but because of Amanda's size there was only room for Laura, Amanda and their luggage. Even the pilot had to be left behind which was just as well; Amanda hadn't liked his looks anyway.

"Pilot's Papers please," said the Star Patrol officer, stepping inside.

"Oh, of course," Amanda said sweetly, digging out her papers.

"Lady, these are way out of date."

"Imagine. Well, I'll take care of it when I get back."

"But lady," protested the officer.

"We're in a rush," said Amanda, gently but firmly pushing him out. "Quick, Laura, buckle up." The doors of the RocketBus closed with a sucking sound as the rockets revved up, clearing the launch pad of Star Patrollers and everyone else.

Amanda couldn't squeeze behind the wheel. "They're sure making these small nowadays." She lay down, prepared to steer with her nose.

"Why don't you make yourself smaller," asked Laura.

"It's easier to be my real size."

"Does it hurt when you get smaller to be with me?"

"Smaller? In some ways I'm not sure I'm as big as you are."

"Can I drive?"

"I saw you with those bumper cars at the Big Beach."

"This is different," Laura said, clambering over Amanda to get to the co-pilot's seat. "What's the big red button for?" She'd never seen so many dials, gauges, levers, switches and buttons.

"Do you know left from right?" Amanda asked dubiously.

"Most of the time."

"This should be an interesting trip."

* * * *

Since nobody enforced the speed limit this far out in space, Amanda put the RocketBus on auto-pilot and they cruised along a little faster than the speed of light. Already in a prone position and lulled by the purr of the engine, Amanda fell asleep.

Laura was too excited to sleep. She looked out the window, making notes in her magic notebook about places they zoomed past in case she wanted to visit them sometime. After a while everything became a blur. She looked around for something to do. Her glance fell on the big red button. Red was her favorite color. She wondered what the button was for.

Amanda had warned her not to touch anything, but the button was such a pretty shade of red. She tried to distract herself but with Amanda fast asleep and everything outside a blur, and the red button so red. It seemed to want to be pressed. Why else would it be so red? Touching just the edge of it, she glanced over at Amanda who was snoring softly. The next thing she knew she had pressed the button.

For a minute nothing happened. Then the engine began to roar, going faster and faster. Everything outside seemed to go slower and slower. The red button got redder and redder. Uh-oh. Maybe it would stop if she pressed it again. Bells clanged. Horns blared. A mechanical voice shrieked, "Abandon ship! Abandon ship!"

Amanda awoke to see a huge red asteroid smack in front of them. Quickly flipping switches to reverse the engine, she grabbed Laura and held her close, managing to find the EjectUs button just before they hit. The RocketBus struck the asteroid with terrible force, smashing itself to smithereens. Blown free, Laura and Amanda landed in a nice, squishy swamp, debris from the collision raining down all around them.

"Kid, are you all right?" Amanda asked anxiously.

"I'm okay," Laura said weakly.

"Thank goodness!" Amanda was greatly relieved. "I never heard of a RocketBus going so crazy."

"Neither have I," Laura said guiltily.

Amanda looked at her suspiciously. "Is there something you want to tell me?"

"I guess, I pressed the red button."

"You little stinker!"

"Are you mad at me?"

"Sure, I'm mad at you! You must promise you'll never do anything like that again."

"I promise," Laura said miserably.

Amanda gave her a half-hug. "Fortunately there are plenty more RocketBusses."

Still wobbly, they climbed out of the swamp onto dry, cracked, red clay and surveyed the damage. Large chunks of the RocketBus drifted in the sky. Feathers, sequins, jewels were scattered everywhere. Except for the swamp, there was no sign of moisture anywhere. In the distance a lone dust devil was doing a whirly dance.

"Do you know where we are?" asked Laura.

"Maybe this is the asteroid the Holier-Than-Thous use to spy on the Club Galaxy. They probably get their kicks that way."

"Probably," Laura said as if she knew what 'kicks' were.

Amanda looked at her, amused.

"Amanda, look!" Laura pointed to two large creatures coming over the asteroid's short horizon. "Giant rats!"

"Then this *is* the asteroid," Amanda decided. "And those must be the Desert Rats, a couple of ancient brothers who farm gold and sell it to the Club for the slot machines."

"What are slot machines?"

"One-armed bandits," Amanda said dryly. "Let's see if these rodents will rescue two damsels in distress."

The Desert Rats, one fat, one skinny, wore dirty overalls, torn straw hats with holes for their large ears and red bandannas around their wrinkled necks. They shuffled back and forth across the dry, cracked earth, slowly, deliberately, their feet worn flat over centuries, occasionally stopping to point things out to each other, gesturing with long, skinny arms, paying no attention to Laura and Amanda.

"Hello there," Amanda called out. "We've had an accident."

Except for swiveling their ears they gave no sign they'd heard.

"Maybe they didn't hear you," said Laura.

"They heard; look at those ears."

When they got within a few feet of Laura and Amanda the Desert Rats stopped, seeming not at all surprised to find a large whale and a small girl in the middle of nowhere.

"Must be showgals," the fat rat said to the skinny rat, taking in the glittering landscape. "Them guys are sure hirin' some strange 'uns nowadays." The Club paid a hefty finder's fee for showgals.

"Big 'uns got a beard," snickered the skinny rat.

"It's stuck on," Laura said, annoyed that he was making fun of Amanda.

"Little 'uns jes' a mud minnow," honked the fat rat. "Oughtta be throwed back in the swamp till she's grow'd."

"I am not a mud minnow."

"Are so."

"Am not!"

"Who asked ya, squirt?"

"I don't like you."

"We've had an accident," said Amanda, deciding things had gone far enough. "Can we use your phone to get help?"

"We don't got no phone," the fat rat said cagily, looking Amanda up and down.

"How do we get to the Club Galaxy?" she asked.

"We'll take ya," said the skinny rat, grinning a gray-gummed, toothless grin.

"In what?" Amanda sniffed, "a pumpkin drawn by five white mice?"

"Pumpkin? Whaddaya mean, pumpkin?"

"She's funnin' ya," snorted the fat rat.

"We got twelve thousand white mice," the skinny rat boasted, "an' a gold-haulin' waggin. Better'n any old pumpkin."

"We'll walk. Just point us in the right direction."

"Too fur ta walk," the fat rat said smugly.

"Too hot, too," gloated the skinny rat. "Desert sun'll kill ya."

They were right about the sun. Amanda was parched, inside and out. "I need some water."

"Sure thing, lady," said the fat rat, as if he was doing her a big favor. "Right this way."

"I'll be right back," she whispered to Laura. "Think you can handle the skinny one?"

"I'll be all right."

* * * *

The fat rat took Amanda the long way around, past various crash sites he and his brother had commemorated with markers and dates.

"Nice lookin' gal," said the skinny rat. "What's her act?"

"Her act?" Laura was puzzled.

"Does she juggle?"

"I don't think so."

"Does she dance?"

"I guess."

"Bet she sings real purty."

"Oh yes, especially underwater."

"Underwater! The Singin' Mermaid?" he exclaimed, dollar signs dancing before his eyes.

"Singing Mermaid?"

"She's a big star."

"Oh, the Singing Mermaid."

"I knew it!" the skinny rat said triumphantly.

Laura was relieved to see Amanda returning; she seemed annoyed about something. The fat rat trailed after her, looking uncomfortable.

His greedy eyes gleaming, the skinny rat ran to meet him. "We dun hit the glory hole! That there is the Singin' Mermaid!"

"You sure?" asked the fat rat, imagining the reward they would get for delivering her.

"Little 'un told me."

Barely able to contain his glee, the fat rat called out to Amanda. "Stay right there. We'll git the waggin'." The two rats shambled off, talking excitedly,

"You look angry," said Laura.

"I can't wait to get out of here," Amanda said irritably. "They act like I'm a piece of cheese. What's got the skinny one so excited?"

"He kept talking about the Singing Mermaid."

"That fake," Amanda said dismissively.

"What fake?"

"The Singing Mermaid. She's no more mermaid than I am."

* * * *

Laura and Amanda rummaged around in the swamp, stuffing what they could salvage into their mud-splattered suitcases. By the time they finished they saw the wagon coming over the horizon, preceded by what looked like a large flow of whipped cream undulating over the ground.

"Well, whaddaya know."

It was the twelve thousand white mice the rats had bragged about, pulling a wagon piled high with gold nuggets. It rolled to a stop a few feet from Laura and Amanda. The mice looked at Amanda. Amanda looked at the mice, the same question in all their eyes. Could they pull the wagon with Amanda in it? There was only one way to find out. Amanda tossed their suitcases onto the wagon and climbed up to the buckboard. The wagon creaked ominously. The mice chittered nervously. The Desert Rats squeezed themselves in on either side of Amanda, the fat rat taking up the reins.

"Hey, what about me?" Laura cried.

"Don't you dare try to leave without her," warned Amanda.

"Okay, okay," grumbled the skinny rat. Climbing down from the wagon he boosted Laura up onto the gleaming cargo. Delighted, she scrambled to the top, feeling like the Little Princess on her throne of gold.

"Are you okay up there?" asked Amanda.

"Oh, yes." The gold felt soft and warm. "I can see everything."

The wagon rolled slowly over the cracked red clay. Laura enjoyed the view. Crowded between two grungy rats, Amanda fumed. The white mice huffed and puffed, barely making it to the top of a low ridge.

"Amanda!" Laura exclaimed from atop her golden throne, "I see the lights! It's the Club Galaxy!"

That's all Amanda was waiting for. Grabbing the reins from the fat rat, she knocked him off the wagon with her right fin. A bump of her left hip sent the skinny rat flying. "Hold on, Laura," she cried, urging the white mice on. "It's a downhill roll from here."

By the time the Desert Rats came to, Amanda, Laura and their luggage were far away and the mice had run off with the gold.

Chapter Seven

Club Galaxy

Laura and Amanda arrived at the grand entrance of the Club Galaxy weary, wilted and bedraggled. Amanda dragged herself up the broad marble steps but Laura hung back, staring owl-eyed at the spectacle of the lights. They twinkled, flared, danced, blinked, chased each other across the sky, turned all colors of the rainbow or shot off into space in sparkling streamers.

The lights were the defining symbol of the Club Galaxy and all it represented. They blazed away night and day, their brilliance so blinding you could only see the dazzle, not the source, giving rise to endless speculation about who or what they were and how it was they never dimmed. It was rumored they were actually alien beings disguised as lights, on the lam from a distant galaxy. Having found this one ripe for the plucking, they clustered together to form the Club, choosing to remain anonymous for tax purposes.

There were other rumors, some created by management, that added to the allure, the mystery, the hint of danger, attracting people whose lives were otherwise mundane, who came in droves to mingle with the demi-monde and revel in forbidden pleasures.

The Criminal Gazette had once sent a photographer with special equipment to capture the lights on film for a feature on *Illegal Aliens Who Made Good*. Neither the film nor the equipment nor the photographer was ever seen again.

Blazoned across the sky was the Club's motto:

THE CLUB GALAXY
WHERE EVERYONE'S A WINNER!
It's In The Cards!
You can bet on it!

Deliberately ignored by the greeters and doormen, Laura and Amanda trudged into the reception area and set down their battered suitcases. The gilt glare of the lobby with its faux crystal chandeliers contrasted jar-ringly with the vast room it opened into, which was drenched in diffuse, sedating light, and where every imag-inable species was engaged in some kind of fascinating game. Frenzied eruptions of glee from winners punctu-ated the otherwise dreamlike atmosphere. ServoRobots bustled about, satisfying every player's needs.

"I've got to get off my fins," Amanda complained, "they're killing me."

"Mine too," said Laura.

"You don't have fins."

"I have..." Laura searched for the right word, knowing there had to be one. "...empathy."

A fat, green toad about four feet tall hopped over to them. Taking in their muddy disarray with a disdainful glance, he sniffed officiously. "Have you reservations?"

"We didn't know we needed any," Laura said, disappointed.

Riff-raff, thought the toad, sneering. "We're booked solid. Everyone who's anyone knows there's a Wizards' Convention in town."

Amanda seized him by his bow tie, lifting him up to her eye level. "We're hot, thirsty and dirty."

"So I see," the toad croaked nervously, finding it difficult to stand on his dignity while dangling in midair.

"Listen, toad," Amanda warned. "I've had just about enough. First your crummy RocketBus crashes, almost killing us, then those slimy rats kidnap us and now we're being snubbed by a flunky. Get us a room, or else!"

The House Thugs, hired from Thugs and Thieves Unlimited to keep things peaceful, began to take notice. The gamblers paid no attention.

"Put me down," squeaked the terrified toad.

"We want a room!" Amanda bellowed, making the chandeliers tremble and the toad blanch gray.

The House Thugs began moving toward them. Some of the gamblers looked up, their eyes glazed from days of rhythmically pulling levers or watching little balls skip around on wheels. Nothing was forbidden at the Club Galaxy except distracting gamblers from their game.

The Floor Boss motioned to someone in the shadows.

Amanda found herself looking up into the eyes of the House Gorilla, the deepest, blackest, most adorable eyes she'd ever seen. It was love at first sight. Releasing the screeching toad, she turned passion purple and fainted dead away, flattening ten poker tables and ruining some mighty good hands.

The big gorilla stood transfixed. Looking down at Amanda as she lay there, her flowers drooping and her long lashes resting trustingly on her delicate purple cheeks, innocent as a babe among poker chips, he too was smitten. With one sweep of his mighty arm, he sent the House Thugs reeling. "Don't nobody touch her!" he boomed. Gathering his newly beloved in his arms, he slung her tail fins over his shoulder and carried her out to the courtyard.

In a flash, the recycle robots had the poker tables repaired and fresh hands dealt out. Except for a few disputes over who had which hand when Amanda landed on it, things returned to normal.

Standing there, dazed, his beloved in his arms, the big gorilla wasn't sure of what to do next.

"Maybe she needs water," Laura suggested.

"Huh?" He looked down, noticing Laura for the first time.

"She's a whale."

"Oh, yeah," he said snapping out of his daze. Carrying his darling to the pool, he dropped her in the deep end, creating a mini tidal wave which washed away the poolside chairs and their occupants.

Amanda opened her eyes, wondering if she was dreaming, but there he was, looking at her with love in his eyes. "I'm drowning," she cried, "Please, won't somebody save me?"

Jumping at the chance, the big gorilla leaped into the pool, feet first, cracking the bottom.

He's so clumsy, Amanda thought tenderly. "Thank you, Big Boy."

"How did you know my name was Big Boy?"

Amanda batted her long lashes. "What else could it be?"

"Are you hurt?" he asked, barely able to hear his own voice over the roar of his emotions.

"I don't think so," said Amanda. "Maybe you should give me a squeeze and see."

Laura had never seen Amanda act like this. "Are you okay?"

"I'm fine," Amanda said dreamily, draping herself half in and half out of the pool.

"You're acting funny."

"Big Boy," Amanda purred, making him quiver. "Do you think you could get us a room? Otherwise," she said, pouting prettily, "we'll just have to leave."

"Leave?" exclaimed Big Boy. "You can't leave. I'll get you a room no matter what," he promised. Unwilling to take his eyes off Amanda even for a moment, he backed into and through a plate glass wall. "I'll be right back."

"He's so sweet," Amanda sighed.

"I hope I don't act silly when I grow up."

"You will, if you're lucky."

A few minutes later, Big Boy returned, beaming. Laura noticed the way Amanda's face lit up when she saw him. "Look at that smile," Amanda said blissfully. "He's everything I've ever wanted."

"Like Pinocchio and Contentment?"

Amanda laughed. "Something like that, only better."

Laura could see how much Amanda and Big Boy liked each other. Maybe he could help them find her father.

"Big Boy," Amanda said sweetly, "were you able to get us a room?"

"I bent the truth a little," he told her, brushing the few remaining shards of glass from his shoulders.

"What does it mean, bent the truth?" asked Laura.

"The Club is full because of the Wizard's Convention so I told the Boss you were a sister act the agency sent."

"A sister act! Big Boy, look at us," Amanda sputtered.

"I didn't say you were twins."

Laura giggled.

"Oh, Big Boy," Amanda cooed, "you think of everything."

"We're kind of like sisters," said Laura.

"Even better than sisters," said Amanda, giving her a hug.

"Then it's okay?" asked Big Boy.

"It's wonderful," Amanda sighed.

"I guess I'd better take you to your room," said Big Boy. "Then the boss wants to meet you."

"We'd better clean up first," said Amanda, taking him by the arm. "Besides, we need time to figure out what to do about an act."

* * * *

The Wizard's Convention, a yearly catastrophe that befell the Club Galaxy, was in full swing. There was no point in barring the Wizards; they would just show up disguised as something else and cause even more trouble. Better to allow the Convention to take place openly, making it easier for management to keep tabs on them and make use of their talents. It was rumored that management was learning sorcery, for what purpose it could only be guessed, possibly to keep one step ahead of the Light Family who supposedly owned it all.

Clean, but not rested, Laura and Amanda passed through the main gaming parlor on their way to meet management. Big Boy ran interference, protecting them from the inebriated Wizards who'd gotten out of hand, turning themselves into flying carpets, weaving drunkenly over the heads of the crowd, dipping down to steal poker chips, throwing cards in the air, shrieking with laughter, bumping into each other, collapsing over the dealers and dragging them to the floor.

An organized band of fuzzy, sticky Sleaze Balls took this opportunity to roll over the gaming tables, picking up all the chips and rolling out the door before the dealers could summon the House Thugs. Working in tandem with the Wizards, the Sleaze Balls handed over the loot to them in a back alley, settling for a small percentage of the take. Since everyone knew the Sleaze Balls had stolen the chips they had to work with the Wizards to get the chips cashed in.

Management knew all about this arrangement. The Wizard's drinks had been laced with scanners so tiny they could enter the blood stream and swim up to the Wizard's eyes, allowing management to keep an eye on things.

* * * *

The solid gold door of the secret elevator was weighty and impressive. Management had picked up the elevator, door and all, at a fire sale when a very exclusive store, *We're Too Good For You*, had gone out of business, having been too good for its own good.

Management loved a bargain but like many bargains this one had hidden costs. The elevator refused to acknowledge its reduced circumstances, haughtily clinging to its former ways. It particularly resented the tacky piece of tape bearing the words "The Boss" that someone had pasted over the executive suite button. The elevator had been trying to work it loose for some time.

* * * *

The elevator door whispered shut behind Laura, Amanda and Big Boy. "Destination please," said the elevator in a condescending *We're-Too-Good-For-You* manner.

"The Boss," Big Boy said, smiling fondly at Amanda, her fin clasped in his hand.

"What department would that be, sir?" the elevator asked haughtily.

"Whaddaya mean department? We want the Boss."

"Is he in lingerie?" the elevator asked archly.

"Lingerie? What kind of question is that?" asked Big Boy, glowering at the control panel. "Quit asking questions and take us up to the Boss."

"I'm sorry, sir," said the elevator in a tone that made it clear it was not. "You must give me the correct department. This is a very large store."

"This ain't no store," Big Boy said angrily. "It's the Club Galaxy."

"You must be mistaken," the elevator said prissily. "I would never work in a place like that."

Laura noticed the piece of tape over the elevator's top button was coming loose. Reaching up, she pulled at it. "Thank you," the elevator said, beginning to ascend. "I'm glad someone finally had the sense to do that."

"I'd like to punch its lights out," growled Big Boy.

"It's okay, Big Boy, it's only an elevator," said Amanda, patting his hand comfortingly. "It's not very bright." The elevator blinked irately and turned off its lights.

When they reached the top floor, the elevator door banged open emphatically. Laura passed through without any trouble but both Amanda and Big Boy tripped over something.

"Thank you for shopping at We're *Too Good For You*," the elevator said sweetly. "I hope you had a pleasant ...*Trip*." Snicker, snicker. The door slammed shut.

* * * *

While Amanda tried to calm Big Boy, Laura wandered down the hallway, stopping in front of a door marked General Management. She looked for a knob or a handle, but there wasn't any. "That's funny," she said to herself.

"Thank you," replied the door.

"Oh!" Laura said, startled.

Management had found the door discarded in a theater alley. After weeks of rehearsal, the comedy it was in had bombed on opening night, traumatizing the door which kept going over and over the lines of the play, which weren't too good to begin with, making a hodgepodge of them in the original actors' voices.

"You may now applaud," said the door.

"Applaud?"

"Thank you. Thank you," gushed the door. "Now say knock, knock."

Laura was puzzled. "Knock? Knock?"

"Who's there? I don't care," giggled the door. "Say knock knock."

"If I do, will you let me in?"

"Jeeves, open this door!" ordered the door in a deep baritone.

Laura wondered, was there was someone behind the door or pretending to be the door? What would happen if she did knock on it?

"That tickles," giggled the door. "It's the maid's day off. Tennis anyone?" it twaddled.

Amanda and Big Boy joined Laura at the door. "It won't open," she explained.

"This happens all the time," said Big Boy.

"The play must go on," declared the door.

"Stand back," Big Boy warned. "It's stuck in scene II where a troupe of acrobats break down the door and rescue the heroine from the mad scientist."

"Big Boy, what are you talking about?" asked Amanda.

"We have to break in," he explained, pushing against the door until the hinges creaked.

"Say knock knock," it grunted, refusing to budge.

"Let me help, darling," said Amanda, stepping between Big Boy and the door, giving it a shot with her hip. The door flew open. "Oh, Big Boy," she cooed, "you're so strong."

* * * *

Management's office was a riot of gizmos, thingamajigs, whatchamacallits and whirligigs — things that wiggled, things that twirled, things that danced, that played music, that popped up and down. Laura was all agog. There were balls, skates, marbles, musical instruments, jump ropes, toy cars, dolls, a magic wand (how it glittered!). Seated on the floor, in the midst of it all, was an egg-shaped man in military regalia festooned with ribbons, medals and gold braid playing with an elaborate set of trains. "Be right with you, Big Boy," he said, not looking up. "This is a tricky curve comin' up."

"Boss, you gotta do something about that door; it's getting crazier and crazier. And the elevator's turning mean."

"Don't take it personal," said the Boss, watching the train come out of the tunnel and chug into the station. "There, that does it," he said, getting to his feet. He was only a little taller than Laura. "How do you do, ladies," he greeted them, tipping his cap. "The name's Management, General Management. Call me Gen." His eyes twinkled as blinking lights on his cap spelled out his name. He reminded Laura of someone she'd seen in a picture book.

"Big Boy, who are these ladies?"

"This is the sister act I told you about."

"Sister act?" Gen looked at Big Boy in disbelief.

"It's not Big Boy's fault," said Amanda. "I talked him into it. We needed a room."

"We had an accident," said Laura. "We nearly got killed."

"Gee, kid," Gen said, concerned, "are you okay? I'll call the house doc."

"I'm okay, Mr. Gen."

"I got a kid about your age; if anything happened to her it'd kill me. Big Boy, did you notify her folks?"

"It's okay," Amanda said quickly. "I'm taking care of her."

"Sure, sure, but I'm a father. Her daddy'll be real worried."

"My father died," Laura explained. "We're looking for him."

"Oh." Gen looked at Amanda questioningly. "How about her mother?"

"She's too busy." Laura said, feeling uncomfortable.

Gen put his arm around Laura, a soft look in his eyes, "Kid, would you like a gizmo?" Laura couldn't help glancing over at the magic wand. It was encrusted with gold glitter and had a large gold star at the tip. "The magic wand!" Gen exclaimed. "You picked the best thing in the joint!" He handed it to her with a flourish.

"Do I get to keep it?"

"It's yours."

"What if your daughter wants it?"

"Nah, she never looked at it," he said wistfully. "Anyway, she's not here anymore."

"Amanda and I could look for her," Laura offered.

"Thanks, kid, but I know where she is. She's with her mother and the Holier-Than-Thous. Her mother said this was no place for a kid. Can you imagine?" he asked, gesturing at all the toys.

"But this is a wonderful place," said Laura.

"You think so?" Gen asked, brightening.

"Oh, yes!"

"Wanna play trains, kid?"

"Yes, what do we do?"

"You never played with trains before?" Gen asked, astonished.

"My father gave me lots of books and a Pinocchio puppet that flies."

"You like books?"

"Especially the books with the golden edges. I used to read them with my father and make up stories."

"Sounds nice," Gen said softly.

"When I see him again I'm going to have lots of stories to tell him about the places I've been," she said waving her magic wand authoritatively.

"I bet you will," Gen said, smiling. "So," he said, turning to Amanda. "What made you pick the Club Galaxy?"

Amanda laughed. "It was Laura's idea. She read about it in the Criminal Gazette."

"Criminal Gazette?"

"It had lots of new words and things," Laura explained.

"I can imagine. Kid, I'm gonna make sure you have a terrific time here. Anythin' special you wanna see?"

"A sugar daddy and showgirls covered with diamonds."

Gen laughed. "They're a dime a dozen around here."

Dime a dozen? Laura wished she hadn't left her magic notebook in their room.

"Come on, kid, let's play trains." But before they could get started they heard loud voices coming from the adjoining office. A man and a woman were arguing. "Aw, nuts," Gen groaned. "Head Light and his Ma are at it again."

"Head Light and his Ma?" Amanda wondered if she'd heard right.

"They own the joint," Big Boy explained. "Boss, what are we gonna tell them about the sister act?"

"I'll figure somethin'," said Gen, rummaging around in his desk. He came up with an assortment of dark glasses. "Here, you're gonna need these."

The door to the adjoining office flew open. An explosion of light blasted the room.

"Don't let 'em throw you, kid," Gen said protectively.

The Lights swept in. "Peons! Ruffians!" hissed Ma Light.

"Gen, I swear, this time I'm going to fire you," sizzled Head Light.

"Now what'sa matter?"

"Have you seen what the Wizards are doing to the Club?" Head Light asked, arcing angrily.

"How dare they behave in such a manner," Ma Light flared indignantly. "Why aren't you out there seeing what they're up to? They're destroying the place."

"Don't flip your switch," Gen said unimpressed. "I got

the scanners working. It's all on tape."

"Who's going to pay for all the damage?" asked Head Light. "Don't forget, Weasel and Crooks cancelled our insurance after last year's debacle."

"Gimme credit for some brains," said Gen. "With all the extra charges we buried in the fine print, the Wizards are payin' through the nose. Even after the cleanup we'll come out way ahead."

Paying through the nose? Laura wondered, yawning. It was hard to imagine such a thing.

"But the benefit's only a week away," said Head Light. "Can we get ready in time?"

"Just leave it to me," said Gen.

"Who are these creatures?" Ma Light asked suspiciously, glaring at Laura and Amanda.

"The talent agency sent 'em."

"For what purpose?"

"For the benefit."

"Oh, for the benefit," said Ma Light, softening to a glow. The benefit was to be the social event of the century and the apex of her career. She'd called in a lot of I.O.U.s for this one. "And what exactly do they do?" she asked benignly.

"We're a sister act," said Laura, waving her magic wand.

Ma Light's glow turned red. "Do you take me for a fool?"

"They're not even the same species!" snapped Head Light.

"Right you are," said Gen. "They're a novelty act. The agency sent 'em for free in honor of the occasion."

"In honor of the occasion..." Ma Light glowed warmly, feeling her position in Society was finally being recognized.

"What does this novelty act consist of?" Head Light asked suspiciously.

"I don't wanna spoil the surprise," said Gen. "It'll knock your socks off."

Knock your socks off? Laura yawned a double yawn.

"You're sure the Club will be ready?" asked Head Light.

"What did I tell you? Of course it'll be ready," said Gen.

"It better be," warned Head Light. And with that, the Lights dimmed and went out.

Big Boy gave a sigh of relief. "That was quick thinking, Boss."

"Anything to do with the benefit and Ma gets soft as the felt on a craps table."

"What's the big deal about this benefit?" asked Amanda.

"Ma's a social climber, big time," Gen explained. "Every gamblin' joint in the universe wants to host the benefit. You get your picture taken hob-nobbin' with celebrities, politicos and such. The famous columnist, Smugly

Simp, writes it up in his *High Life Among The Low Life* column in the Criminal Gazette. Even high-class citizens try to crash this bash."

"Oh," said Amanda. "What's it a benefit for?

"It's like this. Every so often them that's made it in the rackets puts on a benefit to raise moola for them that ain't, meanin' the poor slugs in the slammer who ain't got the do-re-mi to pay enough lawyers to get 'em what they call the benefit of the doubt."

"That's why they call it Benefit of the Doubt," Big Boy explained.

"Benefit of the Doubt!" Amanda hooted.

Do-re-mi, slugs in the slammer, moola, benefit of the doubt. Overstuffed with phrases, Laura was getting sleepier by the moment.

"And we're supposed to perform at this shindig," Amanda said dryly.

"Listen," said Gen, "with all the showin' off them mugs and molls do, and the roulette wheels and slots, nobody'll pay attention to your act."

"That's good," said Amanda, "because we haven't got one."

Pushing a pile of cushions aside, Laura climbed into the lap of a giant stuffed panda.

"Don't worry," said Gen. "With a few spotlights on you and some fancy duds you'll do fine. Do a little shuffle, warble a few bars, or whatever."

"I can help," Big Boy said eagerly. "I can juggle." Amanda gave him a peck on the cheek.

"I'll even hire some stooges from *Anything For A Buck*," said Gen. "They'll hoot and holler and applaud so loud even you'll think you're hot stuff."

"Laura knows a whole poem, *Trees*," said Amanda, "and I can sing underwater. If you don't mind flooding the place."

"That's the spirit," said Gen.

"Well, we've got our work cut out for us," said Amanda. "We better to get to our room before we fall asleep on our feet. In fact," she added, glancing over at Laura, "I think one of us is already asleep."

"Let me carry her," Gen whispered.

"You don't have to carry me," Laura murmured.

"I'd like to," said Gen. "Up we go."

"I'll get the elevator," said Big Boy.

"Not necessary," said Gen. "They're gettin' the penthouse suite."

"You don't have to do that," said Amanda.

"Sure I do. She's collectin' stories about places to tell her father," said Gen, leading the procession down the hall. "I'm gonna make sure her Club Galaxy story is the best."

"What's do-re-mi?" Laura asked sleepily.

"Money," Amanda whispered.

"Oh," Laura said dreamily. "Tastes cinnamony."

They stopped at the impressive double doors of the penthouse suite. "Goodnight, kid," said Gen, handing her over to Amanda.

"Night, Humpty," Laura said softly.

"Humpty?"

"In a picture book. He looked like you," Laura said, stretching.

"Did you like him?"

"Oh, yes, he made me laugh. Could I give you a kiss goodnight?"

Gen's face lit up like the marquee of the Club Galaxy. "Plant one on me," he said, offering his cheek.

* * * *

'Humpty', thought Gen, heading back to his office. What a kid. He touched his cheek where she'd kissed him. "Humpty," he said out loud.

When his wife took off with their kid, he'd felt real low, like he'd failed as a father, but now he didn't feel that way. He felt okay.

Chapter Eight

The Benefit Of The Doubt

The Lights outshone themselves, inviting even the dimmest family members, some not seen for centuries, ferreting out every Light hidden under a bushel, reaching into dark corners, alleys and byways to find them. And they came, from all across the cosmos, faster than the speed of light, illuminating a vast area around the Club Galaxy.

A royal family crest, acquired by Ma Light in a mysterious transaction just a week before, blazed over the entrance. She'd had the crest embroidered on everything in sight.

In honor of the occasion, well-known art forgers who usually applied fake grime of time to the palpably new, worked against the grain, restoring faded gilt to fresh brilliance and removing the authentic dust of centuries from walls, furnishings and art.

Over the objections of Gen and Head Light, Ma Light

had the gaming tables removed from the grand ballroom, replacing them with elegant pink marble tea tables and plush red velvet chairs, obtained at great expense from those who made it their business to supply such things, no questions asked.

* * * *

Gen had taken on the role of stage manager for which he had no aptitude. Finding that his decisions mostly had the effect of rending asunder rather than unifying the production, he turned the job over to the chorines and musicians who at least knew the difference between a pool cue and a baton.

He found his niche as propmaster. A lover of bargains, gimcrackery and gizmos, he enjoyed going down into the storage basement where everything from old scenery to musical instruments to disarmed hand grenades and stink bombs left over from a more boisterous time in the Club's history, gathered dust. He would wander around putting this and that in a large basket he'd found. One day his eye was drawn to an odd shape under a pile of old drapes. Shoving the drapes aside, he discovered a pair of angel's wings. He couldn't imagine what use the Club would've had for them but he knew they would be right for Laura. Not far from the wings he noticed a small harp leaning against the wall. It still had four strings. With a little gold paint and some distance it might do. As an afterthought, he took a few stink bombs and grenades, telling himself they were for Big Boy to juggle, but underneath he knew it was really for old time's sake.

* * * *

The chorines had taken Laura under their wing, calling her "little gypsy." Laura knew about gypsies from the books with the golden edges, but not that dancers were also called gypsies. They helped her with her costume, working in oodles of sequins, rhinestones, spangles, bangles, feathers and glitter from Hot Goods Haven. "More glitter, jewels and sequins, please," Laura said, pointing with her magic wand. The chorines laughingly complied, pretending these appeared like magic, shaken from her wand.

* * * *

Outside, it was a mob scene. Fireworks sprouted in the sky like night-blooming flowers; blaring horns signaled the impatience of incoming guests. Limmo-Rockets were piling up as harried attendants checked every invitation for authenticity. Ma Light was very fussy about who got to attend her benefit. Some of those on her guest list were so hoity-toity they would ordinarily consider time spent at the Club as slumming.

Mugs, molls, politicos, celebrities and the ruthlessly rich poured in from known and unknown places, dressed to kill, in some cases, literally, keeping the hatcheck chicks busy pecking through the cloakroom looking for concealed weapons.

Rare carpets, unintentionally on loan from the best museums, were unfurled. A leftover wizard, disguised as a carpet, amused himself by pulling the rug out from under guests.

The blasting horns, glaring lights and shouting guests contributed to the air of excitement. Anticipating her impending triumph, Ma Light basked in her own glow, a glow only slightly diminished by the last minute cancellation of her arch rival, Palmyra Loveseat. Palmyra had always made Ma Light feel a little déclassé, as if she were

the one living in squalor, though how Palmyra managed
to do this, when her own betting parlor was located next
to the Universal Dump, was something Ma Light could
never quite figure out. She had so been looking forward to
showing Palmyra what a classy benefit she could put on.
It irked her to think Palmyra might be thumbing her nose
at the whole affair.

                              * * * *

     Inside, tension mounted. Many of the mugs felt un-
easy about mingling, unarmed, with others of their pro-
fession. However, to not attend the benefit labeled you a
loser, or even worse, a chump, not to mention how angry
it would make your moll.

     New champagne in old bottles, the most authentic
bottles her bootlegger could find, waited impatiently in
sterling silver ice-buckets. Being of youthful vintage and
very bubbly, some of them popped their corks and giggled
all over passersby.

     While sullen male guests stood around trussed up in
their tuxedos, their female companions acted as if the
Benefit were a debutante ball. Taking the opportunity to
show off their finery and status, they fluttered from table
to table like Birds of Paradise, checking out each other's
plumage, ages, figures and carat value. The losers in this
unacknowledged contest retreated with ruffled feathers,
forming little cliques to peck away at the winners until
they'd reduced them to a rag, a bone and a hank of hair
(dyed of course).

     With the gaming rooms off limits to them till after the
benefit, bored male guests wandered over to the tables
laden with booty to be auctioned off for the benefit of the
slugs in the slammer. A few of the ruthlessly rich recognized items they didn't recall donating. Notoriously un-

willing to part with items of monetary value, they began
to view their fellow guests with some suspicion. Restless
pickpockets, fences and switch-artists amused themselves by testing security, pocketing items they fancied,
mostly gems, checking their authenticity by scratching
them against glass or viewing them through a jeweler's
loupe.

These activities met with the disapproval of their
ladies, other guests, and the House Thugs, who felt such
behavior was antithetical to the spirit of the Benefit,
which promoted honor among thieves, at least for a night.
The only thing that kept the mugs from bolting the Benefit of the Doubt for the benefit of the gaming rooms was
fear of retribution from their molls.

In the midst of all the color and glitter, standing out
like a patch of desert in a tropical forest, was a cluster of
khaki-clad stooges hired to cheer Laura's and Amanda's
act. Gen groaned when he saw them. Across the back of
their jackets were the words *Anything for a Buck*, making
it impossible to palm them off as guests.

* * * *

Backstage, Laura peeked out from behind the curtain, on the lookout for the promised "showgirls covered
in diamonds." She'd been assured the place would be
overrun with them, though once covered in diamonds,
they no longer thought of themselves as showgirls. Laura
overheard one chorine say diamonds were a girl's best
friend, but she couldn't imagine diamonds replacing
Amanda.

Amanda wore a slinky, white, sequined gown that
closely matched her own color; from a distance it looked
like she wasn't wearing anything but sequins. She prac-
ticed walking and talking like someone she'd seen in a

movie. "Come up and see me sometime, Big Boy," she murmured huskily, batting her long lashes. Between ogling Amanda and keeping a jealous watch over any guy who tried to get near her, Big Boy kept dropping whatever he was juggling. If anyone gets fresh, he thought fiercely, I'll slug 'em!

"Big Boy, pay attention to what you're doin'," said Gen. "Them grenades might not all be duds."

"Sorry, Boss, I'm not real good at this. Besides they're sticky; the paint ain't dry yet."

Gen had dipped the grenades and stink bombs in bright colored paint so they'd look more cheerful. "The paint cans said quick-dryin'."

"Maybe you should juggle one at a time," suggested Amanda.

"Never saw anyone juggle less than three," said Gen. "I thought there was some kinda rule."

"Big Boy, when are you getting into your costume?" asked Amanda. She'd heard a lot of buzz about it backstage.

"I don't see why I can't wear my regular clothes."

"Showbiz is illusion," said Amanda.

"But...."

"Won't you wear it just for me?"

* * * *

Laura was delighted with the wings Gen had found.

They looked great with her favorite, cloud-white dress, the one her father made. Gen had even improvised a halo out of scraps of wire painted gold. With her halo and her wings and her magic wand at the ready, she couldn't resist admiring herself in every mirror she passed.

* * * *

"Come on out, Big Boy," coaxed Amanda. Big Boy was hiding behind some crates, self-conscious about his costume. He was dressed as the romantic buccaneer of all her seafaring dreams complete with red satin tights, wide black leather belt with brass buckle, bare chest, purple cape and jaunty hat with a large feather. "Oooo, Big Boy," cooed Amanda, "you're gorgeous!" She wasn't the only one who thought so. Taking firm possession of her buccaneer, she steered him out of chorine range.

* * * *

"I've always wanted to sing opera," said Amanda, taking a breath so deep it challenged the seams of her gown. "I've been told I have the lungs for it."

"Opera!" Gen gasped. "Those mugs won't sit still for opera."

"Talk to my agent," Amanda said airily.

"If she wants to sing opera, she gets to sing opera," Big Boy said firmly. "Anyone don't like it can deal with me."

"Okay, okay. Sing opera," Gen said, unconvinced. "Know any short arias?"

"All my arias are short."

Gen had the sinking feeling he was going to wish he'd paid for a better grade of stooge, and more of them.

"I can play the harp," said Laura. The first violinist of the house orchestra had strung it for her. She had taught herself to play by letting her hands talk with each other on the strings. Sometimes they were playful or teasing, sometimes they argued, their music clashing, sometimes one went silent as though hiding while the other searched the strings, sometimes they made a whispery, private music full of secrets.

"I thought you were gonna fly," said Gen. Against his better judgement, he'd gone along with the routine Laura and Amanda had worked out. Dressed as an angel, Laura was going to recite *Trees* while dangling in mid-air from a pair of Big Boy's hot pink suspenders, the ends of which he was to keep clamped in his teeth. Since he had no spoken lines this made a certain amount of sense, if sense was the word, which Gen doubted.

"I can play my harp and fly at the same time," said Laura, pirouetting to make her wings flutter.

"Our little gypsy angel," a voice called out from up in the flies.

* * * *

Gen strutted around backstage in his costume, fishing for compliments. "So, whaddaya think?" He was especially proud of his red, drum major's hat with gold tassels.

"Oh, Humpty!" Laura squealed, using her nickname for him, "You're like the circus!"

"That jacket's great. Parakeet yellow is very in," said Amanda. "And those peacock-blue tights, well, what can I say?"

"What about it, Big Boy?" Gen asked.

"You look like an Easter egg."

"Get a look at this." Gen pressed a secret button on his jacket. Rainbow colored lights spelled out HUMPTY across his chest. "Pretty neat, huh?"

"Places, everyone," someone called out. The show was about to begin.

THE PERFORMANCE

As the Dancing Flamingos went into their routine, Marvello, the MC, cowered in the wings. Of all the gigs he'd ever had this one looked like it was going to be the worst. Warming up this crowd was going to be tougher than breaking into Fort Knox with a butter knife. What a time for his regular old gypsy to be out sick. Better make sure her replacement told only happy fortunes; put the crowd in a better mood. Marvello felt sorry for the Gorgeous Sisters who were on next. He wondered if they were the same two sisters he remembered from the old days. He'd heard they'd made it in the big time. Maybe they could use him in their act. He'd go backstage after the show and get chummy with them.

Ma Light's grandkids, the Flashes, had been increasing the tension by popping off in people's faces, temporarily blinding folks who were up tight at being in each other's company to begin with, especially unarmed. The popping of champagne corks sounded too much like gunfire for comfort, making everyone even jumpier and Marvello's job harder.

The Dancing Flamingos wound up their routine to grudging applause. "Hey," Marvello cried, bounding out of the wings, "can those flamingos flamenco, or what?" Nothing. "Anybody out there?" he joked nervously, motioning for the replacement gypsy to go into the mind-reading act. There was something odd about her but at least she'd been a quick study, maybe too quick. She'd learned the routine so fast it made him wonder if maybe she really could read minds.

Crossing his fingers, he reminded himself the mind reading act usually put even the toughest audience in his pocket, though he wasn't sure he wanted this audience anywhere near his pockets.

The old gypsy held her gnarled right hand over the head of a beautiful blond. With her left hand she pointed at Marvello. He found himself speaking the blond's thoughts. "Some sugar daddy. The cheapskate. Look at the rocks on that dame over there." The blond gasped. So did Marvello. There was an uncomfortable stir. The blond's companion glowered menacingly. "Just kidding, just kidding," Marvello said nervously.

What was going on? Was he actually reading people's minds? Nothing like this had ever happened before. He watched apprehensively as the old gypsy moved her hand in a circle over the heads of some surly thugs who were glaring at some other surly thugs. Marvello flinched as she pointed to him. Once again he found himself speaking the thoughts of others, only this time he was saying some really outrageous things. Furious, the thugs attacked each other, armed with whatever was available — champagne bottles, long stemmed glasses, finger bowls and such. It would have turned into a riot if it hadn't been for the ear splitting clamor of sirens, bells, whistles and gongs piped in from the main casino, announcing a big winner. Saved by the bell, thought Marvello, fleeing the stage. Gen caught him by the tails of his tux as he rushed past. "If you ever wanna work again get out there and do your job. And cut out the mind-reading!"

Like a lamb to the slaughter, Marvello went back out on stage as a squad of cops burst in. Many of the guests jumped to their feet, looking to make a quick exit.

"Don't panic, ladies and gents," the Police Chief bellowed over his bullhorn. "This is not a raid, I repeat, not a raid." Some of the guests returned to their seats. "I'm sure you'd like to meet some of the poor slobs the Benefit's for. This way they can thank you proper." A motley bunch of mugs in striped uniforms shuffled in, chained hand and foot, some looking mean, some looking mortified. "Say thank you to the nice people," ordered the Chief. "Thank you," mumbled a chorus of disgruntled voices. Many of the guests squirmed in their seats, realizing that there but for the grace of — access to expensive legal brains — went they.

The criminals in stripes were seated on the floor directly below the stage upon which Marvello stood, trembling. They glared up at him. "Go ahead," growled one of them, "entertain us."

Magic, I'll do some magic, Marvello thought desperately. The criminal mind was childlike, right? "How would you guys like to see some magic?"

"Sure," cracked one of the striped ones. "Make the cops disappear."

That got the laugh of the night. "Next thing you'll want the cuffs to disappear," joked Marvello, trying to get something going. No dice. "Moving right along, fellas, ladies, cops, you're gonna love this next act, the Gorgeous Sisters!" A ripple of interest went through the audience. "Two gorgeous dames, double the talent, double everything. They dance, they juggle, they sing, they..."

"Quit talkin' and bring on the dames!" A barrage of

spit-balls, wadded up napkins and champagne corks pelted Marvello. The criminals rattled their chains rhythmically. "Bring on the dames! Bring on the dames!"

"Fellas, the Sisters!" shouted Marvello, running for his life.

* * * *

The conductor pressed a button; the house orchestra rose from the pit on a platform the shape of a grand piano. Usually limited to providing background music for gambling, this was the orchestra's night to shine. Determined to milk the opportunity for all it was worth, they began a seemingly endless pastiche of show tunes, playing louder every time the audience shouted for the Sisters.

Where were the Sisters?

At the last minute Amanda had noticed paint splatters on the front of her gown, probably from Big Boy's juggling. One of the chorines loaned her a large feathered fan to cover the spots. Dropping his third grenade for the tenth time, Big Boy decided to juggle only two objects, one grenade and one stink bomb. The old gypsy from Marvello's act was sorting through the prop basket. Gen dashed about seeing to last minute details. Although he continued to have misgivings about Laura flying through the air from pink suspenders, he tried to help hook her up to them. The old gypsy took over, shooing him away.

Running out of show tunes, the house orchestra dug deeper into the dregs of its repertoire, launching into elevator music — syrupy strings dripping globs of honeyed notes. "Cruel and unusual punishment!" protested one of the prisoners. "Dis is unconstitutional!" shouted another. They began throwing things at the orchestra.

Without missing a beat, the conductor pressed a button, lowering the orchestra out of the line of fire. Showing no mercy, the orchestra piled fortissimo on fortissimo, crescendo upon crescendo.

Gen rushed out to calm things down. Even the hired stooges were booing. "You guys ain't gonna get paid," he hissed. "You couldn't pay us enough to root for this," they hissed back.

Tired of waiting for the Gorgeous Sisters, some of the thugs in tux began amusing themselves by shaking unopened bottles of champagne until they were ready to explode, aiming them at anyone within range. Gen signaled the orchestra to put a lid on it. A final bravura burst of sugary sound rang out, and the curtain went up.

Expecting the Gorgeous Sisters, the audience was stunned to see a giant gorilla in red satin tights, purple cape and feathered hat fidgeting with two colorful, vaguely familiar objects, passing them from one hand to the other like hot potatoes. Next to him stood a great white whale who appeared to be wearing nothing but sequins and a large fan. The gorilla's jaws were firmly clamped on a pair of hot pink suspenders from which a red haired child with a halo and sagging wings dangled. She was clutching a small harp and kicking her legs vigorously to maintain momentum as she swung through the air like a pendulum without a clock.

The spell was broken by the Police Chief. "Ain't you guys got a sense of humor?"

Motioning to Laura, who was to accompany her on her harp, Amanda took a deep breath and began her vocal exercises. But she was so nervous she started an octave too high. By the time she realized this she was afraid to turn back. Giving it her all, she cracked everything glass within ear shot — windows, mirrors, wine glasses, chandeliers, champagne bottles, jeweler's loupes, and a number of supposedly genuine gems.

"These ain't the Gorgeous Sisters! We want the Sisters!"

Flustered, Laura had jumped her cue, launching into her recitation of *Trees* while Amanda was still breaking glass. More preoccupied with Amanda than his act, Big Boy dropped one of the objects he was juggling. It landed with a thud and rolled off the stage toward a burly bodyguard who knew a grenade when he saw one, no matter how colorful. Reaching into the prop basket the old gypsy found a replacement and tossed it up to Big Boy. Some of the guests ducked under the tables.

Well into the final verses, Laura was pumping her legs so energetically one of her shoes flew off and hit a cop on the nose. Her other shoe hit one of the ubiquitous blondes, knocking off her wig which fell into her salad, revealing that She was a He, an undercover cop with his badge tattooed on his bald head. "Behave yourselves, everybody," he shouted. "Remember, we got the guns." That cooled things down to a smolder.

Amanda could tell that her singing wasn't going over very well so she decided to try something she'd seen in movies — a striptease, a few sequins at a time. Her routine elicited a chorus of wolf whistles. Big Boy cried out in protest, the pink suspenders popping out of his mouth, leaving Laura in free fall, unsuspendered. The old gypsy raised her hands as if to catch her, at which, Laura's wings billowed out, releasing a shower of gems and easing her down in a cascade of glitter.

For a finale Amanda tossed handfuls of fake jewelry into the audience.

"Don't nobody touch them rocks!" warned Big Boy.

Amanda held Big Boy back, "It means they like me," she explained.

"I don't want them to like you."

"Bring on the Sisters or we'll wreck the joint!"

The Lights flickered nervously. Wrecking the joint was not part of the planned festivities.

"Bring on the Gorgeous Sisters! This joke is getting old!"

Joke? What did they mean? Amanda drew herself up. "We *are* the Gorgeous Sisters!" she bellowed, gathering Laura close.

This was the last straw. They'd been played for chumps and now the perpetrators were trying to intimidate them. It was against the criminal code!

Concerned, Gen rushed onstage. He knew all about the criminal code and it didn't apply to jokes.

The old gypsy stood by the prop basket, unperturbed, as a stink bomb exploded in the audience, creating a stench so revolting it disabled everyone within smelling distance. It had never occurred to anyone to bring a gas mask to a benefit. Gen was surprised the stink bombs still had any stink; he'd assumed they were all duds. Reaching into the prop basket he came up with some round red objects he didn't recognize. They were neither stink bombs nor grenades. Shrugging, he tossed a couple up to Big Boy and grabbed a few for himself.

Reeling and gagging, their noses running, their eyes streaming, a few of the hardier mugs staggered through the stink cloud, knocking over people and furniture in an attempt to storm the stage.

Gen tossed a couple of round red things their way. They exploded right where they'd do the most good, releasing poufs of thick red smoke that engulfed the attackers. Some of the noises coming from inside the red cloud began to sound like giggles, as if the mugs were being tickled.

Howls of outrage came from the vacinity of the auction merchandise where some of the ruthlessly rich and a few crooked connoisseurs were trying to take advantage of the confusion and help themselves to a few trinkets, only to find them too hot to handle. Lobbing in a few of the red smoke bombs for good measure, Gen turned their howls of outrage into gales of laughter.

"Tickle bombs!" Laura exclaimed, delighted.

One obnoxious mug made a grab for Amanda's fan. Big Boy knocked him into the middle of next week.

Tickle bombs were going off everywhere. In the smoke and confusion they almost seemed to be flying out of the basket by themselves.

Gen was astonished to hear Ma Light laughing at the wreckage of her Benefit. "Woe is me. Woe is me. I'm ruined," she giggled. "I'll have to hide myself under a b-b-bushel!"

People wandered around in the red haze slapping each other on the back, their titters growing into chuckles, their chuckles into giggles, giggles into guffaws into gales of laughter. Mirth stricken guests rolled around on the floor, holding their stomachs, helpless with laughter.

Mysteriously unaffected by the tickle bombs, Laura, Gen, Amanda and Big Boy looked out over the spectacle with relief and disbelief. Catching something out of the corner of his eye, Gen glanced over at the old gypsy, startled by what seemed to be the shadow of a horse slipping out of the prop basket.

"We must have a guardian angel," Amanda marveled.

"Guardian gypsy, you mean," Gen muttered, not knowing what to think.

Part Two

Chapter Nine

A Raw, Fierce Happiness

In the starry dark a wagon waits with two fiery red horses in gold harness stamping and snorting impatiently.

"Where have you been?" they whinny to the old gypsy. "We must reach the encampment by daybreak."

"Have patience, my dears. I have found a treasure worth the waiting."

Laura and her friends watch in amazement as the old gypsy sheds her cloak and with it her ancient appearance, becoming young and beautiful. Her gnarled hands are soft and supple with life, her face glows with health and good humor. Her eyes are bright black, filled with starlight; her long, black hair ensnares the moon.

"You have found her, Magdalena!" exclaims the mighty stallion.

"This very night, as I knew I would."

"As told by the Ancient Ones," says the magnificent red mare, tears of joy in her soft, black eyes.

"Just so," the gypsy says softly. "Come, child, we must leave at once if we are to get there before sunrise."

Laura is silent for a moment.

> *Trust yourself*
> *and your companions*
> *and the goodness of the universe.*

"Can my friends come too?"

"Amanda and Big Boy, yes."

"Why can't Humpty?"

"His destiny lies elsewhere."

"She's right," Gen agrees. "First thing I gotta get my kid away from the Holier-Than-Thous; she's startin' to believe the stuff they tell her." He reaches into his pocket. "Somethin' to remember me by," Gen says shyly, presenting her with a small gold box.

Laura opens it. Inside she sees the phrase *I love you* written in diamonds. It wraps itself around her wrist.

"Oh, Humpty!" she cries, giving him a hug. "I don't have a present for you!" The beautiful gypsy makes a motion with her hand. An identical bracelet encircles Humpty's wrist.

"No cryin', kid, no cryin'," Gen sniffles, wiping his nose on his sleeve. "You'll always be the star attraction at Club Humpty. Now, get goin'."

Big Boy helps Amanda onto the wagon and seats himself beside her, feeling close to heaven.

The majestic fiery horses flick their tails excitedly as Laura takes her place next to the beautiful Magdalena. She snaps the reins and the enchanted wagon rises into the star-filled sky.

"The stars are like fireflies," Laura says, surprised.

"There is magic in this night."

Laura can feel it ...a deep rhythm strummed on distant guitars, the power of flashing hooves, the night drenched in the fragrance of white gardenias, the wild, haunted music of the stars.

* * * *

They reached the encampment just as dark was letting go, running its long fingers languorously through the clouds.

They were greeted by a ring of welcoming campfires, small flaming forces of good that warmed, nourished and protected the gypsies. There was music, deep song from the gypsy soul, and color, the rich dusky hues of their lost world reflected in their clothing, their tapestries, their tents, color with blood meaning, color remembered in the soul of this wandering people.

"Magda!" a man shouted.

"Guitano!" Magdalena cried, love shining in her eyes.

A tall, handsome gypsy swept her up in his arms. "You have found her!" Guitano said joyfully. "Come, everyone, make welcome! Magdalena has brought our lost child home!

Gypsies rushed from their tents. "Magdalena has found her! Magdalena has found her!"

Their tumultuous welcome — the kisses, the embraces, the cries of joy, the freedom and intensity — was unlike anything Laura had ever known, awakening a raw, fierce happiness in her. Not the ethereal happiness she'd felt with the Great Poet but a dark, wild, extravagant happiness which was also strangely sweet, and for which she had unknowingly hungered.

"Come, child, it is time to rest." Magdalena took Laura's hand. "We will sleep in my tent till sunset."

"Unless you want to stay with me," said Amanda.

"I want to stay with Magdalena. Just for tonight," Laura quickly added," not wanting to hurt Amanda's feelings.

"If I know you, you'll have her up all night with questions. At least I'll get some sleep."

"Night, Mandy," said Laura, giving her a hug.

"So, now I'm Mandy. Well, good night, little gypsy," Amanda said lovingly. "If Magdalena gets tired of your questions and throws you out, you can always come snuggle with me."

* * * *

"I promise not to ask too many questions."

"Questions are good, child," Magdalena assured her. "But now we must rest."

Her lips pressed tight together, Laura looked about to burst.

Magdalena laughed. "Ask, little one."

"Why is everyone so nice to me?"

"We have searched for you for such a long time."

"For me?"

"We have a legend."

"A legend about me?"

"Amanda knows you well," said Magdalena, laughing. "When we have rested your questions will be answered."

"Why do you sleep in the daytime?"

"For people who wander, night can be a protection," Magdalena explained, tucking Laura into a bed fragrant with the scent of flowers. "It is good to follow one's own rhythm and not the rhythm of others."

"I like night too."

"That does not surprise me," Magdalena said softly. "Sleep well, little Indra."

"Why do you call me Indra?"

"Shhhh." Magdalena put her finger to Laura's lips.

* * * *

Light from the dying fire danced with shadows on the

tapestries of burgundy and gold that covered the walls of the tent, tapestries depicting scenes of gypsy life, a life that seemed familiar yet unfamiliar, faraway yet close. The rich colors, complex symbols and mysterious designs suggested meanings Laura could sense but not express. A guitar of warm, burnished wood hung next to a zither and a tambourine, instruments she remembered from the books with the golden edges. Feeling she had played them somewhere, long ago, she fell asleep to their imagined music.

* * * *

The sun set fire to the clouds before leaving the sky. The night slowly awakened, lazily stretching its dark limbs over the last of the light. Laura awoke to the laughter and singing of the gypsies.

"A perfect night has begun," said Magdalena, wrapping Laura in a warm robe. "We will go to the river to bathe, but first I have a surprise for you." Opening an old trunk, its ancient hinges creaking, she removed some things. "These are yours now."

They were the most beautiful clothes Laura had ever seen — silks, brocades, velvets in rich, warm tones of wine, gold, crimson, deep green. There was a gold belt with intricate designs, a crimson vest, a necklace of gold coins and a circlet of coins for her head.

"Are they really mine?"

"They have always been yours."

* * * *

The river ran swift and clear through the deepest part
of the forest where it formed a large, quiet pool edged by a
waterfall. Laura and Magdalena slipped into the water.
The night was alive with the sounds of nightbirds, flying
squirrels, singing insects and other nocturnal creatures.
Through the trees Laura could see the brilliant orange
moon climbing a ladder of branches to the sky.

Magdalena cupped some water in her upraised palms,
letting it run through her fingers. "O, Deep River of Life,"
she intoned, her voice dark as night. "Flow and flow and
flow. Wherever you flow, we gypsies shall go."

Resting against the grassy bank, her legs floating in
the water, Magdalena's song flowing through her, Laura
looked up through a lattice of leaves, watching the stars
coming out, wondering if her father was out there somewhere, listening.

"What are you thinking?"

"About my father."

Magdalena was silent for a moment. "Then he must be
nearby."

"Why do you say that?"

"We have a saying: What is dear in your thoughts is
close to your heart." Helping Laura onto the bank,
Magdalena dried her with a soft, thick cloth. "Now you
may put on your rightful garments."

In her gypsy clothes, the circlet of coins on her head,
Laura felt like dancing, felt she had danced in these
clothes before and the clothes remembered.

* * * *

By the time they returned to the encampment, the
moon was a large silver spangle in the sky. Fires were
blazing, pots sizzling, foods roasting; there was singing
and laughter as the gypsies prepared for the feast. "Would
you like to meet our queen?" Magdalena asked, the echo
of something unspoken in her voice.

"Oh, yes!" Laura said eagerly. She had never met a
queen before.

Magdalena led her through the throngs of gypsies who
showered Laura with compliments. "Isn't she lovely!"
"How beautiful our little gypsy looks in her gypsy clothes!"

The tent of the gypsy queen was striking in its sim-
plicity. Spare, graceful, muted in color, unadorned, it
radiated harmony and peace.

Within, there was a living quiet. Things were bathed
in soft, warm lamplight. The tent was sparsely furnished,
yet filled with things beyond things, with whispered secrets, with mysteries only partly revealed. It was the
mother tent from which all the others drew life.

In the shadows under a filmy canopy sat a mysterious, ancient figure.

"Mother Romany?" Magdalena spoke softly. "I have
brought her."

There was the barest rustle of movement. "Let me see
her eyes."

"Go to her, little one. She will not harm you."

The queen's face was hidden in shadow. She took
Laura's small, soft hand in hers. Laura felt its roughness;
it was an honest hand, comforting and strong, like her
father's. Mother Romany leaned forward. In the flickering
light her face was all crevices and shadows, but her eyes

were quick, eager and alive. Laura opened to them like a night-blooming flower, reaching out to touch the queen's cheek. But suddenly self-conscious, she snatched her hand back. The queen laughed a deep muffled laugh. Laura started to giggle. The queen threw her head back, laughing a full, warm, embracing laugh that seemed to come from the core of the earth. Swept up in her laughter, Laura heard her own laughter mingling in it, felt herself floating in a sea of laughter, laughter limitless and eternal, possessed of the joy that is the wellspring of life.

* * * *

Guitano came to escort them to the feast. The look on Magdalena's face told him something wonderful had happened. Silently, he gave thanks for the joy uniting Laura and the queen.

Supporting Mother Romany with his arm, they proceeded slowly through the assembled gypsies who parted in silent homage to their queen. Reaching her place of honor, a velvet couch beneath the stars, she turned to face her people, knowing they awaited a sign.

With a formal gesture of her outstretched arm, she presented Laura. Misunderstanding, Laura took her hand. The queen laughed. They swung hands like playmates as the gypsies exploded with shouts of joy and laughter. And a night of celebration began.

* * * *

The gypsies savored good food as they savored all life's goodness — love, laughter, beauty, music. In their wanderings they had gathered a rich variety of traditions and foods, combining them with traditions and recipes of their

own, flavoring them with gypsy soul, making them
uniquely theirs, yet part of something larger, creating a
harmony of tastes that nourished the body and satisfied
the soul.

* * * *

A good-natured shout went up as Amanda and Big
Boy joined the throng. Amanda was radiant in her green
brocade robe with braided gold trim. Big Boy wore a bold
gypsy shirt open to the waist, a wide leather belt studded
with gems, satin trousers tucked into boots, a red scarf
around his head and a smile as bright as the moon.

"They look so happy," said Laura.

"Very happy," Guitano agreed, squeezing Magdalena's
hand.

Amanda rushed over to them. "Big Boy asked me to
marry him," she said excitedly. "He knows just the place
for us to live, a tropical asteroid with all his favorite trees
and lots of ocean for me."

"Oh, Amanda, that's wonderful!" Laura exclaimed.
Then it hit her. Amanda would be going away with Big
Boy. She loved being a gypsy but she loved Amanda too.

"Hey," said Amanda, seeing her dismay. "We're sisters, aren't we? Even when sisters get married they're still
sisters."

"Besides," said Big Boy, "you can come live with us
after our honeymoon."

"Oh, I'm going to live with the gypsies!"

Amanda was silent for a moment. "You really like
being a gypsy."

"I love being a gypsy so much I could explode!"

"Like the Rocketbus, I suppose," Amanda said teasingly.

"If I did, you'd have bits and pieces of me to take away with you."

Amanda sighed. "I already have pieces of you. Right here," she said, indicating her heart.

"Oh, Mandy, I love you so much!"

Swallowing the lump in her throat, Amanda enveloped her in a hug. "Me too, kid. Me too."

"Do you like my gypsy clothes?" Laura asked, pirouetting.

"Very nice," said Big Boy.

"Gorgeous," Amanda agreed. "And what a beautiful locket."

"It's very old," Laura said proudly. Most of the design had worn away but the name *Indra* could still faintly be seen. "I get to keep it."

"Of course," said Magdalena.

"Being a gypsy is good for Laura," Amanda said thoughtfully.

"And Laura is good for the gypsies," Magdalena said graciously. Guitano whispered something in her ear. Her face lit up. "Amanda, would you and Big Boy like to have a gypsy wedding?"

"Oh," Laura squealed, "that would be great!"

Amanda looked up at Big Boy. "Could we, darling?"

"Whatever you want is okay with me," he said adoringly.

"A double wedding then," said Guitano, putting his arm around Magdalena. "With Mother Romany's permission, of course."

"I'll go ask her," said Laura. "She likes me."

Mother Romany laughingly agreed. "Three times the joy," she said, a look passing between her and Magdalena. "One full cycle of the moon and the ceremonies shall take place."

* * * *

After the feast and the music and dancing, everyone gathered around Mother Romany to listen to the Legend of the Lost Child.

Mother Romany raised her hand for silence. Even the night creatures were hushed.

"There have always been gypsies," she began. "We are old as time, old as the river that flows through all living things.

"Once we had our own planet, the verdant and peaceful Enigma. We were rooted in its soil, planting and reaping in harmony with nature, and content to live so forever. But that was not to be.

"It had been foretold a flame-haired child would be born to us, a child who would embody the goodness of all LivingKind. Her existence would unite every living thing.

"When our queen was blessed with a beautiful red-haired daughter she was called *Indra the Unifier.* Her birth was celebrated by all LivingKind. We went with her from galaxy to galaxy so that, through her, all might know the Unifying Soul, know that we are all part of the same deep river that flows from the beginning to the end of time. And beyond.

"She was a beloved and loving child, pure and trusting, knowing nothing of evil. There was a light within her, a loving light that brought forth love from others. With each passing day she became more beautiful and more precious to the universe, awakening envy in the tormented heart of the queen's childless sister.

"One terrible night, while the queen lay sleeping, her child in her arms, her black-hooded sister came silently into the bed-chamber. Casting a spell over the queen from which she would never waken, she took the child from her arms, intending to destroy her, then and there. But the love in the child's eyes softened even her heart and she could not. Hiding the child in the folds of her cloak, she stole away.

"The queen's spirit was mad with grief and could not rest. She pursued her evil sister, pursues her still, even over the edge of time.

"With the loss of our miraculous child, our Unifier, we were severed one from another. Blood-knowledge of our unity was lost, allowing Evil to walk among us, a hooded figure who steals people's souls.

"Where once everyone would have mourned the loss alike, hatred, blame and divisiveness took root. For the evil deed of one, all gypsies were reviled. We were driven from our home and hounded from place to place. Even now, when the reason for hatred has been forgotten, the hatred remains.

"Thus we became a wandering people searching for the Lost Soul of the universe."

Laura felt the unfairness of their suffering and loss like a deep wound, and began to cry silently.

"Every thousand years the queen's spirit comes to us in dreams, telling us our search is not in vain. In dreams she names our new queen, a queen who will live a thousand years, sustaining us in the hope that somewhere in the vastness of time our lost one will be found, and unity restored to all LivingKind. And so ends our legend."

* * * *

"Did the evil sister steal my father?" Laura asked her later.

"No, child."

"Will she try to steal me?"

"No, no," Mother Romany assured her. "But she has followers. They speak of love but wear a black hood over their souls. Trust what is meant, not what is said."

"But how will I know?"

"Do not be afraid, little gypsy. You have the gift of reading souls. And the courage to trust it." Mother Romany lay back, looking up at the stars through closed eyes. "It is very simple, really. At the core we are alike, ourselves, others, the universe..." Her voice trailed off.

"Come away, child," Magdalena whispered.

* * * *

"She looked so tired."

"She is." Magdalena replied, "Very, very tired. It is the Time of Dreaming. Soon there will be a new queen."

"Who?"

Magdalena did not reply.

"Does the new queen know?".

"Yes," Magdalena said quietly.

"Doesn't she want to be queen?" Laura asked, sensing something.

"It goes beyond wanting or not wanting," Magdalena said gravely. "It is the greatest honor and responsibility a gypsy can be given."

"Why does it feel so sad?"

Oh, child-who-reads-souls! Magdalena cried out inside herself. *How can I explain?* She took Laura in her lap. "Our queen lives a thousand years, ten centuries. Everyone she loves, her husband, her children, her grandchildren, all pass over the edge of time. For her the grieving never ends."

For her the grieving never ends! The words were like hooks, tearing at Laura's heart. She began to sob for her father, deep soul-wracking sobs — able, at last, to release her grief. Holding her close, Magdalena rocked back and forth.

> *Cry, little gypsy, cry.*
> *Fill the River with your tears.*
> *Let it bear your grief away.*

Chapter Ten

A Flurry Of Activity

Holograms, telegrams, cosmograms and mind-to-mind-o-grams went streaming through the galaxies, inviting people to the double wedding, but not to the Naming of the New Queen which only gypsies could witness.

Gypsy coronations were mysterious and rare, occurring only once every thousand years. Even those who disparaged the gypsies wanted to attend. Rumors that the lost gypsy child had been found heightened interest even more. Unaware that only gypsies would be admitted to this most secret ceremony, acceptances had come pouring in, even from those not invited — like Ma Light who wanted to put in an appearance to repair her reputation which had been shattered by the disastrous Benefit of the Doubt. Flocks of pigeon substitutes were loosed, carrying messages to the uninvited, urging them not to come.

Hundreds of lavishly decorated gypsy wagons, each pulled by matched pairs of snow white or fiery red horses, were dispatched to bring those who could not fly or teleport or materialize by other mysterious means.

Mr. and Mrs. Loveseat sent their regrets. Being a distant relative on Big Boy's side of the family, Palmyra Loveseat would have liked to attend but the Moon was behaving strangely, staying away longer, hiding behind clouds, sometimes blacking out entirely. His erratic behavior had changed the odds in his fight with the Sun. Because of the many bets she was covering Palmyra needed to stay glued to the TV.

Claribel and Dolly, two witches who advertised themselves as the greatest chefs in the universe, though no one could be found to verify this, had been engaged to prepare a sumptuous banquet. Laura wondered if they were the same witches who'd made the awful smelling stew at the Universal Dump. "The very ones," she was assured.

Warned by Laura, the gypsies tactfully let it be known stew would not be appropriate for the occasion. The witches interpreted this as a criticism, which it was, and were quite put out, but since no one except gypsies had ever been to a gypsy coronation they were in no position to argue. Besides, it would be a wonderful opportunity to put an end to those nasty rumors about their cooking, so they had accepted, believing they had enough culinary "surprises" up their wide sleeves to pull it off.

Laura sent invitations to the Great Poet, to Humpty and his daughter, and to Pinocchio and Loki, looking forward to having her old friends and her new ones get to know each other. She asked Mother Romany about sending an invitation to her father, or maybe to his hologram. Mother Romany said she was sure he would come if he could but that Laura must not count on it. Laura grabbed her magic wand and rushed out into the night, pointing it at the brightest star in the sky, wishing an invitation to her father with all her might.

The most accomplished musicians and dancers in the gypsy world canceled all other engagements for the great event. The best designers and tailors canceled all other fittings and rushed to the gypsy encampment where they were kept busy day and night creating gowns and other finery for the brides and members of the bridal parties, some of whom had sent their measurements on ahead. Knowing how reluctant some people were to reveal their real size, ample time had been set aside for last minute alterations. Taking advantage of the gypsy preference for bold color and spontaneity, the designers shunned the conventional tuxedo and formal gown in favor of attire far more fanciful and free-flowing.

It was traditional that prior to the coronation of the new queen no one see the old queen in her ceremonial robes. Consequently, Mother Romany's garments were created and fitted in utmost secrecy by the most talented blind designers in the galaxy. Their ancestors had designed ceremonial finery for gypsy coronations since time began.

For the comfort of Amanda's and Big Boy's relatives, the gypsies chose a wedding site near a long stretch of white beach on the western shore of the Great Sea, not far from a deep forest. Giant interlocking tents with complicated symbols were erected. Campfires were kept blazing day and night to welcome arriving guests.

Although something weighed on her mind, Amanda enjoyed herself between fittings, splashing about in the Great Sea with Big Boy. "Sweetums, have you ever considered the possibility that your family might object to our marriage?"

"My folks'll love you."

"I know you think so, darling, but that's because you love me."

"Everybody loves you."

"Oh, Big Boy," said Amanda, putting a flipper around his shoulder, "you're so innocent. Some people may not see beyond the fact that we're different species. They may not want to look beneath the surface and see what kind of person someone is."

Knowing what she said was true, Big Boy became thoughtful. Amanda splashed him playfully. "Penny for your thoughts."

"If anybody hurts your feelings, they'll be sorry!" he said fiercely. "The real problem is going to be how your folks feel about me. They're high society. I'm just a mug."

"You are not! You're my hero, my protector, my darling. Besides, let me tell you a secret. Years ago, before my mother married my father, she had a 'thing' for a gorilla. She almost married him."

"You're just saying that to make me feel better."

"No, really. The women in my family have very strong feelings."

"They sure do," he said, grinning.

Amanda laughed. "Wait till I tell you about Aunt Finnie and the rhinoceros. It made gossip columns all across the galaxy!"

"Time for a fitting, Mandy," Magdalena called from the shore. The past few days the two brides had become good friends. It was Mandy this and Magda that. "Okay, I'm coming," called Amanda as she and Big Boy headed for shore.

"Gosh, I love you," said Big Boy, shaking himself dry.

"Oh, Big Boy," Amanda purred as he swept her up in his arms.

"Come on, Mandy," Magdalena said. "Our temperamental designers are waiting."

Big Boy set Amanda down gently, his eyes black fire, his voice husky. "See you later," he whispered. "Oooo," Amanda cooed, blushing lavender.

"Oh, you two," Magdalena scolded fondly as Big Boy gave Amanda one last kiss. Leaving him glowing, the two brides walked off together, laughing and giggling like old friends.

Chapter Eleven

Heart Of The Moon

The restless Moon hid his face behind the clouds as a man and a woman riding fiery red horses entered the deep forest. Something about the woman intrigued him. He slipped out from behind the clouds to watch her. When they stopped by the river and dismounted, the Moon slipped back behind the clouds so they wouldn't notice him.

"This is no time for sadness, my beloved," said Guitano. "It is a time for rejoicing; our love is forever."

"Forever," Magdalena repeated sadly. For her, the word was haunted.

"Come, little Magda, smile or I will begin to think you no longer love me," he teased.

"Oh, Tano, you know why I am sad." Her melancholy stirred the heart of the Moon.

"How can there be sadness for lovers under a lover's moon?"

"The moon is behind a cloud. Like my heart."

"Poor little cloud-covered heart," teased Guitano. "Magda must marry me, but I am so unworthy she wants to cry."

"Oh, Tano," she laughed.

Smiling, he put his arms around her. "Soon we will be wed. We will have so many years of love."

"And I will have so many years without your love."

Cautiously, the Moon moved out from behind his cover of clouds.

"I wish Mother Romany could live forever," Magdalena said sadly, "that we could run away from destiny."

"My beautiful, foolish darling, think how fortunate we are. We have purpose; how rich this makes our lives. Our love is blessed by destiny."

"I know, I know, but still my heart rejects what must be."

Guitano reached up to the branch of a sturdy oak, swinging from it as he had when they were children.

> *Hey diddle diddle,*
> *Life is a riddle*
> *And Magda lives on the moon.*

He looked so comical, swinging from the branch, mimicking her doleful expression, she couldn't help laughing. He'd always been able to make her laugh. Even as a child she'd had a seriousness about her that set her apart from other children. For Guitano, it was part of the mystery that drew him to her.

"I know you are right, Guitano, but the responsibility comes so soon."

"Think of our marriage instead."

"If only we could be like others!" She looked up at the moon, as though pleading with heaven. "I can't bear that our love will end!"

The Moon was bewitched. He fell in love. He cried for her, for himself. He buried his face in her hair, drowned himself in her eyes, lost his light in her darkness.

Transformed by the Moon's adoration, her beauty became unearthly, making her seem out of mortal reach. Guitano felt a shadow cross his heart, reminding him she was more than mortal, she who would be queen for a thousand years. Taking her in his arms, he vowed to protect her from all unhappiness, even his own.

The heart of the Moon was roiled by powerful emotions. Romantic, impetuous, always falling in love, he had never experienced love so strong. Clouds swirled past him, over him, around him, turbulent as his feelings. Stunned, the Moon pulled back behind the clouds.

With Guitano's arms around her, her head against his chest, the beat of his heart matching hers, Magdalena knew he was right. With his help she would grow into her destiny.

Mourning his impossible love, the Moon went dark.

The man and woman sat together in silence.

Chapter Twelve

Oliver's Dilemma

In his usual, fuddled way, Amanda's Uncle Oliver Octopus III arrived early for the wedding. He stood on the deserted beach at the edge of the shore, all but one of his appendages planted firmly in the sand. With that one he took a gold timepiece from the pocket of his white brocade vest and looked around.

"Humph, no one here to greet me," he said out loud. Being a bachelor and shy, he often talked to himself. "Not very good manners. And I've come all this way to be ring bearer."

Off in the distance he saw what looked like carnival tents. Perhaps that was where the natives lived. Maybe they could guide him to the wedding site.

Being a bit past middle-age, portly and used to living in the sea where he was practically weightless, he decided he'd sit awhile and gather his strength before trying to traverse the great expanse of beach. As he bent his legs to sit, the tug of his trousers reminded him he'd put on weight since he'd last worn them. They were so tight he couldn't sit down.

"I suppose I'll have to go on an all algae diet when I get home," he said sourly. He detested algae. He'd been forced to eat more than his share as a child. Mrs. Parsimonious, the tyrannical housekeeper, served it at every meal. It tasted like mud. His sister Valerie also hated it. When Mrs. Parsimonious wasn't looking Valerie would plunk her serving on his plate and force him to eat both portions. Valerie was even more intimidating than Mrs. Parsimonious.

A sudden gust of wind took his top hat in its arms and carried it down the beach; then, discovering it wasn't good to eat, dropped it in the sea. Oliver had to dive in to retrieve it before the waves got it and started playing hide-and-seek with him, one of their favorite games. They were so playful, those wavelets. Knowing their Uncle Oliver's penchant for absentmindedness, they delighted in raiding his ancestral mansion, Oceana, carrying off things and secreting them in a storehouse of sunken treasure they kept under the ocean floor. Occasionally, they would sneak some of his possessions back into the mansion, putting them in unexpected places which confused him even more.

Oliver checked his other vest pocket for the four rings to assure himself those mischievous little wavelets hadn't absconded with them. To his relief, they were exactly where he remembered putting them. Maybe *Mind Over Matter*, the memory course he'd been taking was finally working. Nevertheless, he'd have to speak to his formidable sister, Valerie, about the wavelets. She was the only one they listened to. Intimidated by her from childhood, he found Valerie positively terrifying now that she was married to the ultra-powerful Marcus Highwater. He supposed she and Marcus would be attending the wedding too. "Oh my, oh my," he muttered, feeling weak in the knees at the thought. Leaning against a large boulder, he pulled out his handkerchief and mopped his brow.

Laura walked along the beach looking for the curved shells that made the sound of the sea when held to the ear. It would be nice to give them to Amanda's relatives so whenever they wanted they could pick up a shell and hear the sea. She was so absorbed in her search she didn't notice Uncle Oliver in the shadow of his boulder.

"Little girl are you a native?" he called out in a high pitched voice.

Startled, Laura dropped her bag of shells, astonished to see a fat green octopus wearing a white suit and vest with a red flower in his lapel. On six of his eight append-ages he wore high-buttoned black and white patent leather shoes. On his other two appendages he wore crisp white gloves. Each gloved appendage was holding firmly to either side of a tall top hat, as if he expected the wind to blow it away although there was no wind.

"I didn't mean to startle you, little girl," he lisped, something he did when he was nervous which was most of the time, especially around females. "Are you a native?" he asked timidly.

"Native?" Laura asked, trying not to stare. She'd never seen an octopus all dressed up before.

"Are you from that carnival over there?"

"That's not a carnival. Those are gypsy tents. They have important meanings."

"Oh, I'm sure they do. I'm sure they do," he lisped, flustered.

"Of course, you'd have to be a gypsy to know that."

"May I ask a question?" he asked timidly. "I mean, if it's not too, too," he stammered, "personal? I didn't know gypsies had red hair."

"Mostly they don't, but every thousand years one does."

"I see," he said vaguely, not seeing at all. "Would you perchance know where the wedding is to be?"

"At our camp. Over there," she said, pointing at the tents. "The gypsy camp."

"Gypsy camp!" he squeaked, shocked. "Oh my, oh my! What will Norville and Felicity think?"

"What's the matter?" Laura asked, puzzled.

"The wedding! I mean, at such a place!"

"But it's a beautiful place."

"Of course, of course," he said distractedly. "I'm, a man of the world, a broad minded man, but Norville and Felicity are such snobs. When they find out, well."

"Find out what?" Laura asked, beginning to feel annoyed without knowing why.

"Well, of course, I'm not one to gossip but the gypsies do have a reputation."

"I bet you don't know anything about the gypsies or Mother Romany or the legend or anything."

"Of course I do. Of course, yes, Mother Romany. Who is Mother Romany?" he asked timidly.

"The gypsy queen."

"Oh. Will she be, er, attending my niece's wedding?" he asked, trying to sound casual.

"She's going to perform the ceremony. Then there'll be the coronation."

"Oh my, oh my!" he exclaimed. He knew Norville and Felicity would insist on their own clergy.

"I get to be in it," Laura said proudly. "The coronation is the most important event in the whole universe."

"Coronation!" gasped Uncle Oliver, turning a sickly green. "You mean my niece's wedding is mixed up with this, this pagan rite?"

"What's a pagan rite?" Laura asked, starting to get angry. "You shouldn't say things about people you don't know."

"Oh my, oh my," lisped Uncle Oliver, swaying back and forth.

"What's wrong with you?"

"Nothing at all, nothing at all," he replied nervously. "I get these spells." She was just being fanciful, he told himself. "You must be misinformed. After all, you're just a child. How would you know?"

"I'm not just a child! And I know lots of things!"

"Oh, yes, of course, I'm sure you do." She certainly had strong opinions for such a small person. He sighed. Females were so intimidating. "I didn't mean to offend you," he said apologetically. "I was just surprised."

"Well, if you really didn't mean it..."

"What's your name, dear?" he asked, taking a nip of

some black liquid. It was such a comfort at times.

"Maybe it's Laura," she said mistrustfully.

Oh dear, he thought, taking another sip. "What a charming name."

"I like Indra better."

"Indra? Who's Indra?" he asked, more fuddled than ever.

"That's my other name."

"Oh, I see." But, as usual, he didn't.

"What's your name?"

"I am Uncle Oliver," he said, tipping his hat.

"You're Amanda's uncle! I know all about you."

"You know about me?" he asked, taken aback.

"Amanda told me."

"Amanda, you know Amanda?" he asked, astonished. Of course she knew Amanda. What could he be thinking?

"She's my big sister."

"Sister? Surely not!" He'd heard the family gossip about Felicity, but there were limits. "You mean that figuratively, of course."

"What does figuratively mean?" Laura asked suspiciously.

"Well, you could hardly be blood sisters, now could you? You're different species."

"What do you mean, different species?"

Oh my, oh my. Her persistence was wearing. "Species are when everyone is like everyone else."

"I think it's more fun when everyone is different."

"What do you know? You're just a child."

"I am not, and what if I am? I wish you'd stop saying that!"

"A slip of the tongue, a slip of the tongue," he lisped, taking another sip of his black liquid. "It's unnerving to be around people who are different."

"What does unnerving mean?"

Oh my, oh my. No let up. "It means a bit frightening." Like you, he thought, wishing she'd go away.

"Why is it frightening to have friends who are different? I have lots of friends who are different."

"Friends are one thing, but for family relationships, well, that's another matter."

"Why?"

Uncle Oliver mopped his brow with his handkerchief. "Every species has its own ways. How would anyone know what was right and what was wrong if everyone was different?" Seeing Laura wasn't convinced, he tried to explain it another way. "I am," he said, pointing to himself with three of his appendages, "a sea species, as are all my relatives and friends. Therefore we all agree our way is the right way."

"A tree species isn't wrong just because it isn't a sea species."

"Well, well, of course not," he lisped, loosening his collar. This was getting to be too much. "But if everybody was mixed up with everybody else, imagine how confusing it would be. Next thing you knew there'd be monkeys with feathers and fish that flew."

"I've met fish that fly."

"Well, yes, yes, perhaps that was a poor example. But if whales could climb trees, for instance. Think how preposterous it would be."

"Big Boy is teaching Amanda to climb trees right now."

"What are you trying to tell me?" he asked, feeling a little dizzy.

"Amanda is learning to climb trees because she's marrying a tree species."

"What!" squealed Uncle Oliver, emitting an inky black cloud that quickly concealed him.

"A tree species," Laura repeated firmly. Amanda had told her all about Uncle Oliver and his black clouds. "Big Boy is a tree species! He's a gorilla!"

There was a groan, a thud and the sound of something tearing.

"Uncle Oliver?" Laura asked tentatively.

"Yeeeessss." His voice was very faint.

"Are you alright?"

As the cloud disappeared back into his mouth with the sucking sound of a Genie going back into a bottle, Laura could see Uncle Oliver was in a terrible state. His appendages were splayed out every which way. His white suit was covered with black dust. His top hat was crushed flat. Four of his shoes had come off. One of his red socks had a hole in it. His face was algae green. "Gorillas that swim, fishes that fly. Oh my, oh my, I've split my britches," he said, fainting dead away.

* * * *

In the soft haze of twilight the gypsy encampment came back to life. The dying embers of campfires were soon blazing anew as the gypsies prepared the first meal of their day. Singers and musicians coaxed the moon from its dark bed below the horizon. Night birds sang in the trees. The sweet, loamy scent of the earth mingled with the scent of herbs and spices.

Uncle Oliver awoke to unfamiliar surroundings. Normally this would have alarmed him but there was a serenity about the place that calmed him. Semi-darkness soothed his aching eyes. What color he could see was warm and comforting. Hushed voices and soft music added to the peacefulness. He lay still, trying to remember what had happened ...something about Amanda's wedding, his black liquid, that annoying red-haired child and, *Oh dear, here she comes, the little troublemaker.* "Where am I?" he wailed, trying to hide under the covers.

"You fainted, so the gypsies brought you here," Laura explained.

"I see," he said weakly. "Does Amanda know where I am?"

"I'll tell Magdalena you're awake."

A lovely young woman with thick black hair, a radiant face and kind eyes appeared. Even in his condition Uncle

Oliver could see she was a person of quality. "Here," she said soothingly, "drink this." Her voice was soft and musical. She helped him sit up so he could drink the brown liquid she offered. It smelled like algae and fermented tree roots, but Magdalena was so friendly and caring he knew she wouldn't give him anything bad. Expecting it to taste terrible he was surprised to find it tasted like fresh mint and licorice. "What is this?" he asked, pleased.

"It is our elixir. It helps us stay healthy and youthful, even into old age."

Uncle Oliver began to feel better right away. His eyes stopped aching and his stomach was no longer upset. "It's really remarkable," he said, noticing again how lovely she was. "Perhaps you should bottle and sell it."

She shrugged. "Wherever we go we offer our elixir, but it is refused because we are gypsies."

"But that's preposterous! Why would anyone refuse a miracle for such a foolish reason?" he wanted to know, forgetting about his former attitude toward pagan rites and gypsies.

"It is a pity. The elixir can do so much good."

Uncle Oliver's mind was teeming with new ideas. "We must do something about this," he said firmly. "My family is not without influence." He tried to rise, but overtaxed, fell back on his pillow.

"The elixir knows when you must rest," Magdalena said soothingly.

He slipped into a deep, healing sleep. When he awoke, several hours later, he felt thoroughly refreshed and years younger.

"Uncle Oliver!" Amanda exclaimed, "how well you look."

"Amanda," he said, delighted to see her, "you look fetching in those charming garments."

His confident affability surprised her. So unlike the fretful, narrow minded Uncle Oliver she was used to. "Then you don't mind they're gypsy clothes?"

"Mind? Why would I mind? They're lovely," he said emphatically.

That elixir really works miracles, thought Amanda, noticing how Uncle Oliver's face lit up when Magdalena joined them. *What do you know, the little dickens has a crush on her!*

Feeling robust, Uncle Oliver hopped out of bed, forgetting he was stark, knobby-knee-naked. "Oh my, oh my," he lisped, diving back under the covers.

Magdalena pretended not to notice, but Amanda being Amanda, laughed heartily.

"Where are my clothes?" he asked, peeping out from under the covers.

"They are being fixed," Magdalena explained.

"How very kind you are," he said, beaming at her.

"If you would not be offended, we have gypsy clothes for you."

"Offended, my dear? Why would I be offended? It would be a privilege and an honor, and, please, call me Ollie."

"May I call you Oliver?" asked Magdalena. "Ollie doesn't seem dignified enough."

"Oh, my dear," he sputtered happily. "Oliver would be perfect."

"But Uncle Ollie," Amanda teased, "I thought you didn't like gypsies."

"Don't be foolish. How could I not like gypsies when I never knew any until now?"

"You must be hungry, Oliver," said Magdalena. "The meal will be served as soon as Mother Romany is ready. We will wait outside while you dress."

"How thoughtful you are, my dear."

Mother Romany, he thought. She was the one who was going to marry Amanda and the tree species. He'd let Norville and Felicity worry about that. After all, Amanda looked so happy and the little red-headed girl did seem to be right about the gypsies. Why couldn't Amanda be right about Big Boy?

Chapter Thirteen

Listening For The Laughter

In preparation for the Naming of the New Queen, Mother Romany had gone into seclusion for three nights, three lonely nights for Laura who missed their closeness. She knew their separation was a necessary part of things, but still it gave rise to an uneasiness in her, something to do with the coronation and the naming of a new queen. Magdalena did her best to reassure Laura but her uneasiness would not go away.

After her seclusion, Mother Romany was different, more lighthearted, younger. There was an ease and grace to her movements. She no longer needed frequent periods of rest. When Laura took her hand, she was surprised to find it was as soft as Magdalena's. The changes were obviously good for Mother Romany but they only increased Laura's uneasiness.

"Why are you troubled, little Indra?" Mother Romany asked as they sat together by the campfire. Even her voice was different, more musical, like Magdalena's.

"You're different."

"I am growing younger."

"How can you grow younger?"

Mother Romany smiled. "Sometimes, when a person is old the weight of life is lifted and they become younger."

"Why didn't my father get younger?"

"He left too suddenly. There was no time."

"What were you doing when I wasn't allowed to be with you?"

"I had to go to places only I could go."

"But you were in your tent the whole time."

"I went back to my beginning and forward to my ending."

Ending! Laura felt a coldness she hadn't felt since the night her father died. "You're going away," she said, her voice flat.

"It will be different for you this time," Mother Romany assured her. "You will not be alone. There will still be many who love you."

"If only my mother…"

"Sometimes people who love you are locked up inside themselves with no way to express their love."

"She was always worried something was going to happen."

"Worry was your mother's prison. It will never be yours, little Indra. Trust your happiness and always listen for the laughter in things."

"That's what my father used to tell me!"

"He gave you a foundation in joy, not sorrow."

"He used to say he was holding open a secret door so I could hear the laughter of the universe."

"And did you hear it?"

"Yes."

"Can you still hear it?"

"Sometimes," Laura said wistfully. "Mother Romany, why do people have to die?"

Mother Romany was silent for a moment, looking into the fire. "Life is meant to be a wonderful adventure. And when we are done, it is good to go home, like children after play."

"Maybe if I could have made my mother hear the laughter."

"You cannot give happiness to someone who has none. It is a gift shared by those who already possess it." Mother Romany rose to put more wood on the fire. "You have created a new family, born out of your joy and love. Pinocchio, Loki, Amanda, Humpty, Big Boy, Guitano, the Great Poet, Magdalena."

"And Mother Romany."

Mother Romany laughed. "And Mother Romany. There will be others." She stirred the fire. It flared back to life, her face catching the light.

"You look like Magdalena!"

"I am Magdalena!" Mother Romany said exultantly, stretching her arms toward the sky. "Life is good, little gypsy. So many wonderful things, so many surprises."

She took Laura's hands in hers, looking straight into her eyes. "I make you a promise. When I journey over the edge of time I will linger for a moment on the threshold. And when I do, I promise you will hear the laughter."

Chapter Fourteen

Evert's Dream Of Glory

For Evert J. Snidely, or Ever-Snide, as he was called behind his back, owner and publisher of Cosmic Communications and the Galactic Gossip Syndicate, the double wedding and gypsy coronation were a journalist's dream. He intended to cover the once-in-a-millennium coronation personally. He needed something stupendous to revitalize his gossip empire which was suffering heavy losses from increased competition — scandal sheets were proliferating like fungi.

Looking over the guest list for the wedding, he gnashed his shark-like teeth with relish. It contained such luminaries as the scandalous mermaid, Great Aunt Finnie and the ultra-powerful, oh-so-social, Marcus Highwater, to name just two.

Furthermore, no journalist in the history of time had managed to crash the mysterious and secret gypsy coronation. There were rumors about those who'd tried and were never heard from again, which made the challenge even more exciting. After spending two days with his research department getting the lowdown on the gypsies, Evert was confident he knew as much about them as anyone not a gypsy.

He'd show those stuck-up "intellectual" publications a thing or two. Once he'd won the Galactic Pullover Prize for his coverage of the coronation they wouldn't be able to treat him like a sleaze anymore.

He'd used all his influence and a bundle of Lorelei's bucks to acquire two perfectly bogus invitations. A person had to be careful. Every two bit forger in the galaxy was trying to cash in on the coronation.

Never having seen a real invitation, some of them were letting their imaginations run wild. The funniest was the guy who, having heard the invitations had the gypsy "seal" of approval on them, had embossed his fakes with the face of Sebastian Sea Lion, the famous gypsy impersonator. Evert had been so amused, he'd paid the guy a few of Lorelei's bucks just for the laugh, telling him to use the money for a refresher course at the Forger's Academy. Now he had a good story to tell over cocktails at the Columnist's Club, which he still resented having had to buy his way into. None of the members would sponsor him because they thought gossip was beneath them, as if what they printed wasn't just gossip dressed up as "news". They'd sing a different tune when he scooped the whole prissy lot of them and copped the Pullover Prize. None of them could afford a bogus invitation as good as his; they'd never get in. "Pay for the best and steal the rest" was his motto, especially when he paid with someone else's money, Lorelei's, for instance.

She'd been bugging him for a chance to show what she'd learned about photography at the big feet of that bombastic, self-promoting charlatan, Montgomery Tusk. Great artiste of film, hooey! Distinguished cinematic dynasty, rubbish! Evert had seen the guy's work, a lot of artsy gauze and fancy lighting. And Lorelei thought it was swell. Dames. Now she wanted to use Tusk's technique on this assignment. Didn't she realize this was Journalism, not Creative Camera 101? Why did these rich dames always think they had to have a career? You'd think shopping would be enough.

But Lorelei knew she had him behind the eight-ball because "Crazy" Vern Light, his best photographer, the best in the galaxy, had disappeared while photographing black holes. That crazy guy, always taking risks. Why black holes and why now, he wanted to know. With Vern missing, he'd have to give Lorelei the assignment or she might get angry and break off their engagement, and with it his expensive lifestyle.

Of course, if the rumors he'd printed about Lorelei being the love child of Reginald Rhino and Great Aunt Finnie were true there might be some advantage to having her cover the wedding.

Rumors, rumors, rumors, how he loved them. To him they were as clay to a sculptor, words to a poet, strings to a violin. Once published, they took on a life of their own. They became true. At least until proven false.

Besides, if the rumors about Lorelei were true, that would make her first cousin to the bride, in which case she would have a real invitation, and as her escort he would be accepted without question.

If Reggie and Finnie really were Lorelei's parents, having Finnie as his prospective mother-in-law would have obvious advantages. She was already one of his best sources of gossip even if sometimes her stories were so improbable she had to be pulling his leg. No matter, her stories always looked good in print.

Marrying into the Oceanus family would open all

kinds of doors for him. Once inside, he'd slam them shut on the competition. Smiling, Evert let himself into Lorelei's mansion, *Le Grotto*, to tell her she had the assignment.

Chapter Fifteen

Making newThings

Laura rushed to the Designer's & Tailor's workshop for a fitting. As a participant in both ceremonies, the wedding and the Naming of the New Queen, she needed different costumes. She spent a lot of time at the workshop watching, fascinated, as their skilled fingers lovingly transformed silks, velvets, satins, spun gold, tiny jewels and glitter into garments that dazzled the eye and flattered the figure.

Soon she began attempting creations of her own, sketching an idea for a dress on a scrap of pattern paper or spontaneously draping material on anyone willing to stand still for a moment. She would run outside and drag someone in to try out a new idea — an unusual belting, the perfect jewel in the perfect spot, a dramatically flaring collar or sleeve.

Sewing was another matter. Magdalena and Amanda watched, amused, as Laura worked feverishly, her small hands tangling the threads, her face scrunched up, the tip of her tongue sticking out, trying to make the pieces fit the way she wanted, not the way they wanted, resulting in sleeves attached to hems, collars to legs, pockets to cuffs. Something in her rebelled against doing things by pattern. When she held up a "finished" garment the look of astonishment on her face sent Amanda and Magdalena into fits of laughter.

Frustrated and bored with clothes, she began using materials because of their textures, colors, shapes and relationships to each other — juxtaposing a soft curve of silk against a hard square of linen, the scratchiness of wool against the smoothness of satin, a sprinkle of gold on a swatch of dark indigo. Freed of the practical, she delighted in making things for their own sake, odd, whimsical, free-form, strangely beautiful things, things that flowed, pulsed, sparkled and glowed with inner harmony, creating a kind of music for the eyes. You couldn't wear them or eat them or do anything with them, but just looking at them, touching them, holding them, gave her a delicious feeling.

"Gee, kid, these are neat," Amanda said admiringly. "What are they?"

"They're *doThings*," Laura explained.

"Do things?"

"They're always doing things," said Laura, picking one for Amanda that twinkled in a friendly way.

"Gee," said Amanda, cradling the *doThing*, "do I get to keep you? Forget about sewing, kid, these are great!"

"I've never seen anything so beautiful," said Magdalena.

Laura stood among her creations, touching them, trying to decide which one to give Magdalena. Watching her, Magdalena saw a Laura she'd not seen before. An important transformation had begun. Her face was emerging from the soft beauty of childhood, becoming more defined, more confident and self-aware, reflecting the lineaments of her soul.

* * * *

Laura took over an unused utility tent for her workshop. Feeling limited by the materials she'd been using, she went in search of better things, scouring the beach for interesting shells, poking about the witches' kitchen where she found all kinds of interesting implements. At the dump she found rusty metal things, bits of lumber, clumps of plaster and other wonderful things. Everywhere she went things cried out to her, "Take me! Take me!" For a moment she considered using Magdalena's burnished musical instruments but she hesitated, sensing that would be wrong. They were already everything they were supposed to be.

People passing her workshop could hear her arguing with herself and her materials. There would be a "Wow!" or an "Oooops!" or a "Whoopee!" and she would rush out, hair flying, and drag someone in to see what she had done.

One day she decided to have an exhibition so everyone could see. Then maybe Maurice, the snooty decorator Amanda's parents had hired, would include some of her creations in the wedding décor. When she'd approached him he'd snarled at the suggestion, little spears of fire shooting out from between his clenched fangs. Maurice was a dragon. Laura knew from the books with the golden edges that dragons were always spitting fire, so she'd give him another chance. From the look of his dismal seaweed arrangements, he needed all the help he could get.

Chapter Sixteen

From The Heart

Laura meandered through the forest, listening to the soft rush of wind through the trees, breathing in deeply the sweet scents of moist earth, mosses, tropical flowers and dewy grasses. She loved taking the magic of things into quiet places inside herself, collecting feelings and impressions for stories to give her father, much as she collected shells or phrases or bits of fabric for her *doThings*.

She was jarred out of her reverie by a loud, friendly voice coming from somewhere overhead.

"Hello, dearie."

Looking up, Laura was startled to see a large orange creature seated on a thick branch. She was wearing a hot pink mini-skirt which was far too tight for her, coupled with a noisily clashing bright yellow blouse tied carelessly around her hairy midriff. On her head, which was too large for her body, she wore a floppy, broad-brimmed hat of day-glo green with purple polka dots and an enormous lopsided red flower that made it sag down on one side. She propped it up with a gloved hand (zebra stripes, gold fringe), her other hand gripping the handle of a battered straw suitcase. She had long arms and short, hairy legs. Her wide feet were squeezed into bright yellow plastic wedgies with cork bottoms. Everything clashed with everything else, but Laura could see her outrageous outfit suited her. "Are you here for the wedding?"

"That I am, dearie. Phew!" She sniffed herself unselfconsciously. "I'd better freshen up. Any place around here a lady can take a swim?"

"There's the river. I could take you there."

"Well, aren't you nice," she chittered merrily, dropping down from the tree, landing on her very sturdy, very bowed legs. "I'm Aunt Myrtle. That's what everyone calls me. What do they call you, dearie?"

"Laura. Or Indra, sometimes, because of my locket."

"Isn't that interesting. Mind if I call you Laura? First names are so much friendlier, don't you think?"

Laura started to explain but decided it didn't matter. "Laura is okay."

"Good, let's hug on it."

Laura hugged her back.

"I don't usually get hugged back," Aunt Myrtle said, pleased. "Sometimes people act like I slapped them instead of hugged 'em. I guess I'm too friendly or something."

"I don't think so. I liked that you hugged me."

Delighted, Aunt Myrtle rummaged around in her suitcase for something to give Laura, coming up with a heart-shaped red plastic locket on a string. It was something she'd been saving for the wedding. "Hearts mean love."

Laura couldn't help comparing it with her Indra locket.

"I guess maybe it's kinda junky, huh?"

"Oh no, Aunt Myrtle," Laura said quickly, not wanting to hurt her feelings. "It's the best red heart in the whole universe!"

"Thank you, dearie," Aunt Myrtle said cheerfully, tucking her suitcase under her arm. "Let's go for a swim."

By the time they reached the river Aunt Myrtle was more than ready to drop her suitcase, toss her hat and blouse onto a tree branch, wriggle out of her skirt and jump into the water with a "Yowie," attracting a school of curious fish. She paddled among them, playful as a porpoise.

Laughing, Laura sat on the bank with her feet in the water, as delighted with Myrtle's antics as the fish were.

"Hey!" someone shouted. Two black bears wearing fishing gear, waders and all, waddled toward Laura. The bigger, mean looking one, was smoking a cigar. "Keep it down!"

Unaware of the bears, Aunt Myrtle stood under the waterfall, singing loudly.

"It's okay," Laura explained, trying to be friendly. "We're just having fun."

"Your friend's makin' such a racket she's scarin' off

the fish," growled Herbert, the big bear.

"She is not," said Laura, sticking up for her new found friend. "Fish aren't stupid. They know you want to catch them."

"You callin' me stupid?" Herbert's eyes narrowed.

Essie, the other bear, tugged at his arm. "Please, Herbert, don't make no trouble. If they take away our license again we won't be able to fish no more."

"Butt out!" snarled Herbert.

"We can go upstream," Essie suggested.

Sensing something was wrong, Aunt Myrtle stopped singing.

"We're not movin'. They're movin', if they know what's good for 'em," Herbert said menacingly.

"Please, little girl," said Essie. "You and your friend better go."

"We got here first," Laura said stubbornly.

Herbert took a swipe at her. Aunt Myrtle exploded out of the water, landing on Herbert's back and began pounding the top of his head. Trying to shake her off, Herbert took another swipe at Laura, losing his balance. Aunt Myrtle swung up onto a tree branch overhead.

"Herbert, please," Essie pleaded.

"Lemme at her!"

"Pick on someone your own size!" shouted Aunt Myrtle, cuffing Herbert on the ear. He yowled in pain, trying to get a his claws on her. "Run for it, Laura!" she hollered.

"Yes, run away, little girl!" Essie urged.

"Make him stop!" Laura insisted, scrambling up onto a large white boulder just as an earthshaking roar thundered through the forest.

"Yippee!" Myrtle shouted. "Duke!"

A huge, handsome gorilla came toward them, shouldering trees aside, batting boulders out of the way.

Herbert froze.

"Hi ya, Myrt," Duke said laughingly, flashing a perfect set of formidable white teeth. He brushed a few stray tree limbs from his well-tailored white linen suit. "You ladies in trouble?"

Laura liked his deep laugh, his easy-going way, his white suit. He was like a hero in the books with the golden edges.

"This one's a troublemaker," said Myrtle, indicating Herbert. "Herbert, say hello to Duke."

"Excuse us, ladies," said Duke, tipping his white fedora. "Herbert and I need to talk."

"We was just fishin'," Essie said timidly. "We heard this noise."

"Shut up," Herbert interrupted. "I'll tell how it was."

"That's no way to talk to a lady," Duke said, frowning. Putting a massive hand on Herbert's shoulder, he pushed him about four inches into the ground. "You want to apologize, don't you?"

Herbert was too scared to speak.

"He don't have to 'pologize," Essie said wearily. "I'm used to it."

"But he wants to," Duke said pleasantly, leaning a little harder on Herbert's shoulder, pushing him a little deeper into the ground. "Isn't that right, Herbie?"

"I'm s-s-sorry," Herbert mumbled.

"Doesn't that feel better?" said Duke, taking his hand off Herbert's shoulder. "Now, Herbie, tell Duke what happened."

Herbert tried to think fast. "Like Essie said, uh... we heard this noise and come to see what it was."

"That's not true!" Laura said indignantly. "He tried to hit me. Aunt Myrtle was taking a bath."

"That's right," Myrtle chimed in. "The guy's a bully."

Lifting Herbert by his waders, Duke brought him up, up, up to eye level. "It's not nice to take advantage of people who are smaller than you. Sometimes they have friends who are a whole lot bigger than you." Herbert trembled before Duke's fearsome black eyes, afraid to look down or even move.

Laura was very impressed. Duke had never even raised his voice.

"Please, mister," Essie pleaded. "Don't hurt him."

"That won't be necessary, ma'am," Duke said calmly, setting Herbert down. "Herbie and I understand each other perfectly now." Herbert's eyes darted about frantically, looking for an escape route.

"Thanks, mister," said Essie, picking up the fishing

rods. "Come on, Herbert, let's go." Before the words were out of her mouth, Herbert was gone.

"I'm sure glad that's over," Myrtle said, relieved.

"Thank you, Sir Duke," said Laura, curtsying from atop her boulder.

Duke bowed chivalrously. "My pleasure, Princess."

"She's a very brave princess," said Myrtle. "You should've seen the way she stood up for me."

"That was brave, alright," Duke said, smiling. "But sometimes, Princess, it's better to run."

Laura stared up at him, her eyes like saucers.

Myrtle could see Duke had made another conquest. "Where's Lilli?" she asked.

Duke laughed. "That wife of mine. We'll be lucky if she gets here in time for the wedding."

"That's our Lilli," Myrtle chuckled. "Laura, this is my kid brother Duke. He's Big Boy's daddy. Duke, this is my friend Laura."

"Pleased to meet you, Princess."

"I'm not really a princess," Laura said, mesmerized.

"Oh, yes you are," said Duke, bending down to kiss her hand. "Now, you ladies must excuse me. I'm anxious to see my boy and meet his bride."

"Sure, Duke," said Myrtle. "Mind taking my suitcase? It's getting kinda heavy."

"Glad to, Myrt. See you ladies later," he said, striding off into the woods.

Laura looked after him long after he was out of sight.

Chapter Seventeen

One Thing Leads To Another

As Laura and Aunt Myrtle strolled along, Laura was thoughtful.

"So, dearie, tell me about my nephew's bride-to-be."

"Amanda's wonderful."

"Big Boy's kinda shy. What's she like?"

"Oh, she makes him laugh a lot."

"That's real good. Is she tall? Big Boy takes after his daddy, you know."

Laura frowned. Big Boy was very nice but she didn't think he was anything like Duke.

"Did I say something wrong?" asked Aunt Myrtle.

"I was just thinking."

"Bet they make a real nice couple."

"How tall is Duke?"

"You got a crush on him, don't you?"

"No, I don't," Laura said, blushing.

"It's okay, dearie. Our ma was always having to shake his girlfriends outta the trees. Women just naturally like him. He's so easy to talk to, so relaxed."

"Is he always so nice?"

"Only time I ever saw him upset was a couple of months before he married Lilli."

"You won't tell that I like him?"

"Course not. What's Amanda look like?"

"Well, she has beautiful eyes."

"Eyes are important. They tell a lot about what's inside a person."

"Eyes are the windows of the soul."

"That's very nice. Did you make it up?"

"I don't think so."

"Isn't that interesting. Now dearie, tell me more about Amanda."

"Well, she's got lashes long as willow branches and the cheeriest smile and flowers on top of her head, like a hat."

"You certainly got a knack for describing things," Aunt Myrtle said admiringly.

"Should I describe some more?" Laura asked, pleased.

"Sure.

"Her eyes are blue like the sea and her skin is satiny white, and..."

"A white gorilla?"

Laura giggled. "Amanda's not a gorilla. She's a whale."

"A whale? Now ain't that something. Big Boy and a whale. Imagine that." Aunt Myrtle got a funny look on her face. "Amanda wouldn't be from the Oceanus clan, would she?"

"You know them?"

"Only what I hear."

"I met Amanda's parents. They were very nice."

"I don't suppose you'd happen to remember their names by any chance?"

"Felicity and Norville," said Laura, wondering what she was getting at.

Aunt Myrtle let out a whoop. "Felicity and Norville! Wait till Lilli hears about this!"

"Hears about what?"

"About her son marrying Felicity's daughter."

"What about it?" Laura wondered if this had anything to do with the species stuff Uncle Oliver had been talking about. "You mean because Amanda's a whale and Big Boy's a gorilla."

"Shucks, that don't make no difference. My last husband was a sea lion, Sebastian Sea Lion, best gypsy impersonator in the universe."

"Then what?" Laura was perplexed.

"It ain't just Lilli that'll be upset. Wait till Felicity finds out her Amanda is marrying Duke's son."

"Amanda's and Big Boy's parents already know each other?"

"Gossip says they do."

"Who's Gossip?"

Aunt Myrtle laughed. "It's not a who. It's a what. Gossip is when folks say things about someone."

"What kind of things?" Laura asked, intrigued.

"All sorts of things. Things they make up, or things nobody else is supposed to know about."

Gossip sounded interesting.

"All kinds of things about folks you'll likely never even meet. Funny," Aunt Myrtle chuckled, "when it comes to foolishness, it don't seem to matter; rich or poor, famous or not, we're all the same."

Laura had an idea. "Maybe we should have a newspaper with gossip stories for the wedding so all the guests could find out things about each other. We could interview them, like on TV."

"Well," Aunt Myrtle said hesitantly, "I don't know..."

"We could put in lots of 'intimate' details," Laura said enthusiastically, using a phrase she'd seen in the Criminal Gazette.

"Intimate details? How intimate?"

"Things like what you said about Felicity and Norville, and Duke and Lilli. We could put copies everywhere so everyone could get to know everyone else."

"They sure would," Aunt Myrtle said, chuckling. "Would those intimate details of yours include what they call affairs of the heart?"

"Of course," Laura said confidently, sensing they must be very important.

"You know, dearie, some folks might not want everyone to know everything about them."

"Why not?"

"Well, maybe they got reasons. Sometimes people pretend things about themselves."

"But if we put everything about them in our newspaper they wouldn't have to pretend."

"Some folks don't feel comfortable unless they pretend."

"But how can anyone get to know what they're like?"

"Lots of times they can't."

"Don't they feel lonely?"

"Never looked at it that way," Aunt Myrtle said thoughtfully.

"Anyway, I think people would like gossip stories."

"It would be interesting to see how some folks react," said Aunt Myrtle, a mischievous gleam in her eye.

"It'll be like they're celebrities. Everyone will talk about them."

"I'll say," Aunt Myrtle chuckled. "In this case you won't need anything but the facts, dearie, the facts of life."

"That would be a good name for our newspaper, the Facts of Life."

Aunt Myrtle laughed. "I think that one's been used before."

"Oh," Laura said, disappointed.

"Laura, honey, sooner or later a person's bound to say something someone else said first."

"It doesn't sound very newspapery anyway."

"You'll think of something else."

"I know, let's call it the Wedding Gazette."

"That sounds very dignified."

"The Wedding Gazette." It sounded very professional.

"You could put in lots of the describing you like to do. Trot out those words and make 'em dance."

Laura laughed, imagining rows and rows of words high-kicking, like chorines at the Club Galaxy.

Chapter Eighteen

Duke Reflects

Enjoying the break from his usual routine, Duke strode through the forest, tickled by that little girl, Laura's, pluck and fancifulness. He was glad he'd taken a leisurely detour instead of going directly from Starport to the wedding site. He needed times like this, away from Lilli's charming but watchful presence. An early worry of hers about his interest in someone else had made watchfulness a habit with her.

Glancing up at the sky, he reminded himself how much he was looking forward to his retirement from the Space Corps. No more breaking in starships for hot shot young pilots, who got to take them off into the unknown. Each time he got into a new ship he fought the urge to head out for the Unexplored himself. But he'd made a bargain with Lilli before they were married, a bargain he wouldn't have made if he hadn't returned from his first assignment with his confidence shattered by something more dangerous than space flight — falling in love with someone way out of his league. Lilli, smart lady that she

was, never asked what had happened, only making him
promise that if she married him he would take a perma-
nent assignment close to home.

But now that he was about to take early retirement he
would be free to do what he'd always wanted, if he still
had the courage. After Big Boy's wedding he intended to
find out.

It was a little disconcerting to realize he had a son old
enough to get married when he still felt young enough to
follow a young man's dream. He hoped Big Boy wasn't
making any compromise with his dreams. In a way, he
was proud of his son for having the sense to walk away
from the Space Academy when he realized it wasn't for
him. Hopefully, he'd used the same good sense picking a
mate.

Not that his life with Lilli hadn't been good. Lilli was
the best. She was just going to have to accept that he
wasn't putting off his dream any longer. Somehow, meeting that little girl Laura had strengthened his determina-
tion. Maybe it was her spunk or the way she held out her
hand for him to kiss. He saw many of the romantic no-
tions in her he still had inside himself.

Chapter Nineteen

Finnie Arrives

Great Aunt Finnie, a mermaid of indeterminate age, rose from the sea like a goddess, astride her escort, a very young, very muscular, wet-behind-the-ears seahorse. Her extravagantly red, lamé gown, which matched her plush red lips and long red fingernails, clung to a body that could still drive males of every species to foolish excess. Her long, blond hair was piled atop her head; wispy tendrils drifted around her face emphasizing her long graceful neck.

"Tibor, darling," she said huskily, managing to make her command sound like a seductive request, "go find Amanda for Mama."

"How will I know her?" asked Tibor, his voice fluctuating between manhood and adolescence.

"Tibor, darling, how many white whales do you imagine you'll find at a gypsy encampment? Think, darling,

think, before you speak. Now go," she said, throwing him
a kiss.

Finnie was often fashionably late, not because it was
fashionable, but because she'd be having such a good
time wherever she was. But this time she was early because Reggie's space yacht had been grounded by a
starstorm on that dreary planet, Misery, home of the
Holier-Than-Thous. She couldn't wait to get away from
the place.

Just thinking about those sanctimonious hypocrites
infuriated her. Why did some people feel it was their
mission in life to inflict their sour sublimations on everyone else? And that pompous, fake, Holy Man of theirs,
what nerve! She'd been sleeping an innocent sleep when
he slipped into her cabin and tried to remove her satin
penoir and replace it with that scratchy sackcloth negli-
gee. What could she do but smack him with her bed
lamp, grab the baubles Reggie had just given her and slip
into the nearest ocean?

It wasn't long before she noticed a very attractive
seahorse and decided to call for help. It didn't occur to
him that being a mermaid she couldn't be drowning.
Tibor was a charming boy. A little young perhaps, not too
bright perhaps, a little inexperienced, but such an eager
pupil.

What was taking Tibor so long? Finnie glanced down
the beach. No sign of him. In the distance she could see
the welcoming campfires and realized she was a bit
chilled. Normally, a luxurious wrap would be placed upon
her shoulders at the slightest sign that she was cold, but
this time she'd given her usual retinue of suitors the slip.
She didn't want them pulling any of their stunts at
Amanda's wedding. They were so boisterous, always trying to outdo each other, piling on gifts, competing for her
affection. Much as she loved gifts, it spoiled things when
her worshipers became unruly. "Boys," she would scold in

her best sultry voice, "Mama will banish you if you misbe-
have." Lately, she'd begun to wonder if the fuss they
made over her, their mad pursuit, wasn't just a sport for
them, like water polo or surfing barefoot on waves of light.

She hoped she'd also managed to give those parasitic
gossip columnists the slip. They were worse than her
suitors. And they didn't give presents even though her
every indiscretion was a gift to them. They'd made a cot-
tage industry out of her escapades. True, she did derive a
certain amount of pleasure from embellishing things. The
columnists didn't seem to care whether what she told
them was true or not, so long as it looked good in print.
Celebrity did have its rewards — the best tables at the
best restaurants, the best designers vying for her patronage, proposals from millionaires she'd never met, but at
times it could be inconvenient; like now, at Amanda's
wedding. Amanda's parents, Felicity and Norville, would
be horrified at the thought of being written up in a gossip
column. Those insufferable Goodie-Two-Prudes, it was a
miracle that they'd managed to have even one child, never
mind one as down to earth as Amanda who, she was
sure, would take it all in good humor.

Not that Felicity had always been so proper. There
had been something, way back when. Her family had
hushed things up and sent her away to 'recover'. There
was a skeleton in a closet there somewhere.

Finnie wondered what was keeping her little sea pony.
Shivering in the cold wind whipping in from the sea, she
headed for the welcoming warmth of the campfires.

Chapter Twenty

Maurice Mistakes Himself

Having restored his seaweed arrangements to perfection after that nasty incident with the red-headed child, Maurice glowed with satisfaction. Hopefully she wasn't anyone important. If he'd been sure she was a mere nobody he would have cheerfully incinerated her. What nerve she had wanting the Great Maurice to share the spotlight with an amateur, and a child at that. He could just imagine the kind of things she'd want to include in his magnificent décor, little cuddly dolls, yo-yos, mudpies and such.

His seaweed centerpieces were a stroke of genius. And how apt for an Oceanus wedding. Sometimes he was so good he scared himself. The mystery was why it was taking the rest of the universe so long to catch on. He was certain this wedding would finally catapult him into intergalactic fame. Then he could drop Felicity and the whole Oceanus family with a splash. Too bad about the groom's plebian background. Tree species were a trifle déclassé. It might take some of the luster off his achievement. He wouldn't be at all surprised if they wanted bananas added to his elegant seaweed creations.

Hmm. Did Felicity and Norville know the groom was a gorilla? Probably not. It would be delicious to witness their embarrassment when the truth came out. For years Felicity had treated him like a performing lizard instead of the great artiste he was, trotting him out to impress her rich, empty-headed friends. Lately, she'd made it quite apparent she was disappointed that her "pet" hadn't won any blue ribbons. Not half as disappointed as he was, considering all the doors her patronage had opened for him. The universe was apparently even more insipid than he had supposed, forcing him to behave obsequiously for a lot longer than he'd planned.

Felicity's impatience was frustrating, but Norville's indifference was infuriating. After all his years with them Norville still mistook him for a butler or waiter, forever asking him, the Great Maurice, to mix him a drink or light his pipe. He would never forgive Norville for the humiliation he'd suffered the night he'd insisted on being treated as the genius he was, pointing out the magnificent décor he, the Great Maurice, had created. Norville had glanced up from the Financial Times to select a bon-bon. "Felicity, get rid of this junk and hire a decorator instead of letting the waiter do it."

Maurice vented his pent-up fury by harassing the servants, among whom his petty tyrannies were legend. His fiery outbursts made it necessary for them to be ever on the alert, fire extinguishers at the ready, interfering with their chores and creating a constant state of emergency. Their hostility had become so extreme Maurice made a practice of switching place cards at the dinner table, afraid his food might be poisoned. So far, no one had suffered anything worse than a stomach ache.

One way or another this wedding was going to put an end to his obscurity and frustration. Once the scandal of an Oceanus marrying a gorilla was out in the open, he'd allow himself to be interviewed standing next to one of his creations, tinkering with it as he spoke. Acting the part of the loyal retainer, he would let slip that he had not allowed his patron's humiliation to effect his artistic obligation, however offensive the situation might be to him personally. The photographers would snap away and his reputation would be made.

Just thinking of it made his squinty red eyes crinkle with glee, his fire ducts twitch, his livid red tongue coil like a cobra ready to strike. A venomous smirk exposed his sharp white fangs. No one would dare call him 'waiter' again.

"Oh, waiter," a husky female voice called, "have you seen a seahorse wandering about?"

Maurice stiffened. "Are you calling me waiter?"

"I don't see anyone else, do you?" Finnie's glance swept the room, coming to rest on one of his dingy seaweed ensembles. "How original, seaweed for an Oceanus wedding."

"Of course," Maurice said haughtily, temperature rising, "one would have to be a professional to appreciate the finer points of decorating."

"I see," said Finnie, picking up one of the smaller arrangements with just two well-manicured fingers as if fearing contamination, dropping it disgustedly after a moment's inspection.

Maurice began exhaling smoke by the cloudful.

All that smoke and no fire, thought Finnie. No wonder he was so testy.

"Madam," said Maurice, little slivers of flame darting

out between his clenched fangs.

"That's better," said Finnie. "Smoke without fire is very unhealthy, you know."

"Madam!" Maurice shrieked, beside himself. "I am the decorator!"

"Poor dear," Finnie said sweetly, jumping back to avoid being incinerated. "Temper, temper," she admonished, "toodle-oo."

Chapter Twenty-One

Things That Matter

Wrapped in solitude by the incoming fog, Laura sat at her thinking place, a cliff high above the endless sea, her notebook open in her lap. Every now and then she would jot down an idea for the Wedding Gazette. Her word collecting was starting to bear fruit. The right words were popping up just when she needed them, along with a lot of their tag-a-long friends, neighbors and relatives. All she had to do was listen and there they were, quivering with anticipation, eager to be chosen. She couldn't possibly use them all in the Wedding Gazette, but she admired them nonetheless. Like Magdalena's musical instruments, they were beautiful in their own right, waiting only for their chance to shine.

She planned to begin the Gazette with a description of Amanda, how tall she was, her flowers, her lovely smile. Of course this wouldn't tell what Amanda was like inside, which was what Laura really wanted to write about. For that she would have to tell how she and Amanda became friends and about their adventures together, which would

take up more space than she'd planned for her whole
newspaper, leaving no room for Mother Romany, Big Boy,
Magdalena, Guitano or the Naming of the New Queen.
And what about Duke? She wanted to write a whole story
about Duke. And then there were the guests. Some of
them were bound to be interesting.

It had all been so easy when she was just thinking
about it but when it came to writing things down she
found she had much more to say than would ever fit into
the Gazette. Putting her notebook aside she picked up the
copy of *THEM!*, a popular gossip magazine she'd borrowed
from Aunt Myrtle to see how they handled the problem.

THEM! What a silly name — as if the people they
wrote about were different from, or better than, or led
more interesting lives than anyone else. Actually, it didn't
tell very much about the people at all. It was mostly pictures with a few words explaining the pictures which
showed famous people and their 'escorts' doing this or
that uninteresting thing, wearing this or that designer's
clothes. And for some reason, it always said how old they
were. Laura couldn't understand why *THEM!* was so
popular.

> Yvonne Sharktooth, 29, heiress, fell off her yacht last night
> at Star Harbor while wearing a stunning strapless creation
> by Alphonse of the House DuJour. We wonder, is our dear
> Yvonne hitting the bottle again? Her fiancee, Sir Laurance
> Lobster, 22, an Earl, no less, was seen earlier in the evening
> at the Snakepit, wing in claw with a gorgeous white swan, 19,
> who, according to our source, 23, refused to be interviewed.
> 'Just friends', Larry?

It didn't make sense. Why didn't they find out who the
swan was and how she and Larry became friends? How
could hitting a bottle make Yvonne fall off her yacht,
whatever that was? *THEM!* left out all the interesting
things. Disappointed, Laura put the magazine down. The
fog had lifted. Sparkling little waves were dancing playfully on the surface of the sea. She looked out to the far

horizon, thinking of the things she really wanted to write about.

"Hello, Princess."

"Oh, Sir Duke," she said, pleased.

"Mind if I join you?"

"You may sit beside me on the royal rock."

"I'm honored," he said, seating himself. He was surprised to see her with a copy of *THEM!* instead of a book, of poetry maybe. "Is this yours?"

"Oh no," Laura said with a look of distaste. "I borrowed it from Aunt Myrtle to see how they told about people."

"From the looks of things you don't like it very much."

"It's okay if you don't care about the people."

"But you do care."

"Yes."

They sat in silence for a while, listening to the soft, whispery sound of the sea caressing the rocks. The wind picked up, rustling the pages of Laura's notebook.

"What are you writing?" asked Duke.

"I'm trying to write a newspaper for the wedding, but it's hard to fit everything in unless I do it like *THEM!* does."

"Journalism's not very good, is it?"

"Journalism?"

"That's what it's called when you write newspaper stories."

"Is journalism bad?"

"Not bad, exactly," he said reflectively. "Good journalists try to be accurate and tell the whole story about the people and the events they're describing."

"That's what I'm trying to do, but there's too much to fit in."

"Well, you could put it in a book."

"Would that still be journalism?"

"Books are more about imagination and dreams."

Imagination and dreams! Like the books with the golden edges. She didn't have to put everything in the Wedding Gazette. "I could write lots of books!" she said excitedly, picturing shelves and shelves of books, a book for each person she wrote about, full of all the wonderful things she felt and imagined. It would be like telling things to her father when he came home at night, only the books would always be there. They would have golden edges and satin ribbons and lots of pictures and covers with gold letters and beautiful designs, in warm, gypsy colors.

Aware that something very important was going on, Duke sat silently beside her. As they watched the changing colors of the sea, Laura thought about the things she would put in her books — about how beautiful it was out among the stars, about how much she liked the gypsies and how glad she was to have people like Duke, Amanda, Magdalena and Mother Romany to talk to, about her *doThings*, about seeing her father's hologram that day on the beach. She could write down all the stories she'd been saving to tell him. Maybe she could even write ways to find him. She gave a start. Writing could help her find her father!

"Anything wrong?"

"Duke, do you ever have dreams you wish for so hard you feel like you can make them come true?"

"Yes, Princess, I do."

"Big dreams?"

"Real big."

"Big as the whole universe?"

"Even bigger," he said, smiling.

"Bigger? What could be bigger than the whole universe?"

"Sometimes, Princess, what's in your heart."

Part Three

Chapter Twenty-Two

Lorelei Gets Her Way

As soon as Evert was out the door Lorelei let out a screech-laugh. She'd spent most of the evening listening to the poor boob go on and on about how generous it was of him to give her the plum assignment of photographer for the wedding, as if she didn't know about Vern Light being missing, lost in some black hole somewhere. Actually, she found Evert's pathetic attempts to manipulate her rather endearing.

She yawned, stretching her opalescent arms luxuriously and reached for the holophone. Instantly, her father's feisty face appeared, ivory horn and all. It looked dashing on him, but it was the only feature she'd inherited from him that she didn't like. She'd had hers removed, at his expense, naturally. "Reggiedaddy," she cooed.

He grunted. "How much is it going to cost me this time?"

"Oh daddy, what a way to say hello to poor Lorelei."

"Poor you ain't, kiddo."

"Oh daddy." He was the one man she couldn't bamboozle, for which she loved him all the more.

"So? How much?"

"Only a billion, but I need it today."

"A billion!"

"But, daddy, I have to buy a whole new wardrobe for Amanda's wedding, and presents and..."

"Since when have you been a billion friendly with Amanda?" he asked, his penetrating black eyes boring into hers.

"But, daddy," said Lorelei, her large, sea-green eyes open wide, "Amanda and I have always been close."

"You haven't seen her since you were kids."

"Well," she said, "I think about her a lot."

"Lorelei, this is daddy you're talking to." He sat up in bed, swinging his feet around onto the floor. "You want it for that idiot you're engaged to, that Evert Snidely."

"Oh daddy!" she squealed, "you're wearing the pajamas Mom and I gave you!" They had pictures of Finnie and Lorelei all over them; cavorting at the pool, playing croquet, trying on hats. "You look adorable."

He gave a short, snort-laugh. The little minx could always get around him.

"Daddiepoo, would I lie to you?"

"It's one of the things I can count on," he said ironically. "If you stopped I'd get worried."

She laughed. "Are you coming to the wedding? Momsie will be there."

"That's no recommendation," he said sourly. "Your mother jumped ship on me the other night. Left me stuck on that flea bitten planet, Misery. I was up half the night worrying about her. She's totally irresponsible."

"But loveable, like me."

"Yeah, right."

"I have to go now, daddikins. Hair, nails, facial, massage, shopping, you can't imagine."

"I don't have to imagine. I get the bills. What's that hairdresser, Ferdinand, using for dye these days, real platinum?"

"Daddy, what a thing to say about your Lorelei. Everyone knows I'm a natural blond."

"Listen, Pookie, I was there when you were born."

"Well, maybe the light was bad," she said, flouncing her long, platinum blond hair. "Will I see you at the wedding?"

"Not if those idiots who follow your mother around are going to be there."

"She told me she'd given them the slip."

"Whose slip?"

"Oh daddy. What about the wedding?"

"I'll be there," he grumbled.

"Ta-ta, daddikins. Don't forget about the billion. Remember my account number?"

"How could I forget. I know it better than my own."

Lorelei hung up, smiling to herself. He was so tough and loveable. How would she ever find anyone like him? She rang for the butler. Gustave bounded in on his springy, kangeroo legs. "You rang, Lorelei," he said eagerly.

"Really, Gustave. I've told you a thousand times, it's over between us. I am engaged. You must address me properly if you are to remain in my employ."

"Yes, ma'am," he said contritely, his large ears drooping.

"You know I can't stand it when you do that," she said, trying to be firm with him. "Take this to Mr. Snidely at Cosmic Communications at once." She handed him a small gold box tied with a diamond studded ribbon.

"Do I have to?" he asked, his big brown eyes filling with tears.

"Oh, Gustave," she sighed. "Alright, huggy-huggy. But this is the last time."

One short hop and he was in her arms.

Chapter Twenty-Three

Magdalena's Dream

A sliver of lavender in the purple dark, the Moon watched intently as Magdalena entered Mother Romany's tent.

"May I come in?"

"Of course, Magda. I have been expecting you."

Though Magdalena knew about the mystical transformation of the old queen, she still was not prepared for the shock of seeing her mirror image in the person of Mother Romany. She felt angry, as though her identity had been stolen from her, that she was merely part of a continuum of what had been, was, and would be. "Mother Romany," she said, her voice shaking, "I am not ready. Not ready."

"Fate is deaf to our anger," Mother Romany said quietly. "It hears only its own voice."

"I know..."

Remembering her own distress at encountering her own twin self, ten centuries before, Mother Romany waited for Magdalena to continue.

"I am no longer me. I feel I have lost my soul."

Mother Romany's healing sympathy reached out to her. "Could it be you have lost an illusion, that your soul is in your destiny?"

Magdalena felt the rightness of Mother Romany's words stir something inside her. "I have had the Dream of Confirmation. It has given me some peace, but..."

"Tell me your dream."

The two women sat facing each other in the flickering light. Magdalena began, hesitantly, at first. "I am on an urgent journey, moving through a misty, barren landscape, obsessed with getting somewhere, but I don't know where or why it is so urgent. I am grim, relentless. I look neither right nor left, only straight ahead into the featureless distance. Then, all at once, off to my left, I hear the most astounding music. It is so compelling that I abandon my driven course and go toward the music, intently, as though my soul depends on it." She fell silent, rehearing the music in her dream as Mother Romany gathered stillness around them to help her concentrate. "It is music the stars make when they sing to each other across the distances, cool, without beat, a crystal sound like breaking ice, but warm and voluptuous too, shimmering like a corona of mist around the moon."

"Yes," Mother Romany said softly, remembering.

"I go toward the music. It is my soul singing to me, guiding me to myself. When I reach the place I see three dark-skinned boys in brilliant robes. Eyes closed, they are twirling, dancing, twisting, pressing places on their bodies with nimble fingers, creating the music, celebratively, effortlessly, each movement, each touch creating miracles of sound. They are utterly absorbed in the music they are making, in the music which they are." Magdalena paused, overcome by her recollection.

"And then?" Mother Romany prompted, knowing there was more.

"Then I see their faces." Magdalena's face was suffused with wonder. "I shall never forget their faces, the ecstasy, the love. They were the soul made visible, the soul and its music made one. We are each of us our own instrument."

"We and the music of ourselves are one," they said in unison.

The two women sat in silence, gripped by the miracle, all the light in the tent gathering around them.

"You have been given the greatest gift, the gift of experiencing the music of your own soul."

"Till now, I had thought my destiny my prison," Magdalena said wonderingly.

"I understand," said Mother Romany. "At some point in life we are given a vision of great potential. We have a choice to refuse it and continue as before, looking neither to the left nor to the right, or we can change our direction and follow the music our soul sings."

"Can you always hear it?"

"Sometimes it is not easy," said Mother Romany, a shadow crossing her face. "Other voices will make their way into your song. The strongest will be the voices of those you love, Guitano, your children, your children's children, the voices of your people. Through all these you must listen for your own true song. It will guide you in your life as it guides me now, as it can guide each of us to the place where all songs are one."

Chapter Twenty-Four

When Bad Things Happen

The minute he saw Amanda, Duke knew fate had thrown him a curve. She was Felicity's daughter all right. The resemblance was so strong he pulled back a little when she kissed his cheek. He hoped she hadn't noticed; it would be awkward for him to explain why. Even her voice and the scent of her flowers reminded him of Felicity, but he could see right away Amanda was more sure of herself. Nothing was going to stop her from marrying Big Boy.

The look of pride and love on Big Boy's face reminded him of what loving Felicity had been like for him. It almost broke his heart. It surprised him how strong the hurt still was, the hurt, and the undertow of still caring. What a time to discover Felicity and his dreams were still tangled up together, almost as if he couldn't have one without the other. No sooner had he decided to change his life than fate sent it spinning like a top.

He hoped his hurt and confusion hadn't spoiled any-thing for Big Boy and Amanda. As soon as he could he headed for the sea to sort himself out. He was glad to find Laura there, looking out at the water, her red hair tousled by the wind. Their talk about her writing, and her upbeat attitude about things had strengthened his confidence in his own dreams. It was good to watch her sort through various possibilities, see her turn them over in her mind like multifaceted jewels. "Hi, Princess, mind if I join you?"

"Oh, hi," she said, delighted.

"Are you writing?"

"No, I'm dreaming."

"I could do with some of that."

"What's the matter?"

"Nothing important," he said, stretching himself out and looking up at the clouds.

She reached out and touched his cheek. "I know when someone's sad."

"And how would you come by such knowledge, O-Princess-of-happiness-and-dreams?"

"When my father was sad I would kiss him and make it go away." She was quiet for a moment. "Sometimes I'm sad too."

"Like now?"

"I haven't kissed my father for a long time," she said wistfully.

"I bet he feels kissed every time you think about him."

"Do you think so?"

"I bet he's smiling right now."

Laura stared out at the horizon. "Duke, why do bad things happen?"

"You mean, like your father?"

"Other things too."

"I wish it were different," he said soberly. "But we'll be okay Princess, you and I. We've got something deep inside us the bad things can't touch."

"That's right," she said, her spirits lifting a little.

Chapter Twenty-Five

Business As Usual

Reggie punched the holophone button in his usual forceful manner, reaching his private presidential suite at Rhino Enterprises. The sorrowful face of his second in command, Beesely Bowser, appeared. Beesely's long, droopy ears, baggy eyes and sagging jowls gave him a look of perpetual woe.

"Yeah, Boss," Beesely said wearily, his eyes fixed on the column of figures in front of him. "I'm in the middle of something here."

"What's wrong?"

"Nothing's wrong."

"Why so grumpy?"

"Unlike some people, I have work to do."

"What's that supposed to mean?"

Beesely sighed. This was going to be one of *those* conversations. "It means I'm busy."

And I'm not; that's what he really means, thought Reggie. "Do I have to come in today?"

"Why should today be different?"

"Very funny."

They'd been through this so often it was choreographed. They both knew Reggie hated routine details. That's why he'd hired Beesely. Beesely loved details.

"Listen," Reggie said, seriously, "transfer a billion to Lorelei's account."

"Why not put it directly into Snidely's? There'd be less paperwork that way."

"Beesely, you're a cynic."

"If you say so."

Of course, Beesely was right about Snidely. He was always right. That's what made him so valuable. It also made him annoying. "And Beez, send a space-dozer to pick up the yacht. It's stuck on that godforsaken planet, Misery."

"This is the third time in a month you've gotten stuck somewhere. This is getting expensive. You've got to start paying more attention to where you're going."

"It was a star storm. Why do you always assume the worst about me? Sometimes you're wrong."

"Yeah, sometimes," said Beesely, unimpressed.

"So," said Reggie, changing the subject. "How's our

undersea prospecting project going?"

"Pretty good. Nothing big yet, but enough to keep things interesting."

"Do I need to sign anything?"

"It would only confuse the accounting department. They're so used to my version of your signature they'd probably call the cops and have you arrested."

"I see you've thought of everything," Reggie said sardonically.

"What's up? All of a sudden you don't trust me?" said Beesely, pretending to be hurt.

"What makes you say that?"

"This wanting to come to work, sign things, asking about things — it's not like you."

"Maybe it should be. Maybe I should pay more attention to things," said Reggie, needling him a little. "Maybe I shouldn't leave everything to you."

"Maybe you shouldn't. Of course, things are running great around here. Money is pouring in like water. Your investments are sound. Your trust funds are up to the brim, tax free. You'd probably just screw up the system."

"Whaddaya mean?" snarled Reggie.

Beesely snorted, wondering if maybe he'd gone a little too far this time. "You haven't been in the office for years. We've got a well-oiled machine here. Start monkeying with the engine and you never know what'll happen."

"Oh yeah? Don't forget who built that engine."

"I know, I know," Beesely said wearily. "You built Rhino Enterprises from nothing. You found the investors. You made the market. You did it all. Now you deserve to relax, enjoy life and leave the drudgery to me."

"That's right," agreed Reggie. "But I'm getting bored. Maybe I need to ride herd on Rhino again."

"What for?" Beesely asked cautiously. He didn't want Reggie looking over his shoulder, poking his nose in things, disrupting routine. Beesely had been running things too long to be content with being second in command. Rhino Enterprises was his life. "Boss, you need a new challenge," Beesely said craftily. "That fancy space yacht you got stuck on Misery, maybe you should take off for the Unexplored in it and discover things, like in the old days. Take Finnie with you."

Unbeknownst to Beesely, Reggie had already outfitted the ship for just such a voyage. Like most self-made tycoons he relished control but didn't want to be trapped behind a desk. "Beez, you've hit on something," he said, letting Beesely take credit for the idea. "After all, Rhino was built on stuff I brought back from the Unexplored."

"That's right," Beesely said encouragingly.

"You're a good man, Beesely. It's a great idea." Reggie knew Beesely would be loyal as long as he felt he was in charge. "I might be gone a long time. Think you can manage without me?"

"Always have," said Beesely, managing to keep his hangdog expression despite his elation.

"I'll take off right after the wedding."

"Good idea."

Chapter Twenty-Six

Look Grim/Feel Grim/Be Grim

"I don't see why I have to go to a stupid wedding," Sheila whined, scrunching up her small face into an ugly scowl.

"Sheila, try to be nice. They're my friends," Gen pleaded with his daughter.

She glowered, unmoved. "Your friends," she said contemptuously, sounding just like her mother.

"Honey," Gen said placatingly. "It'll be good for you to be around real people for a change."

"They're probably scum of the earth," Sheila sneered, rattling off her condemnation by rote.

"Where do you learn such things?" Gen asked, dismayed.

"I won't go."

"Listen, Sheila, while your mother is at that seminar on Misery you're gonna be with me, and where I go, you go. Got it? I'm gonna make you human again if it kills me."

"I suppose you think gambling and carousing is human," she said loftily.

They sure work fast on a kid, Gen thought unhappily, hoping it wasn't too late to undo some of the damage. "Sheila, somewhere in you is my real kid and I'm gonna get her back."

"Oh father, really."

"Don't oh-father me; I'm still in charge. You're gonna meet that great kid I told you about. You're gonna love her."

"I'm going to hate her. I already hate her."

Gen sighed. She hates so quickly. "What's happened to you? You used to love people. You used to be so much fun. Every waiter, dealer and gambler at the Club Galaxy was wrapped around your finger. What a black jack dealer you were, a regular child prodigy. Now, look at you."

"That was before I learned the truth," she said primly.

"What truth?"

"It's our duty to be miserable," she said, running the words all together. "Look grim, feel grim, be grim."

"Sheila!" Gen exclaimed, horrified. "You can't believe that!"

"I do so. I learned it at Misery School."

"Everybody knows that's crazy."

"Everybody is wrong."

This ain't gonna be easy, thought Gen. She seemed to like this misery stuff. Sure, she was just a kid, but who knew how deep it went? Maybe Laura could get through to her.

As they approached the gypsy encampment, Sheila stopped, aghast. "Father, this is a gypsy camp! I couldn't possibly set foot in such a place!"

"Then we'll leave your foot behind," Gen said, exasperated, "and just take the resta you with us."

"You can't make me."

"Wanna bet?" Gen asked, slinging her onto his shoulder and marching into the camp.

Chapter Twenty-Seven

Laura's First Interview

On her way back from the sea Laura wandered
through the hustle and bustle of the wedding area, looking for someone to interview. So far, everyone had been
either too busy or not interesting enough. Then she heard
a hearty, female laugh and turned to see a gorgeous mermaid, dressed all in red. She was making fun of Maurice's
seaweed arrangements to an athletic young seahorse.
Laura was intrigued. Notebook in hand, she marched over
to the mermaid, determined to get an interview. "My name
is Laura," she said, trying to sound professional. "You
look very interesting. Could I interview you for the Wedding Gazette?"

"The Wedding Gazette," said the mermaid, amused.
"Let me think, I don't believe I've ever heard of it."

"It's new."

"I see, and out of all these people you've chosen me."

"Yes. You're wearing my favorite color and I like the way you laugh."

"Very good reasons, I'm sure," she said, charmed by Laura's directness. "I predict great success for you and the Wedding Gazette."

"Thank you," said Laura, opening her notebook. "Would you mind telling me your name and how old you are?"

"My, my, my. Well, my name is Finnie."

"Amanda's Aunt Finnie? The one who's so beautiful?"

"How well informed you are. That's a sign of a good reporter, you know," Finnie said pleased. "And believe me, I know what I'm talking about; I've been interviewed hundreds of times."

Pleased with her choice of someone to interview, Laura was determined to make the most of it. "I'll start with how beautiful you are."

"I have never met a more charming reporter. Please convey my compliments to your publisher."

"What's a publisher?"

"Why, the person who runs things, the one who puts out the paper."

"Oh, then I'm the publisher," Laura said matter-of-factly.

"That's a great responsibility for one so young."

"Yes, it is," said Laura. "Can I ask some more questions now?"

"Of course," said Finnie.

"Is this young man your son?"

"Tibor is my protégé."

"Protégé?" asked Laura, wondering how to spell it. "What's a protégé?"

"A protégé is someone who is being trained."

"What are you training him to do?"

Tibor snickered.

"Tibor," Finnie ordered, "go tell Amanda I will be along shortly."

"Aw gee, Finnie."

"Go, go." She waved him away.

"Did I ask something wrong?" Laura asked, sensing there was more to the situation than Finnie wanted her to know.

"Not at all, dear, not at all."

"Okay," said Laura, going on to other things. "You were laughing at the seaweed decorations. Would you like to comment on them for the Gazette?"

"How very observant you are."

"Thank you," said Laura. "How about the decorations?"

"That's right, the first rule of good reporting is persistence. Never let the person you're interviewing off the hook."

"Won't you answer my questions?"

Finnie laughed. "To tell you the truth, I think the decorations are awful."

"Me too," said Laura.

"No color, no dash, no verve."

"No nothing."

Finnie gave her an appraising look. "That's right, getting down to brass tacks is what good reporting is all about."

"I have more questions. Can I ask them now?"

"Of course, it's your job."

"Have you ever been to a double wedding?"

"Once or twice."

"Did you have fun?"

"I hadn't really thought about it that way, but yes, I did. Marriage is so hopeful, don't you think?"

"Are you married?"

"Is this for the Gazette?"

"I don't think so."

"In that case, I'm not married."

"Didn't anyone ever ask you?"

Finnie laughed. "Dozens, but at the time I had other

offers that were more interesting. Besides, I wasn't sure
marriage was for me."

"But how can you be sure of something unless you try
it?"

Finnie gave her a wary look. "You ask very interesting
questions for a child ...if you are a child."

"Of course I'm a child," Laura said, puzzled.

"Actually, I've been thinking about marriage a lot
lately," Finnie confided.

"Why?" Laura asked, curious.

"I'm tired of being alone, I guess."

"Don't you have any friends?"

"Yes, dear, I have many friends."

"I think friends are like getting to pick your own family."

"You mean instead of being born into one?" Finnie
asked, sensing something.

"Yes."

"Wouldn't you have picked your family?"

"I would have picked my father."

"But not your mother."

"No, I don't think so."

"If I were a family member would you have picked
me?"

"I already picked you."

"That's right, you have," said Finnie, giving her a hug. "Be sure and tell that to my daughter, Lorelei."

"Is she beautiful like you?"

"Yes, especially since she had that horn on her forehead removed."

"Just one? Like a unicorn?"

"Like a rhinoceros. Her father is a rhinoceros."

"Oh," said Laura, disappointed Finnie's daughter wasn't a unicorn. "How do you spell rhinoceros?"

"Is this for your paper?"

"Yes."

"I don't think you should put that in."

"That he's a rhinoceros?"

"No, dear," Finnie said, laughing, "that he's Lorelei's father."

"Doesn't he know?"

"Well, yes," said Finnie, getting flustered. "Of course he does. Everyone knows. It's just that the family wants to keep it a secret."

"But if everyone knows, who are they keeping it secret from?" Laura asked, perplexed.

Who indeed, thought Finnie. Reggie and Lorelei didn't care. The problem was with Finnie's family, the Oceanus clan and their snobbery. They refused to acknowledge Reggie was Lorelei's father. "You're a very good interviewer, Laura. Your questions make a person think."

"Then it's okay to put it in the Gazette about Lorelei and her father?"

"Yes. And long overdue."

"I want to tell the truth but I don't want to hurt anyone's feelings."

"That's a dilemma journalists often face."

"Maybe I shouldn't be a journalist."

"But you're a very good journalist. Your questions are very good."

"But it's so complicated, and it's hard to get everything in."

"Maybe you should write books."

"Oh, I'm going to, but first I have to do the Wedding Gazette. I promised Amanda and Magdalena."

"It's a big job for one person," Finnie said sympathetically. "Would you like me to help?"

"That would be great!"

"Of course, you'd have to teach me the tricks of the trade, how to ask questions as good as yours."

"You could be the art critic and interview Maurice. He's the decorator. He doesn't like me because I tried to get him to use my *doThings* in the decorations."

"Do things?"

"I make things that do things."

"What kinds of things?" Finnie asked, interested.

"Lots of things. Beautiful things. You'll see."

"I'd like to."

"I can show them to you right now," Laura said eagerly.

"As the art critic I could write about your *doThings* as well as about Maurice."

"That's right," Laura said, pleased, "but be careful around Maurice. He's a real dragon and he spits fire a lot."

"I know. We've met. As far as I'm concerned, Maurice is more smoke than fire."

* * * *

On their way to her workshop Laura heard a familiar voice calling her name. It was Pinocchio rushing toward her, his arms open wide. Loki was bounding along beside him, his tail in the air. Laura squealed with delight and ran to meet them.

It had been such a long time since she'd gone adventuring with Amanda. Pinocchio and Loki often thought of her, wondering where she was and what adventures she was having. They asked everyone who visited Contentment for news of her. Someone mentioned seeing her at the Big Beach in the company of a white whale, but that had been some time ago.

By coincidence, they were having one of their "I wonder about Laura" sessions when their invitations arrived.
The gypsies had considerately included a LightBeam to
bring them to the festivities, knowing Pinocchio's ability
to fly to distant galaxies had dwindled because he never
left Contentment. The speed of the LightBeam frightened
Pinocchio at first. What with nothing solid to hold onto
and everything whizzing past so fast it was all a blur.
Only his eagerness to see Laura again kept him going.
More composed and philosophical, Loki had enjoyed the
experience.

Waylaid on their arrival by a rude, wild-eyed dragon
with hot, bad breath and glaring red eyes, they'd begun to
wonder if they were on the wrong planet. The dragon had
tried to force blistering hot metal calling cards on them. *I
am the great Maurice. Beware, all Ye who enter the workshop of that amateur, redheaded upstart! You have been
warned!* They guessed he meant Laura and were concerned. But now, finding her looking taller and more sure
of herself, safe in the company of a lovely, important
looking mermaid, they were delighted and relieved.

The three old friends kissed and hugged and laughed.
Laura introduced them to her new friend, Finnie.

"Who was that nasty dragon?" asked Pinocchio. "He
seemed to have a grudge against you."

"Oh, that's Maurice. He's just jealous."

"Jealous of what?" asked Loki.

"My *doThings*. Come on, I was just going to show
them to Finnie." As they approached her workshop Laura
felt a twinge of uncertainty. Would they like her
doThings? What if Maurice was right? But the instant she
saw them she knew there was nothing to worry about.
"Here they are," she said proudly.

Her friends were stunned by the dazzle of colors and shapes, the light dancing off embedded jewels, the soaring sound of color.

"No wonder Maurice is jealous!" Finnie exclaimed.

"Color music!" Loki said wonderingly.

"Gee," said Pinocchio, "it makes me want to fly through rainbows."

Chapter Twenty-Eight

At Home With The Highwaters

"Mandrake!" Valerie Highwater yelled into the intercom.

In the kitchen alcove where he and the head of housekeeping, Mrs. Parsimonious, were playing chess, Mandrake looked up from the board. "Drat and double drat!" he exclaimed, crinkling his nose in distaste at the sound of his employer's voice.

"Mandrake!" screeched Mrs. H. "Get the H in here, pronto!"

Offended by her shouting, the intercom smothered her voice with static.

Mandrake sighed. "I wonder what she wants now."

Mrs. Parsimonious had the impulse to shrug but remained motionless, her eyes glued to the chessboard.

She never wasted anything, not even a gesture.

Still crackling with indignation, the intercom threatened to quit on the spot. It was unaccustomed to being screeched at, having until recently been blissfully employed by a monastery steeped in vows of silence.

Mandrake tried to soothe its jangled nerves. It saved him many trips back and forth through the vast, watery depths of the Oceanus family estate. Four intercoms had already quit because of Valerie's abuse. And being notorious gossips, they were spreading the word, making it harder and harder for Mandrake to find replacements. "Please don't quit. I promise to answer on the first call and Mrs. Parsimonious will feed you extra tidbits of electricity for dessert every day."

Not one watt more, thought Mrs. Parsimonious, unwilling to waste the energy it would have taken to speak.

Appeased, the intercom ceased its static.

Relieved, Mandrake left the alcove and swam through the long corridor to the sunroom where Valerie Highwater waited, her dorsal fin twitching impatiently.

"What took you so long?" she asked, exasperated.

Mandrake had been with Valerie's family since before she was born. He'd diapered her and seen her through endless tantrums. "I was detained by a distressed intercom. We must learn to take their feelings into account," he said reproachfully.

"Get rid of the ungrateful so and so," Valerie snapped.

"Madam, I am an elderly catfish, not one of those mechanisms," Mandrake sniffed with a disapproving twitch of his whiskers, alluding to the AutoServants she had introduced into the household. "Unlike mechanical retainers, I would expire from exertion without the services of an intercom."

"Humph." So far all the AutoServants had been duds but Valerie kept them around to remind the staff that they could be replaced.

"If you wish to rid yourself of things I suggest you dispose of those noisy, unreliable mechanisms." Their unreliability was largely due to the staff's campaign of sabotage, which at times reduced the mechanical interlopers to the electrical equivalent of tears. "You called," said Mandrake, changing the subject.

Valerie gave him an imperious look which would have been more effective if her newly dyed, pink lashes hadn't clashed so garishly with her blue skin. "Tell Mr. Highwater that Mrs. Highwater wants to speak to him. Right here. Now."

Mandrake sighed. "Madam, why not just phone him?" He was tired of being a pawn in their endless war of wills. He was far too old for all this back and forthing. If only they would spend more of their time in the same part of the estate. Did they really need to sit at opposite ends of a mile long dinner table? Did their bedrooms have to be at different undersea levels, keeping him up way past his bedtime carrying their angry messages back and forth? "The phone is such a marvelous invention," he said, knowing she would ignore his suggestion.

"Mandrake, I did not ask your opinion. I gave a command."

Mandrake sighed again. Whenever either of them got into the 'command' mode, it was useless to reason with them. Turning tail, he swam off creakily to deliver her message to Mr. Highwater in his study miles away.

Life at Oceana was becoming more exhausting with every passing day. When Mandrake had first heard Valerie was going to marry Marcus Highwater, he'd hoped it would moderate her formidable temper, or maybe Marcus would cart her off somewhere, but alas, it was not to be. Instead, Marcus had moved in, taking on the role of Lord-of-the-Manor, burdening the already overburdened staff with unreasonable demands of his own.

Because of his access to King Triton, Marcus Highwater was one of the most feared and powerful men in the galaxy. Valerie brought social status to their marriage. He brought power. Their constant war of wills made it a marriage of inconvenience for everyone else.

Suppressing his irritation, Mandrake tapped discreetly on the glass door of Marcus' study. Deference had been his life and he was not going to change now. However, he had recently found an outlet for his discontent in the form of a murder mystery he and Mrs. Parsimonious were writing. He particularly liked working out the details surrounding the mysterious disappearance of the aristocratic employers.

"Yes?" said Marcus, opening the door a crack.

"Mrs. Highwater requests your presence in her sunroom," Mandrake said wearily.

"What for?" Marcus asked suspiciously. Mandrake was a cagey old codger, not nearly as deferential as he pretended to be, not by a long shot. Marcus didn't trust anyone. Not even himself. He hadn't gotten to the top by trusting people. He was forever spinning tangled webs to ensnare others, sometimes getting tripped up in his own traps. "Tell her I'm busy."

"May I sit down for a moment? I'm too old for this."

"Mandrake, how long have you been with the Oceanus family?"

"Forever, Sir.

"Tell me, have I missed anything interesting lately? Any visitors I should know about?"

So, thought Mandrake, that was it. "No one special, Sir," he said blandly.

"But there have been visitors," Marcus said, concealing his feeling of triumph. "I thought so."

"Many visitors," Mandrake said calmly. "Will you be going to see the Mistress now?"

Maybe he'd better. Mandrake was obviously hiding something. "Yes, I believe I will. This big new project of Triton's," said Marcus, casually dropping Triton's name into the conversation, "I need a break from it."

"To be sure," said Mandrake.

Marcus checked his slender frame in one of the many full-length mirrors in his study, combed his long green tresses, brushed his walrus mustache, honed his smile to perfection and made a last minute adjustment to the folds of his toga. Infinitely vain, he was particularly proud of his iridescent, sea-green skin. His mother was a water goblin and his father a gob of pure sea matter. He loved being admired for his exotic good looks as he floated by dressed in the pale colors he so favored. Blowing a kiss to himself in the mirror, he set out on the long trek to Valerie's sunroom, Mandrake leading the way.

"Mr. Highwater, Madam," Mandrake announced, worn out by the journey.

"I can see that," she snapped.

"Valerie, darling, you look so well," said Marcus, kissing her cheek as coolly as she presented it.

"I can't imagine why," she said, sounding martyred. "I've been under such a strain."

"Is that a new dress?" asked Marcus.

"Yes, it is," she responded, surprised by the flutter of pleasure she felt at his noticing.

"It's stunning," he said smoothly, aware of her reaction. "It compliments the blue of your complexion. And you've lost a little weight. Not that you needed to," he added quickly.

She shot him an angry look. "Cut it, Marcus! Is Triton coming or not?" When Valerie wanted something, she wanted it bad, and what she wanted now was for Triton to attend her niece, Amanda's, wedding.

"We'll see." Access to Triton was Marcus' trump card. He maintained his leverage with her by keeping Triton just out of her reach.

"Dinner is served," squawked the intercom. "Come at once. Mrs. Parsimonious says there's not a moment to waste."

"We'd better go, dear," said Marcus, grateful for the interruption. "You know how she is."

"Marcus, I warn you, I'm not letting you off the hook. I'm sitting right next to you at dinner."

Mandrake preceded them into the dining room, making a perfunctory attempt to shield them from the redoubtable Mrs. Parsimonious, who stood rigidly at attention by the door. Most sea hens were plump and benign. Mrs. Parsimonious had no desire to be either plump or benign. Her scrawny neck jutted up from her bony shoulders; her face, from which she'd had the 'frivolous' feathers removed, making her beak look sharper, was pointedly severe. Her reproving glance made strong men quail. "Too many for dinner," she said flatly, as they entered the dining room.

"But they're family," Valerie whined.

"Too many," Mrs. Parsimonious repeated, eliminating two unnecessary words.

"We'll all just eat less," Marcus offered.

"Right."

Breaking precedent, Valerie insisted on being seated next to Marcus, forcing everyone on her side of the table to shift one seat to the right.

Actually, Valerie had lied. Not all the dinner guests were family. Mrs. Parsimonious took note of this, serving them nothing but empty plates. Family got their usual dollop of algae which Mrs. Parsimonious considered the perfect food, nutritious, tasteless and disgusting. No one was going to be tempted to excess at her table. She'd been serving algae since Valerie was a child. She was able to purchase it for a song, a squawk, actually, since the Algae Man, a glutton for punishment, had a crush on her, to the amusement of everyone but Mrs. Parsimonious who didn't waste a thought on it.

"Again?" Valerie poked at the rubbery algae with her fork, wishing her brother, Oliver, were there so she could dump it on his plate like she had when they were children.

Motionless, Mrs. Parsimonious stood guard over the table, her sharp eyes watching, ready to condemn anyone who wasted a morsel.

No one dared to ask for more. Or less.

Finishing quickly, the guests dashed away, each to their own private stash of goodies, leaving the Highwaters alone, side by side, in unaccustomed proximity. The feeling was not totally unpleasant, bringing back memories of courtship when finding a place to be alone had been all they thought about.

"Valerie," Marcus said hesitantly.

"Yes, Marcus," Valerie said shyly, noticing how broad his shoulders were, how long his back was. She'd always loved a long back. She ran her fingernail slowly down it.

"Don't do that."

She did it again.

Later that evening in the privacy of Marcus' suite, it was agreed. He would get Triton to attend the wedding.

Chapter Twenty-Nine

Girl Talk

Floating in the deepest part of the river, Amanda stretched herself full length. "Finnie, this picnic was a great idea."

"We needed a break," said Magdalena from the bank where she and Laura were munching fruit and dangling their feet in the water

"Can I have an apple?" asked Myrtle from a branch overhead.

"Here, catch," said Laura, tossing her one.

"I'm glad to get out of this," said Finnie, undulating out of her tight red dress and diving into the water.

"Finnie, you are a knockout!" Amanda exclaimed, admiring her Aunt's well-toned body. "I wish I had a waist like yours."

"Amanda, darling, you're a whale, not a mermaid. You're not supposed to have a waist."

"You're beautiful the way you are," said Laura, "that's why Big Boy gets so jealous."

Amanda smiled, remembering Big Boy's reaction when she did her mock striptease at the Benefit of the Doubt.

"You are absolutely perfect," Magdalena assured her.

"You've got nothing to worry about. My nephew is a lucky boy," Myrtle said emphatically.

"I'm worried Big Boy's father doesn't like me," said Amanda. "He acted kind of funny, like he couldn't get away from me fast enough."

"Maybe it's your personality," Finnie teased, giving her a hug.

"Duke is a wonderful person," Laura insisted. "He wouldn't hurt anyone's feelings."

"Laura's got a crush on Duke," Myrtle explained.

"Aunt Myrtle, you promised you wouldn't tell!" Laura wailed.

"Oops, so I did. I'm sorry." She jumped down to put a motherly arm around Laura. "It's nothing to be ashamed of, dearie."

"That's right," Amanda agreed. "Duke's handsome and very nice. It just shows you've got good taste."

"You should have seen me when I fell in love with Guitano," Magdalena chimed in. "I blushed. I stammered. I dropped things. I made a fool of myself."

"Laura, honey," Finnie declared, "we've all had so many crushes I can't begin to tell you."

"Well, I haven't," said Laura, feeling a little less embarrassed.

"Forgive me?" asked Aunt Myrtle.

"Yes, I forgive you, but everyone has to promise not to tell."

They promised.

"Now that's settled does anyone have any idea why Duke flinched when I kissed his cheek?" asked Amanda.

"You just imagined it," said Magdalena. "He was meeting his son's bride for the first time. That's enough to make anyone feel awkward."

"Maybe," Amanda said doubtfully. "He did say something about being stunned by my beauty."

"Well, there you are," said Finnie. "You must learn to accept compliments. They make life so much more pleasant."

Amanda couldn't put her finger on it but she knew something was wrong. "Maybe he's prejudiced, against whales, I mean."

"Duke's not like that," Laura said earnestly.

"Laura's right," said Myrtle. "Duke's first big crush was a whale."

"Really?" said Amanda.

"Tell us more," said Finnie, all ears.

"Nuthin' more to tell," Myrtle said evasively.

"Come on, Myrtle," Finnie cajoled, "you can't start something like that and not finish it."

"Aunt Myrtle," Laura asked, "does this have anything to do with what you told me about Amanda's and Big Boy's parents knowing each other?"

"What did she tell you?" Amanda asked apprehensively.

"I bet I know," Finnie sang. "There were rumors about Felicity and a certain handsome gorilla, la, la."

"A gorilla," Amanda said slowly.

"There, see how worried you've made Amanda. You simply must tell," Finnie insisted.

"Alright," said Myrtle, wishing she'd kept her big mouth shut, "but everyone has to keep it secret."

"Oh, we will," they chorused.

"Well, the story goes, when Duke got out of the Academy his first mission was an undersea one and he fell in love with a gorgeous whale. He used to write to ma about her, but when he got back everything changed. He wouldn't talk about it. So, I peeked into his letters, and guess what?"

"Felicity," Finnie said, dropping her name like a stone into a pond.

"That's right," Myrtle confirmed. "Felicity."

"Mother!" Amanda gasped.

"A few months later he got married to Lilli," said Myrtle.

"Maybe he's still in love with her," Magdalena speculated. "Maybe you reminded him of your mother."

"You look a lot like her, you know," said Finnie.

So, that was why Duke had been so unhappy, Laura realized.

"Do you think Lilli knows?" asked Magdalena.

"She knows something," Myrtle answered.

Finnie asked the crucial question. "Amanda, does your mother know that Big Boy is Duke's son?"

"Are you kidding? I haven't even told her or dad that Big Boy isn't a sea species, never mind a gorilla. You know how they are."

"So, Norville doesn't know either," Finnie mused. "Very interesting."

"I just keep putting off telling them," Amanda said worriedly. "I guess I figure the closer to the wedding the less time they'll have to upset things."

"Whoooeee," whistled Myrtle.

"Maybe someone should arrange a meeting between Amanda's and Big Boy's parents," Magdalena suggested.

"That would be something to see," Finnie said dryly.

Laura wondered if she ought to write about it for the Gazette, but then she thought of how sad Duke had been that day at the sea and how hard everything must be for

Amanda and Big Boy, how upset Norville and Felicity would be, not to mention Lilli...

Chapter Thirty

Lilli's Distress

Wearing a new outfit and more makeup than she normally put on in a month, Lilli drove her trusty old Stratocar through the massive bronze gates of Cosmic Allure, the fabled beauty spa, rolling to a reluctant stop before the entrance to that precious, pink marble, pseudo-palace. A liveried parking valet opened her door, sniffing disdainfully at her car.

Everything at Cosmic Allure had been designed to intimidate, from the elegant complexity of the formal gardens into which one dared not venture without permission from on high, to the elaborate mystique surrounding the Gold Tower where the cosmic elite were privileged to be remade, to the demeaning sorting process the less privileged went through to determine whether they qualified for a private room or were herded into the main salon with the common folk. And then there was the intimidating price you were expected to gratefully pay the reigning Gods of Beauty who, upon accepting your humble offering, would deign to make you over into something more acceptable to them — any failure to do so being due to the poor quality of material they had to work with, namely you.

Ordinarily Lilli wouldn't have put up with such nonsense but she wanted to look her best for her son, Big Boy's, wedding. She allowed a pompous majordomo to usher her through great bronze doors into a large anteroom that gave off onto the main salon. A haughty ostrich with a diamond tooth presided over the appointment podium, deliberately ignoring everyone. Several women, looking like plants that hadn't been watered in days, waited meekly on uncomfortable chairs. Something told her she'd better check on her appointment.

"Yes?" said the ostrich, looking down his beak at her.

"I'm Mrs. Treetop."

"Have you an appointment?" he asked in a tone that implied she couldn't possibly have one.

"Have you an appointment book?"

"Of course I do," the ostrich squawked huffily.

"Then look it up," she said coolly. "My name is Lilli Treetop."

"What was that again?" asked the ostrich, as if he hadn't heard.

"Perhaps you should see a doctor. I understand selective hearing loss in ostriches is a sign of impending mental collapse."

Ruffling his feathers in annoyance, he pretended to look through his appointment book. "Lilli Treetop, Lilli Treetop. Oh, there you are, all the way down there. Lilli Treetop, 2 p.m. It will be a two hour wait," he said, oozing satisfaction. "Mr. Vincent is with someone *important*."

"My appointment is for 2 p.m. and 2 p.m. it will be!"

"Madam, lower your voice, please."

"My voice comes down when Mr. Vincent comes out!" Lilli's powerful mezzo cut through the reverent hush, making heads turn in the main salon and private room doors pop open...*Darling, you look awful...What have you done with your hair?...We'll have to do something about that chin...*

"Madam," said the ostrich, grimacing, "your behavior is unacceptable." He fumbled around for the trouble button, finding it at last. Four giant armadillos thundered out.

"Triton will hear about this," Lilli said mockingly. At the mention of that fabled name, everyone froze. Little was known for certain about the mythic and reclusive King Triton. Rumored to live in unfathomable luxury on a vast, undersea estate called Paradisio, he was said to possess mysterious powers, including the ability to be everywhere at once disguised as anything from a door knob to a Greek God.

There was a stir as a bosomy flamingo in flowing robes and a tiara appeared. Her feathers fluffed up and her long boa flying, she swept toward Lilli, creating waves of awestruck whispers ...*Madam Fong ... Madam Fong...*

So, this was the famous Madam Fong, thought Lilli.

"Triton? What's this about Triton?" Madam Fong asked imperiously, narrowing her heavily mascared eyes to little slits.

"You know, one word from him and it's all over," said Lilli, looking Madam Fong straight in her slitted eyes. She hadn't intended things to take this turn, but they had, and she wasn't going to back down now. "Perhaps you should teach your staff some manners."

Having parlayed style, chutzpah, tyranny and a canniness about people into a formidable beauty empire, Madam Fong knew and admired self-possession when she met it. There was, of course no way for her to know whether Lilli knew Triton, but she did know how much Cosmic Allure stood to gain from the appearance of being associated with someone who did. And in Madam Fong's world, appearances were everything.

Without missing a beat Madam Fong went from imperious cosmetic queen to scolding employer. "Be gone," she ordered the armadillos. "As for you," she said, snatching the appointment book from the astonished ostrich, "apologize at once." Giving him no opportunity to do so, she turned to Lilli. "It's so hard to get good ostriches these days. He had you confused with another important client."

"I see," Lilli said dryly. "Another Lilli Treetop scheduled for 2 p.m. with another Mr. Vincent, what a coincidence."

Madam Fong clamped her beak shut, determined to avoid a scene. "It was Lilli Tree<u>Frog</u> at 2 p.m. with Mr. Vincent. Your appointment is in the Gold Tower with Mr. Ferdinand, our very best esthetician." She paused, hoping the honor of this would sink in.

"Li'l ole me, in the Gold Tower? I'm sure that's too rich for my blood."

Brushing aside Lilli's objections Madam Fong insisted. "You must allow me to make amends for your unpleasant experience. You are to be my guest. All the miraculous services of my famous Gold Tower are at your command."

"Thank you," Lilli said graciously.

"We wouldn't want King Triton to think we are inhospitable." Stepping over to a large gong, Madam Fong took her anger out on it with two resounding whacks, summoning a bejeweled gondola with brocade curtains to whisk Lilli off to the fabled Gold Tower before her independent attitude caught on and other clients started thinking they had a right to say "Ouch!" or "No!"

* * * *

An entirely different atmosphere prevailed in the Gold Tower, where one's presence alone indicated one's great status. Servants both live and robotic scurried happily about attending to the unreasonable demands of the clientele. An easy camaraderie existed between staff and patrons, for theirs was a symbiotic relationship. Being "done" by estheticians in the Gold Tower meant you were crème de la crème because they "did" only the crème de la crème. What could be simpler?

Having been alerted by Madam Fong of the newcomer's connection to King Triton, the Gold Tower was abuzz with curiosity. Into this mutual admiration society came Lilli, wanting nothing more than to sit quietly and get her run-in with Madam Fong and the ostrich out of her system. The mannered camaraderie of the Gold Tower with all the phony kissing, patting and sweetums grated on her.

Mr. Ferdinand, a well preserved, middle-aged lion, pranced over to greet her, his handsome red mane coifed in the latest eccentric style (his own invention) which Lilli found utterly ridiculous. She might have felt some sympathy for him had she known he felt the same way. In fact, the stress of having to continually come up with something outrageous to maintain his mystique was beginning to wear him down.

"You must be Lilli," he enthused automatically, kissing her hand.

"I am Mrs. Treetop," she said, withdrawing her hand in a way that let him know she was not going to be flim-flammed.

Having spent so many years immersed in the world of phoniness, Ferdinand had almost forgotten how refreshing honesty could be. "Forgive me, Mrs. Treetop. We get so used to first names around here I sometimes forget it's not to everyone's liking."

Lilli accepted his apology.

"Call me Ferdie," he said out of habit. "All my friends do."

"What do acquaintances call you?"

"Oops, I did it again, didn't I?" he said, looking both amiable and contrite, even a little sincere. What an interesting woman, he thought. "I have a lovely private dressing room if you would like to change and relax. I'll be done with my present client shortly."

Passing through curious looks and whispers of "*Triton... Triton...*" Lilli was shown to the dressing room by Ferdinand. How inviting the chaise lounge was, she thought, wanting to lie down and get back to herself.

"The servants will prepare you and fetch whatever you need."

"I can prepare myself, thank you. But I would like some tea."

"Not champagne?"

"It makes me sleepy."

"Of course, whatever you say." Turning to leave, he paused. "May I say something?"

"Yes," she said cautiously.

"I admire your style. I promise not to pull anymore phony routines on you."

"I'd really appreciate that," she said smiling.

"I'll be right next door if you need me."

Relieved to be alone, Lilli changed into the lovely oriental robe provided and began removing the makeup from her face. And a very exotic face it was — a pleasing combination of chimpanzee on her father's side and homo-sapien on her mother's. She seldom wore makeup. Duke liked her better without it. Suddenly, the incongruity of being in such a place made her want to laugh. What am I doing here, she asked herself, putting on my best outfit and coming to this palace of pretense?

Amused, she studied her face in the mirror. The eyes aren't bad, a nice almond shape, large; the nose a little too cute maybe; smooth tawny cheeks; full dark lips that needed no artificial color. Her sleek black hair was the one thing she was vain about. Most of the time she wore it in a French knot. Hugging herself with pleasure, she thought of how Duke liked to undo it and brush her hair.

Preparations complete, she lay back on the couch. In the stillness she realized she could overhear everything being said in the adjoining room.

"Ferdie," a woman whined, "do something about this bump where my horn was. It's growing back."

"Lorelei, there is no bump. You're imagining things."

"Do you think so?" she asked poutily

"I know so," he said firmly. "I'm looking right at the spot and it's not growing back."

"I love Reggiedaddy, but I don't want his horn."

"Speaking of Reggiedaddy, your father sent a note with his check, asking if I use real platinum. I do, of course, but let it be our secret."

"He really is a dear old monster," Lorelei said fondly. "You should have heard him when I asked for a billion."

"A billion!" Ferdinand exclaimed. "That's pushing it, girl. And it's all for Ever Snide, I suppose."

"You sound like my father," Lorelei complained. "It's not all for Ev. It's for Amanda's wedding."

Amanda? Lilli's ears perked up. That was her future daughter-in-law's name.

"Sure it's not for Ev," said Ferdinand, laughing. "By the way, what's with Amanda anyway? I haven't seen her in ages."

"She's preoccupied with her fiancé. Nobody's even met him yet. She's being very secretive."

"Maybe she's just trying to keep him out of the clutches of a certain mermaid," Ferdinand teased. "I wouldn't call that being secretive."

"We don't have the same taste. And she is so being secretive. All we know is his name. Big Boy."

Startled, Lilli sat up.

"Big Boy," Ferdinand said thoughtfully. "Never heard of him."

"Neither has anyone else. With a name like that he's probably an elephant or a gorilla or something."

"I can't imagine a member of the Oceanus family marrying a gorilla," said Ferdinand, laughing.

"What a juicy scandal that would be," said Lorelei. "Imagine Amanda marrying some dumb gorilla."

Lilli burst into the room. "Big Boy is my son!" she shouted, outraged.

"Mrs. Treetop, I had no idea!" exclaimed Ferdinand.

"Where did she come from?" Lorelei asked, startled.

"How dare you talk about Big Boy that way!" Lilli raged, choking with anger. "What kind of people are you soulless petty gossips maligning someone decent and good as Big Boy! You, you empty-headed phonies! You fakes!"

"I'm so sorry," said Ferdinand, genuinely distressed.

"You're just dragging him down to your level. Well, I've got news for you, nobody else can get that low!" She rushed from the room, beside herself.

"Wowee!" Lorelei exclaimed. "What a temper!"

"I feel terrible," Ferdinand groaned.

"Hey, wait a minute. If she's Big Boy's mother then Big Boy probably is some kind of ape. Wait till Felicity hears about this!"

Lilli burst back into the room, Felicity's name going right past her. "And as for you, Miss Mermaid, Ferdinand is lying! Boy does that bump show!" She stormed out of the room and was bundling her things together when Ferdinand stuck his head in, trying to apologize. "Get a haircut!" she said angrily, slamming the door in his face.

But even in her anger, something else was gnawing at her. Felicity...Felicity... Possessed by a sickening, nameless dread, she tore out of the place as if she could outrun it.

Felicity...Felicity...Felicity...

Part Four

Chapter Thirty-One

A Place For Her *doThings*

Ever since Laura realized she was more interested in doing the Wedding Gazette than making more of her *doThings*, she'd felt a little guilty. Not that she didn't love them. After all, she'd brought them to life from a place deep inside herself and was very close to them, but both she and they knew they were at the end of something and the beginning of something else. Only what? Maybe they needed exposure to a bigger world, to experience more variety, to be seen and heard by more people. If so, where better to begin than at the banquet where they could meet all different kinds of people from all over the cosmos? Of course, she had already offered to lend them to Maurice to liven up his dismal décor, but he had turned her down. By now he must have heard how wonderful they were and was probably sorry he'd been so nasty. Maybe she should give him another chance.

Maurice was becoming more peculiar all the time. He'd taken to dressing as a waiter and going around with a tray of metal crackers covered with melted cheese, as

though they were canapés. When tooth, fang or beak met
metal, Maurice would cackle and disappear in a puff of
smoke. So far he'd managed to escape retribution because people tended to notice the uniform, not who was
in it. By changing from a waiter's garb to the robes of a
decorator Maurice could circulate freely among his vic-
tims, chuckling to himself, while the real waiters got
blamed.

Feeling it would be safe to approach Maurice in pub-
lic, Laura sought him out at the banquet area where he
was currently holding court dressed like a queen bee,
complete with a paper crown and tin scepter. He'd had to
bring in giant bees to do the work for him because he'd
alienated everyone else. "I am the queen bee and you are
the drones," he proclaimed, mistaking worker bees for
drones who never worked a day in their lives. Unable to
stop once they got started, the real worker bees dashed to
and fro arranging seaweed and strings of dead fish while
Maurice amused himself by shooting spears of fire at
them.

"Maurice, why are you so mean?" Laura shouted from
a safe distance.

"So," he hissed, glaring at her through his pince-nez,
"it's you."

"You can't use dead fish! What if they're Amanda's
relatives?"

"Have a canapé, kid," he said slyly.

"I'm not hungry."

"In that case, I'll burn a bee," he cackled.

"I'm going to put in the Gazette what a rotten person
you are!"

"Gazette? Gazette?" Maurice said angrily, switching his tail back and forth. "Never heard of it."

"It's famous," Laura yelled, edging away. "I'll tell everyone what a rotten decorator you are too!"

Maurice lunged at her.

Laura took off, running through the forest toward her favorite place overlooking the sea. She knew lots of places to hide there. She ran and ran and ran, with Maurice in hot pursuit, his fiery bolts glancing off boulders and singeing trees. Looking over her shoulder she tripped and fell against something big. "Duke!"

"Where are you going in such a hurry?"

"Maurice is after me!"

"I see this time you took my advice and ran," Duke said, laughing. Grabbing Maurice behind his fire ducts, Duke swung him around and tossed him far out over the sea where he went down in a plume of steam.

"Can dragons swim?" asked Laura.

"Who knows?"

* * * *

With the help of the grateful bees, Laura and her friends gathered up Maurice's seaweed arrangements, dead fish and other yucky things.

"Let's feed this stuff to the Fire-Who-Eats-Junk."

"Fire-Who-Eats-Junk?" asked Laura.

"Come on," hummed the bees. "We'll show you."

Dragging Maurice's nasty things behind them, they trudged across the encampment, over a hill and down a ravine where the Fire-Who-Eats-Junk burned hungrily. There was so much Maurice stuff the Fire burped three times before polishing everything off.

* * * *

With Maurice's things gone and Laura's *doThings* replacing them, the banquet area came alive. They sprawled about, draping themselves over and under things, singing happily to each other and anyone who happened by. Attracted by the wonderful sounds, a troupe of master musicians who had been invited to play at the gypsy ceremony dashed over. Taking up their instruments, they began improvising beautiful, singing chords, shimmering glissandos and soaring arpeggios, engaging the *doThings* in glorious musical conversation.

Inspired, the *doThings* began to experiment with new combinations of shape, color and sound, radiating splendor in all directions. The musicians were ecstatic. Laura was ecstatic. The *doThings* were ecstatic. They had found their place in the world.

Chapter Thirty-Two

Getting To Know You

Guests began arriving from sea, sky and forest. Some even materialized out of the ether. Hospitality kiosks had been set up around the perimeter of the encampment to welcome invited guests and to turn uninvited ones away with consoling souvenirs. Greeting Guards were instructed to sound the alarm when anyone showed up with a bogus invitation.

Realizing she couldn't meet all the arrivals by herself, Laura enlisted the aid of friends who were not otherwise busy preparing for the ceremonies, assigning each of them a group of kiosks to cover. They were to jot down the names of all arriving parties, their relationship to the brides or grooms, and whether they were unusual enough to warrant an interview in the Gazette. She gave each of her sentinels one of Mother Romany's *Telling Tablets* which she had been allowed to borrow for the occasion. The *Tablets* had an insatiable appetite for information.

At the end of the day, they liked to be placed in a circle

touching each other so they could tell one another what they'd learned, rearranging their information in the telling to make it more interesting. In fact, they enjoyed talking so much if they ran out of things to report they made things up, which made them very entertaining if somewhat unreliable. Mother Romany had also given Laura a *TruthPhone* so she could tell what was true and what wasn't but Laura enjoyed the made up parts so much she hardly ever used it.

* * * *

Taking care to keep her *Tablet* from touching the branches, which it would record as senseless babble, Myrtle swung through the trees on her way to her assigned post, hoping she would meet some guests interesting enough to be featured in the Gazette. Too bad I'm not smarter, she thought, but here I am, who I am, and that's that.

Catching a glimpse of something peculiar on the ground, she swung down to get a better look. Some sort of squat, many-legged creature in a gypsy robe was spying on something from behind a big rock. Perched on a branch directly overhead, Myrtle could see it was wearing white gloves on some appendages, spats without shoes on others and a circlet of coins on its head, if that was a head. Oh, my goodness, it was an octopus! What was it doing in the woods? The nearest body of water was the river. The octopus made a low moaning noise. Maybe it was hurt. A wispy black cloud began to rise from it. Alarmed, Myrtle dropped to the ground. The octopus let out a shriek.

"Oh, I'm sorry. I didn't mean to frighten you."

"Why did you sneak up on me?"

"I didn't mean to. You sounded like you were sick and I wondered if you were okay."

"I'm not sick," the octopus said miserably.

"What's wrong?"

"Nothing's wrong. Leave me alone."

"This black smoke stuff doesn't look very healthy."

"It's my tonic," he said lamely.

Myrtle knew all about tonics. "A gentleman like you shouldn't use such stuff."

"I'm not a gentleman," he groaned. "I'm nothing."

"Don't say that," she said, concerned. "Anyone can tell you're a gentleman."

The octopus sniffled and looked away.

"You're just feeling sorry for yourself," Myrtle said firmly. "What's the matter?"

"I've been deceived," the octopus wailed, piling his arms and legs on top of his head.

"Who deceived you?"

"She did," he said pointing in the direction of the river with the tip of a tentacle. "Over there."

Squinting, Myrtle could just make out Magdalena and Guitano. They were sitting on a rock with their feet in the river, kissing. "You mean Magdalena?" she asked, surprised. Magdalena couldn't be unkind to anyone.

"I thought she liked me."

"What makes you think she doesn't?"

"She's letting him kiss her."

"Of course. They're in love."

"But I thought she loved me."

"Did she say she loved you?"

"She was nice to me."

"She's a nice person. Hasn't anyone ever been nice to you?"

"Most of the time people make fun of me, especially females."

"I'm not making fun of you."

"That's right," he said thoughtfully. "At least you don't seem to be."

"Sometimes people make fun of me too. I know how it hurts," Myrtle said sympathetically.

The octopus looked at her with new eyes, noticing for the first time that she was a tree species, and a female one at that. His habitual mistrust returned. From the looks of her garish outfit she was a rather common sort of person. Not someone who traveled in the Oceanus set. "Who are you anyway?" he asked, unable to keep from sounding rather snobbish.

"I was just trying to help," Myrtle said, hurt. "I guess I better go."

"No, please," he said apologetically. "I didn't mean it that way. I'm just no good with women."

"I thought maybe you didn't want to be friends with someone like me, being such a distinguished gent."

"Not at all, not at all," he said hastily, trying to make amends. "You have very kind eyes."

"Thank you," Myrtle said, pleased. "Would you like me to stay?"

"Well, yes, I would," he said, surprising himself. "My name is Oliver, and what, dear lady, is yours?"

"Myrtle," she chirped, giving him a hug.

"Oh my," he sputtered. "I'm not accustomed to being hugged."

"Well, it's time you got used to it," she said, hugging him again.

"You're doing this because I'm unhappy, aren't you?"

"Doing what?"

"Being nice to me."

"I'm being nice because I like you."

"You do?"

She nodded.

"You may not like me when you get to know me better," he said, worriedly.

"I'm sure I'll like you even more."

"I'm forgetful sometimes. Do you mind?"

"You don't seem forgetful to me. You just need someone to talk to, someone smart like you."

"You're very smart and you're a nice person besides."

"What a nice thing to say," Myrtle said, beaming.

Her smile made Oliver feel wonderful inside. If his sister, Valerie, had been there he would have dumped algae on her. "Miss Myrtle, you've made me feel so much better."

"Thank you, Oliver. I'm glad."

"Would you do me the honor of having lunch with me?" he asked, not thinking twice about it.

"Oh, Oliver, I would love to, but I can't," she said, remembering the assignment Laura had given her.

"I've been too forward."

"No you haven't. It's just that I'm supposed to be somewhere else."

"With someone else," he said, crestfallen.

"It's nothing like that," Myrtle assured him. "I promised to help my friend Laura with her interviewing."

"Oh, " he said, relieved. "Interviewing, did you say?"

"For her newspaper," Myrtle explained.

"You look worried."

"Well, I am kind of worried," she confessed. "I don't know if I'm going to be any good at it."

"Miss Myrtle," Oliver said reassuringly, "you have absolutely nothing to worry about. You have a very nice way with people. I'm sure everyone will want to be interviewed by you."

"Do you think so?"

"Would you like me to help?"

"Oh, Oliver," Myrtle said gratefully, "would you?"

"I would be delighted," he said cheerfully.

"Maybe I could start by interviewing you."

"Oh my."

"You'd rather not, I guess."

"Oh no, Miss Myrtle, I want to be interviewed by you. It's been lonely, talking to myself all these years."

Chapter Thirty-Three

The Witches' Kitchen

Their black robes flapping, Claribel and Dolly flew jauntily about the kitchen, bouncing off the ceiling and the walls, haphazardly tossing whatever was on hand into a humongus iron cauldron of brown fungoid stew. "This should be tasty," they chortled, plunking in a ball of green ooze. "Ooooo," cooed Dolly, "I just love the slurpy sound it makes when we do that." Joining hands, they did a somersault, not even noticing when their hats fell into the brown guck and were gobbled up.

"Uh oh, I feel someone coming," warned Claribel. "Get ready to rhyme."

"Do we have to?" Dolly whined. "It's hard."

"We wouldn't have to if you didn't blab all our secrets."

"I don't blab."

"You don't even know when you're doing it. At least

when you rhyme you have to think before you say anything."

They took their places at the cauldron. "Cackle, cackle, fire crackle," chanted Claribel, pointing a claw-like fingernail at the wood under the cauldron, instantly setting it ablaze.

"Yummy, yummy in my tummy," chanted Dolly, levitating over the pot to taste the contents with a long spoon.

"May I come in?" asked Laura, peeping in at the door. "I'd like to interview you." She knew everyone would be interested in reading about the witches.

"No way, go away. Go away, no way," they sang.

"Don't you want to be famous?"

"Famous, schmamous," said Claribel.

"Shamus, famous," Dolly said airily. "Wasn't that good?" she whispered to Claribel.

"Please, can I come in?"

The witches went into a huddle to decide whether Laura should be allowed to interview them.

Laura made a note on her *Telling Tablet* about their heads being pointy. She'd always assumed it was witches' hats, not their heads, that were pointy.

"Do we two know you?" asked Claribel. "Not that we care, but tell us from where."

"We didn't exactly meet," said Laura edging her way in. "I saw you at the Universal Dump outside Mr. and Mrs. Loveseat's betting parlor."

"Oh yes, let me guess," rhymed Claribel.

"No tail, so she can't be the whale," Dolly pointed out, very pleased with herself.

"That was my friend, Amanda," Laura explained. "How come you always rhyme?"

"Why do you ask? Is it your task?"

"Yes, it is. I'd like to do an interview with you."

"Hey there! That's not fair!" Dolly protested.

"What's not fair?" asked Laura.

"Rhyming. It's what we do, not you!"

"Can't you talk without rhyming?" Laura asked impatiently.

"We won't tell," said Dolly.

"But isn't it swell?" Claribel asked smugly.

"That's what you think," Laura muttered, wishing they'd answer her questions.

"We heard that. Don't be a brat."

"Do you want publicity or not?" Laura demanded to know. "I have lots of other people to write about."

"Of course we do," Claribel said grudgingly, "but first, who are you?"

"I'm the publisher of the Wedding Gazette," Laura said proudly. "Thousands of people will read it."

"Thousands, you say? In that case, okay," Claribel

decided, "but we have things to do while you interview."
She waved her hand at the door of their enormous oven.
It flew open, revealing pans of throbbing gray blobs with
hot orange veins pulsating through them. Dolly tossed in
a pair of old shoes. Claribel waved the oven door shut.

"Yuck!" Laura exclaimed. "What were those?"

"Our special bread. People must be fed," chirped Dolly.

"Why did you throw in the shoes?" Laura asked a little
queasily.

"Unto every season, there is a reason," Claribel said
mysteriously.

"We never tell what makes our bread swell."

The *Telling Tablet* in Laura's hand buzzed impatiently,
wanting to get on with things. "In a minute," Laura promised, adding loudly enough for the witches to hear, "but if
all they want to do is make up rhymes and not answer
questions we'll go interview someone else."

"Double dare," the witches chorused. "We don't care."

"They probably can't cook anyway," Laura told the
Tablet. "The stuff they're making is ugly and it smells bad.
Besides, they have pointy heads."

"Uh oh," said Claribel, realizing she'd lost her hat.
"Don't go."

"Will you stop rhyming and answer my questions?"

The witches flew up to the ceiling to confer. "We don't
want her telling people about our pointy heads and our
cooking when she's angry," Claribel cautioned.

"Can we stop rhyming now?"

"If I can trust you not to blurt out everything that pops into your head."

"I never blurt," Dolly said indignantly.

"Well?" Laura called up to them.

Their robes billowing out like parachutes, the witches descended. "Okay, no more rhyming."

"Thank you," said Laura. "Now, how did you become..."

"Here, have one of our pamphlets," Claribel interrupted.

> *Sisters Under the Skin,*
> *Our True Story*
> *by Claribel and Dolly,*
> *Greatest Chefs in the Universe*

"Open it," she urged.

"I'd rather ask questions," said Laura.

"You'll be able to ask better questions if you read it."

"It says you're the greatest chefs in the universe. Did you win a contest?"

"Don't be silly," said Claribel. "Only amateurs enter contests."

The word "amateurs" annoyed Laura. It reminded her of the way Maurice talked. "If you didn't win a contest or something, how can you say you're the greatest chefs in the universe?"

"Everybody knows it," said Claribel.

"How does everyone know it?" Laura persisted.

"It says so in our pamphlet, doesn't it?"

"I've never met anyone who's eaten your cooking."

"You will, at the banquet," said Claribel.

"That's not proof," said Laura, refusing to be side-tracked. "That hasn't happened yet."

"A mere technicality," Dolly said breezily.

"What are you writing down?" Claribel asked suspiciously.

"Just what you said."

"What did we say?" Dolly asked, worried she might have said something she wasn't supposed to.

"You said it was in your pamphlet, only it's not."

"What's she talking about?" asked Dolly.

"That there's no proof you're the greatest chefs in the universe."

"Oh, really," said Claribel. "How can you prove there's no proof?"

Trying to come up with an answer, Laura was distracted by a glob of stuff that materialized out of nowhere and began rubbing against Dolly's leg. "There, there, you nice thing," said Dolly, giving it a pat.

Claribel waved the oven door open. The glob jumped in, closing the door behind it.

"Are people going to eat that?" Laura asked, aghast.

"What kind of witches do you think we are?" Dolly asked indignantly. "We don't eat our pets!"

"Pets?"

"Now, don't try to pretend you've never seen a pet glob before," Claribel chided her.

"But, if it's a pet, how could you put it in the oven?"

"We didn't. It jumped in," Claribel reminded her. "Didn't you see?"

"It likes to be warm," Dolly insisted.

"I don't know..." said Laura, somewhat disconcerted.

"That's right, you don't," Claribel said smugly.

Trying to decide what to ask next, Laura glanced at the pamphlet. "According to this, you're supposed to be sisters."

"We're not really sisters," Dolly blurted out. "We met at Kitchen World in the Universal Mall." Claribel elbowed her in the ribs. "Oops, forget I said that."

"Go, season the fungoids!" ordered Claribel.

Using a giant spoon, Dolly pole-vaulted into the cauldron. "Needs a dash of mildew," she called out. Dripping brown sludge, she pulled herself up over the rim of the cauldron. "Okay?"

"Okay." Claribel said irritably. "Go wish yourself clean."

Dolly slid slowly down the outside of the cauldron, chanting her chant.

"I wish I was clean, I wish I was bright.
I wish, I wish, with all my might."

It worked.

"Why do you pretend you're sisters?" Laura asked, ignoring Dolly's prestidigitations.

"Why does anyone pretend anything?" Claribel asked philosophically.

"Don't you ever pretend?" asked Dolly.

"Yes, lots of times, but that's different. That's for fun."

"Well?"

"What you're doing is different," said Laura. "Telling everyone you're sisters is a lie."

"It's an illusion," Claribel corrected, "not a lie. There is a difference, you know."

"Anyway," Dolly added, "we're sisters under the skin."

Laura sighed. "What does..."

"You'll understand everything better when you've read our real story," Claribel assured her.

"Our real story?" Dolly asked, puzzled.

"You know, the pamphlet story."

"Oh THAT real story," said Dolly, understanding at last. She dug out a pamphlet with a nice glossy cover.

beWITCHery,
Our REAL Story
by Claribel and Dolly.

Laura tucked it away for later.

"Aren't you going to read it?" Dolly asked, disappointed.

"Yes, but first I'd like you to answer some of my questions."

"But this pamphlet is special," said Claribel with a flourish. Another copy dutifully fell out of her sleeve. "It tells lots of our secrets. Listen to this."

> *Alas, we were born with pointy heads full of dreams. We wanted to play heroines in light comedies but always wound up as the Witches of Endor or something, mostly in failed productions, leaving us stranded between parallel universes, sometimes with nothing but the costumes on our backs, our empty stomachs and the power of imagination.*

"I didn't know you were actors," Laura said, surprised.

"What else?" Claribel asked dryly.

"Read her the part about the hot dog wagon," Dolly said excitedly.

"Ah, yes," said Claribel, "those were the good old imaginative days. We told a hot dog man we were writing a book called *Puttin' on the Dog* but that his didn't look like they would taste very good."

> *These hot dogs of yours have a sour disposition. Obviously they were snipped from the vine when the temperature of the moon was off by one degree.*

Dolly chuckled. "He kept asking us to try another and then another, hoping we'd find one we liked so we'd give him a good write up."

"Did that really happen," asked Laura, "or are you making it up?"

"It doesn't matter if you're between parallel universes, now does it?" Claribel said brusquely.

"Anyway," Dolly added, "it was fun, so who cares?"

Parallel universes? Laura was intrigued, but her newspaper was only supposed to tell about real things.

"There's far too much reality as it is," said Claribel, as though reading Laura's mind.

"And too little magic," Dolly said with a sigh.

Too much reality. Too little magic. Laura felt like she was being tickled by a big feather.

"Far too little magic," Claribel echoed wistfully.

It was true. In her heart of hearts, Laura knew it was true. But she was supposed to be a journalist. "Why did you go from being actors to being chefs?" she asked, struggling to keep the interview going.

"Because we wanted to eat," said Claribel. "Anyway, actors, chefs, food critics, witches, what's the difference?"

"Why don't you ask how we became witches?" Dolly suggested.

"You weren't you born witches?"

"We were born with the potential to be witches," Claribel explained. "Everyone is born with a potential for something. It's what you do with your potential that counts."

"Of course, not everyone can be a witch," Dolly said

proudly.

"It takes a lot of pretending, which you're very good at," Claribel said slyly, giving Laura another brochure.

beWITCHery, Part II
A Handbook:
Fake It Till You Make It.

Always wear black *2*
Get pointy hat (especially if you don't have pointy head) 4
Practice on broomstick 5
Firing up with fingernails 11
Learning to levitate 7
Learn to fly 9
Get cat that likes to fly 6
Get large black cauldron 3
Get an agent 10
Be mysterious 1
Hire a publicist 8
          pretend...pretend...pretend...

"Can I learn to fly?" Laura asked eagerly.

"Don't believe everything you read," said Claribel, her eyes twinkling. "People expect all sorts of things from witches."

"But I saw you fly," Laura protested.

"Imagination is the frosting on the cake of reality," said Claribel, brushing Laura's objections aside.

"Look at us," Dolly blurted out. "We can't even cook."

Somehow, Laura wasn't surprised. "How did you get from being food critics to being chefs?" she asked soldiering on.

"How does anyone get from anything to anything?" Claribel asked expansively. "Sometimes, life dumps a hot dog wagon in your lap. If you're hungry, you go for it. Next thing you know, you're an expert on hot dogs. You get some ghost to write a cookbook under your name. You materialize on a few talk shows. Presto, you're a great chef."

"Read this," said Dolly.

The Truth About Illusion
or
How To Repair Reality So It Works
by
Claribel and Dolly
Greatest Chefs in the Universe.

Reality is illusion with the magic removed.
Cooking with the mind — for yourself or for a crowd.
Imagining is believing.
Truth is a tricky word.
Illusion is reality, once removed.
Reality is a whistle-stop on the highway of imagination.
How to get your story into the Book of Life.

Laura was intrigued. She certainly wanted to get her story in the Book of Life, even if she didn't know exactly what that meant.

"Yoo, hoo, remember us?"

"Oh!" Startled out of her reverie, Laura tried to collect her thoughts. "So, if you got to be witches by pretending, and you got to be food critics by pretending, and you got to be great chefs without doing any cooking, except maybe at home when no one was watching because you got hungry and had to cook something..."

"What? Us, cook?" Dolly was aghast. "That would have ruined everything."

"It would?" Laura asked, bewildered.

"If we had become real cooks," Claribel explained, "we wouldn't have needed to create an illusion."

"Think of all the fun everyone would have missed," Dolly chimed in. "People need legends and myths. They need to have magic in their lives."

"Magic!" Laura was thrilled with the idea. Making life magic was more important than the Wedding Gazette, more important than anything. Magic was books with golden edges. Magic was being with her father listening to laughter and music no one else could hear. Magic was making *doThings*, or watching the changing colors of the sea, or traveling through galaxies of ice crisp stars. Magic would be the books she was going to write.

"Your attention, please," said the witches, linking arms with Laura. Lifting her off with them, they sailed in circles high above the kitchen, singing exuberantly.

Truth Is Not Uncouth
by Claribel and Dolly

If, because of the legend
we've created,
the taste of our food
is upgraded,
and people savor
the flavor,
who would be so uncouth
as to claim it is not the Truth?

If someone writes a book or a poem
        that makes you feel less alone,
or reveals what you never have known,
        or gives you insight,
or elicits delight,
        or confirms what you feel is alright,
good or bad,
        happy or sad,
who would be so uncouth
        as to claim it is not the Truth?

Chapter Thirty-Four

The Voice No One Else Can Hear

Now that guests were showing up in larger numbers, Laura's friends were filling their *Telling Tablets* two or three times a day, bringing her information on new arrivals, who had invited them and snatches of conversation. Her master *Telling Tablet*, Amanuensis, who claimed to be descended from a long line of ancient scribes, absorbed it all and added embellishments of his own as he deemed appropriate.

In the evening Laura would gather the *Tablets* together and listen as they spoke to each other, becoming very familiar with their individual voices.

"Sing. SING! sing."

"Ssssinnnnnnng."

"Tweet La. Tweet La."

"Laaaaaaaa."

The *Tablets* had a wonderful time, rearranging their facts in so many pleasing ways. Laura's questions encouraged their natural inclination toward fancifulness so their facts became stories, stories became fables, fables became myths, all in a giddy blur of beginnings and endings till they couldn't distinguish fact from fable and who cared anyway? "Ah," they sighed in satisfied harmony, "Aaaaaaaahhhhhhhh."

But in between the ideas, facts, bits of conversation, words, phrases, questions, Laura sensed something else, something there and not there, a flicker in the mind, elusive, always in motion. Hummingbird thoughts, she called them.

Finnie's *Tablet* began to speak:

> *Lorelei, meet Tibor.*
> *Mom, if they get any younger...*

> TRIVIAL TALE
> trivial tale...

"Amanuensis, wait," said Laura, hearing a new voice. "Who said trivial tale?"

"I heard only *Lorelei, meet Tibor. Mom, if they get any younger,*" said Amanuensis.

"Please repeat 'trivial tale'. I want to hear it again."

> *Mom, if they get any younger...*

> IS HE COMING?

"Did you hear that?" asked Laura.

"What?" Amanuensis asked cautiously.

"Is he coming. Someone said, is he coming."

"Perhaps it is The Voice No One Else Can Hear."

"What's that?"

Loki's *Tablet* burst in:

> *I hate this place. I'll get even.*
> *But Sheila, please...*

WHEN WILL HE COME?

"There it is again!" Laura exclaimed. But when Amanuensis reluctantly went back to the spot, it wasn't there. Yet, Laura knew the voice was real, like certain voices she heard in dreams, not so much in the dreams as standing outside, observing and commenting on them, their words reverberating in her long after the dreams were forgotten.

Pinocchio's *Tablet* interrupted:

> *Please tell Veronica I am here.*

Who was Veronica, Laura wondered?

> *Tell her Augustus is here.*

WILL HE COME?

There was something worrisome about The Voice No One Else Could Hear, something distressing about the longing in it. Who was the Voice expecting and why should it make her so anxious?

Chapter Thirty-Five

The Locket Of Dreams

"Augustus," Mother Romany said delightedly, "come see what Laura has written about us."

The Great Poet scanned the sheets of paper. "A play, I see. She has used some of my early poems to you."

"She's so fond of poetry, and you."

"She has used them very well."

"Once she began making her *doThings* her progress was quite rapid."

"She is almost ready, isn't she?"

"Yes, very close," Mother Romany agreed.

"There is still the riddle of her father."

"She will solve it," said Mother Romany. "Now, let us read her play. She's eager to get our reaction."

AUTHOR'S STATEMENT

I've never written a play before. I was only going to write a newspaper called the Wedding Gazette but after a while I decided I'd rather write books and poems and plays so I could put in what I feel.

THE LOCKET OF DREAMS
A play by Laura

The Characters:

MOTHER ROMANY/QUEEN ROMANY.
(Until she becomes queen she is called VERONICA.)

AUGUSTUS/THE GREAT POET

THE LOCKET OF DREAMS

EARLY POEMS OF THE GREAT POET

Act 1-Scene 1

Time: *The past. A young, handsome, intense Augustus is pleading with his beautiful Veronica who has just become queen.*

AUGUSTUS: Come with me, Veronica. Go where I go.

VERONICA: Veronica would go joyfully but Queen

Romany cannot. The hope of my people is in my hands. The Dreams have foretold that our lost child will be returned during my reign.

AUGUSTUS: If I try to live in Queen Romany's shadow, my soul will die.

VERONICA: And if I, as queen, go with you, my soul will die.

AUGUSTUS: *(anguished)* There is no way for us.

HE

A shadow passes over the moon.
In the play of light and dark
I cannot find the ends of my fingers,
the separation between you and me.
My hand is not mine but yours;
thoughts pass like smoke between us,
all my dreams are made of you.

SHE

Distinguish yourself from me
for I cannot.

HE

I play in the craters of the moon,
streamers of silk bind me to you
like a kite to its flyer,
bits of colored glass fall from your hair
covering me with your reflected light.

SHE

But it is you I love,
not my reflection.
You are not clay to be molded
into the shapes of my imagination.

HE

"Beloved," you call
and I slide down, down, down,
like molten bronze
into molds you have created.

In your presence I am suspended,
caught in the shadow
and light of your moods.

In your presence
I can only be
what you see,
what you hear
what you touch.

In your presence
I am your creation.

SHE

I want to feel
force against my force,
a heart beside my heart,
a will that is not my will,
a soul that is not my soul.

If I cannot touch
the solid shape of you,
there is nothing to love

but sand through my fingers.

*It can never be enough
to love your own creation.*

AUGUSTUS: *(very sadly)* I must be my own creation.

VERONICA: *(takes her locket from around her neck, runs her finger over the surface, magically removing the name Veronica)*

From this day forward Veronica ceases to exist. Everything Veronica cherishes, her love for you, all her hopes and dreams are in this locket, the Locket of Dreams. *(she gives it to him)* Keep them safe.

- Curtain -

Act 1-Scene 2

Time: *The present, just before the wedding and gypsy coronation. Evening. Half moon. A wooded glen. A carpet of autumn leaves, the sound of nightbirds, wind, star songs. In the distance, the sea.*

The Great Poet enters looking for Mother Romany. He sees her leaning against a majestic tree. She is wrapped in a lace shawl, her face is lifted to the moon. She has gone through the transformation and looks just like she did when he last saw her, long ago, when he was young.

THE GREAT POET: Veronica, I have come.

MOTHER ROMANY: Augustus, how wonderful!

THE GREAT POET: I knew it was time. I heard your
                   heart calling. *(he takes her hands
                   in his and kisses them)*

MOTHER ROMANY: How good to be called Veronica! I've
                   been Mother Romany for so long.

THE GREAT POET: *(still holding her hands he steps
                   back and looks at her very lovingly)*
                   Your beauty astounds me, just as it
                   did then.

MOTHER ROMANY: *(they embrace)* It has been so long.

THE GREAT POET: Time stopped for me until now.

MOTHER ROMANY: How I hoped you would return
                   before the end of my time.

THE GREAT POET: Had I not been so young, so un-
                   formed, so in awe of Queen Ro-
                   many, I would never have left.

MOTHER ROMANY: *(sadly, a catch in her voice)* You had
                   to go. I understood. It was the only
                   way.

THE GREAT POET: If only I'd been wiser. My heart
                   never again found its twin.

MOTHER ROMANY: Nor mine. Never. I have cherished
                   the poem you wrote that told of
                   your love...and your anguish. It has
                   become a part of me.

I scooped a silver cup of moonlight
from the River
and it trembled
as love does,
when mortal;
and I thought of how the ocean felt
when I left it
knowing it was too much itself
for me to hold.

I tried to tame a wave
but its force on the rocks
left me foam
with a handful of seaweed
and the terrible roar of my dream.

THE GREAT POET: *(ruefully)* How melodramatic. You
must have thought me a fool.

MOTHER ROMANY: Oh no, Augustus, knowing you
loved me became my sanctuary.
That and knowing the Locket of
Dreams was always with you.

THE GREAT POET: *(softly)* Yes, the Locket of Dreams.

MOTHER ROMANY: *(she looks at him lovingly)* I have
followed your accomplishments.
You have achieved what you
dreamed of. Your work has inspired
generations, inspires me.

THE GREAT POET: *(thoughtfully)* Yes, I have accomplished the work. But not all I
dreamed of.

MOTHER ROMANY: *(she looks at him curiously)* Not all? I
am in awe of what you have done.

THE GREAT POET: Awe is passion once removed.

MOTHER ROMANY: *(she laughs)* How like you. You still want it all. That hasn't changed.

THE GREAT POET: *(laughing at himself)* With you I am still a boy who wants everything, you, my work, freedom. *(he looks at her searchingly)* And you, your reign, has it made you happy?

MOTHER ROMANY: As queen, yes. I have helped keep the gypsy soul alive. There is much love between me and my people.

THE GREAT POET: And as Veronica? *(he looks deep into her eyes)* The love of your people has been passion once removed?

MOTHER ROMANY: *(she laughs)* You always know what I have not said.

THE GREAT POET: That is because, in a sense, I am still your creation, whether in flight from you or by your side. *(they embrace. He takes out the Locket of Dreams and holds it in his open hand. The name Veronica has been restored)*

I am returning the Locket of Dreams. My love for you, my dreams, are intertwined with yours. *(her eyes fill with tears. He places the locket around her neck and kisses her)* When you open it you will find our lifetime together.

MOTHER ROMANY: I shall not open it until you join me over the edge of time and we can open it together.

CURTAIN

(that means it's the end of the play)

signed,
Laura.

Part Five

Chapter Thirty-Six

Oops The Cops

Things had been pretty quiet at the headquarters of Cosmic Officers Patrol Satellite (COPS) and its affiliate, Operating Officers Patrol Station (OOPS) except for the night Yvonne Sharktooth fell off her yacht. The accident had been covered by a large contingent of gossip reporters, photographers and film crews. *THEM!* had given it front page treatment, featuring many OOPS & COPS personnel, lifting morale and whetting their appetites for celebrity.

Officers began adding theatrical touches to their uniforms, a scarlet scarf, a feather in a cap, a bit of fringe on a sleeve. Encouraged by the Chief, they began taking classes in acting, singing, dance and staging mock choreographed crimes to display their newly acquired talents. Posters of Macho Mahoney, formerly an OOPS officer, now a movie star, went up in all the squad rooms.

When a call came in that the largest, most luxurious yacht ever built had been stolen from its moorings, the news was met with jubilation. The publicity would be stupendous, and this time they would be camera ready.

"There may be a kidnapping for ransom too," the Chief announced over the loudspeaker. "This could be a dilly!"

"Yea Chief! Yea Chief!" chanted COPS & OOPS, as though he had personally arranged the crime for their benefit.

"Now, now," the Chief said modestly, "I don't deserve all the credit. Let's hear one for the crooks! We couldn't have done it without them."

"Hooray, crooks!"

"And the best part," crowed the Chief. "Guess who was on board?"

"Who Chief?" asked a chorus of senior officers. They knew their part.

"You're seasoned law enforcement celebrities," the Chief chortled. "Figure it out."

"Macho Mahoney," someone called out.

"Yvonne Sharktooth," shouted another.

"The owner," someone ventured.

"Who said that?" the Chief demanded.

"Mason, Sir," answered a fledgling officer, expecting to be praised for guessing correctly.

"Mason, you must be new."

"Yes, Sir," Mason said proudly. "I am."

"Don't interrupt a superior officer. Didn't you learn anything at officer's training?"

"But I thought..."

"You thought, you thought. Mason, you're a member of OOPS now. You don't think — you act, like in actor! Get it? Act!"

"Right, Chief. We act!" shouted COPS & OOPS in chorus.

"Now, guess who was aboard," said the Chief, pausing dramatically. "The owner!"

"Wow! The owner!" everyone shouted.

Everyone but Mason.

"And guess who the owner is," the Chief said gleefully.

"Who?" they shouted in unison.

"King Triton, I bet," Mason whispered into the shell-pink ear of officer Sharon Softlee, his partner and classmate from officer's training.

"Shhhh," she whispered, holding a finger to her full pink lips. "You'll get in trouble."

"The owner is King Triton!" the Chief boomed triumphantly.

"Wow! King Triton!" everyone shouted.

"You really did it this time, Chief!"

Officer Softlee looked at Mason admiringly. "How did you know it was King Triton?"

"It wasn't all that hard," he said, blushing. "Who else would have the biggest yacht in the universe?"

"You're so smart."

"Now, go get 'em!" the Chief ordered. He sat back, basking in his fame to be. Rescuing Triton would make him Eustace P. Marlin, Chief Superstar.

OOPS & COPS went into action, preparing for the event by parading before imaginary cameras, pretending to be interviewed, practicing standing tall and smiling photogenically.

"But we're supposed to pursue the criminals," said Mason.

"Not yet," said one of the officers. "That's for after the media leaves."

"Anyway," said another officer, "something as big as Triton's yacht is going to be impossible to hide so why waste time looking for it?"

"But it's our job," Mason protested.

"Sure, kid, sure," agreed a senior OOPS.

"Hey, fellas, look at this," another officer shouted, flourishing his jacket like a matador's cape. A fellow officer charged it like a raging bull. Dodging adroitly, the matador took a bow amidst a shower of papier-maché roses.

"Mason, don't pay attention to them," Sharon Softlee said sympathetically. "They're media drunk. You should go after the yacht-nappers. And I'll go with you."

"That's right," said Mason, heartened. "It'll be better this way. We'll be less conspicuous than a whole squad."

"Gee, you think of everything," said Sharon.

"I do?"

"This could be our big chance."

"That's right, it could."

"I don't know about you guys," Mason declared, "but I'm going to rescue that yacht."

"Me too," said Sharon.

"So go, already!" everyone shouted, pelting them with leftover roses.

Chapter Thirty-Seven

The Great Gameplayer

Aboard his yacht, the *Premonition*, King Triton, master of the mutable, was preparing for a long voyage during which he would often assume his favorite disguise, that of Sebastian Sea Lion, the great gypsy impersonator. Impersonating an impersonator appealed to his sense of irony, but more importantly, if he traveled the cosmos in his true identity he was met with fear and awe, whereas traveling as Sebastian he was greeted with affection and delight.

The real Sebastian benefited from the situation by miraculously appearing in two places at the same time, a feat no one else could duplicate. In this Triton recognized, with some amusement, the hand of Life-The-Great-Game-player. Trying to outwit that Old Trickster was one of the few challenges that still engaged him.

He was looking forward to spending his first night with the *Premonition*, getting the feel of her, testing her secrets, sounding the engines of her heart. She had come to him

in a dream — first her name, then the vision of her form
— demanding to be born. Much of him had gone into her
creation, his sense of beauty, his wit, his cool remove, his
mythic qualities, his longing, his loneliness. With her
there would be no need of distancing himself, no need of
disguises, for in a sense she was himself.

Designed to keep his secrets as her own, her cool,
polished surfaces deflected inquiry. Her blueprints were
infused with Triton's natural elements of fluidity and
change, turning to gibberish at a glance or touch by anyone else — as certain greedy shipwrights had learned too
late. They were now fleeing for their lives, pursued from
galaxy to galaxy by the Pirate's League which had paid a
king's ransom for a set of incomprehensible plans.

At the urging of his brother, the Moon, Triton had
agreed to attend the gypsy wedding. It would be the
Premonition's maiden voyage. By coincidence, if there was
such a thing, Marcus Highwater, his useful if somewhat
duplicitous aide, had also asked him to come to the very
same wedding. It amused Triton to see the look of suspicion that had crossed Marcus' face when he'd accepted
the invitation so readily. Unlike Triton who could disguise
his form, Marcus prided himself on being able to disguise
his thoughts, or so he thought. Triton sometimes fed him
small victories like this, allowing Marcus to believe they
were of his own making.

Triton's thoughts turned back to his impulsive sibling,
the Moon, who was once again hopelessly in love, this
time with another man's bride and practically on the eve
of their wedding. That she would live a thousand years,
giving her a touch of immortality, made his brother's
futile obsession with her all the more poignant. Triton
sighed. More and more he longed for the time when he
had known nothing of immortality, nothing of being a
myth, nothing of being worshipped as a god.

Reaching into its nestling place, he lifted the *Pastviewer* from its ancient cradle. The sight of the worn family crest gave rise to bittersweet memories of a time when worlds were being born and he ran free, naked and undisguised.

Peering into it he saw himself as he had been, a luminous, otherworldly child, unfettered by destiny, his wild hair spuming, his clear eyes shining — laughing, always laughing — he and his brother, the Moon, playing amidst newborn galaxies, his brother tugging at him with invisible cords, pulling him close, then letting go, sending him swirling back into the sea of himself in tides of delight — again and again, night after night — never tiring of the game.

The *Premonition* interrupted his reverie to tell him scores of intruders were climbing aboard. Triton reluctantly put the *Pastviewer* back in its nestling place and, assuming his Sebastian Sea Lion disguise, went above decks to see what was going on.

The ship was littered with revelers of various species in various stages of intoxication. Their brightly colored togas made them look like large, wilted blossoms strewn helter-skelter after a rowdy bon voyage.

"What took you guys so long?" Triton asked in his Sebastian Sea Lion basso profundo.

"How'd you get here before we did?" a bleary-eyed lizard wanted to know.

"I took a short cut," said the Sebastian.

"Oh yeah?"

"Yeah," said the Sebastian.

"Some tub," said a woozy simian, weaving from side to side.

"Wait'll you see below decks," said Sebastian. "This boat's really somethin'." Led by himself, an unruly procession stumbled down the stairs as best they could.

"Wow!" someone exclaimed, impressed by the opulence.

"This guy must be rich as Triton!"

"You could say that," Sebastian agreed.

"Look at this joint!"

"I'm trying to," said a muzzy muskrat, making an effort to focus both eyes at once.

"So now what?" asked Sebastian, wondering what they were up to.

"Hey, I don't remember you," sibillated a slippery saurian. "Who are you anyway?"

"Who do you think I am?"

"King Triton," snickered the saurian.

"If I were, I'd turn your cold blood warm just for being here." A rumble of suppressed laughter from deep within shook the *Premonition.* Some of the celebrants lost their balance and fell over, asleep when they landed.

Why was it, Triton wondered, that the less imaginative males of any species always thought falling down drunk together made them brothers for life.

"Hail, fellow suitors!" a wobbly wizard called out, staggering toward them. Grinning foolishly, he fell at Triton's feet, changing into a plush, blue carpet before he hit the floor. "I don't feel so good," fluffed the carpet, changing itself back into a wizard, then back to a carpet. "Hey, where's Finnie?"

So that was it, Triton realized. These were the rambunctious suitors who followed the beguiling Finnie everywhere. He understood her allure all too well. Once, in the guise of a winged stallion he'd had a memorable encounter with the lovely mermaid.

"Hey down there, give us a hand. We gotta get the cannon and the fireworks on board."

Triton-Sebastian followed them above decks. "Anyone know how to make this ship go? Where's the bridge?"

"Huh?" asked a puzzled possum.

"How come this thing doesn't have a sail?" asked an addled aardvark.

"It has a different kind of power," Sebastian said mysteriously.

"Feels kinda spooky to me," grumbled a gibbon, looking at the smooth, unyielding surfaces as if noticing them for the first time. "Somethin' funny about this ship."

"It's scarey," Sebastian said in a way that made it seem really scarey.

"Like it was haunted," the gibbon agreed, shuddering.

"There's definitely something weird about this ship," a morose mongoose muttered.

"Luckily for you, you don't own it," Sebastian said dryly.

"Yeah, we're just stealin' it."

"Stealin' it," parroted a parrot.

"Yeah, right," hiccuped the wizard.

This absurd invasion had to be the work of Life-The-Old-Gameplayer, thought Triton with a sigh. It was too improbable to be anyone else's. Sometimes he felt sympathy for the Old Trickster, sensing that behind its baffling inconsistencies lay a measure of his own boredom and loneliness. He understood Life's dismay at trying to befriend living things only to find it could no more keep from imposing its will on them than rivers could run backward to their sources, or rain fall back into the sky, or people stop believing *such things could happen, if only...*

"Let's get going," someone shouted.

> *To the gypsy wedding*
> *To the gypsy wedding*

Triton made his way through snoring drunks, semi-conscious babblers and fools loading cannon. Taking the helm, he felt a twinge of sadness for them. They understood so little, and he perhaps understood too much.

* * * *

"Hey, look at Sebastian!"

Standing on the bridge, stars drifting past him, Triton guided the *Premonition* into the dark sea of space. How glorious she was in her element.

"A toast to Finnie," a suitor called out.

To Magdalena, murmured the Moon

To the wedding, hummed the Wind

To the gypsies, sang the Stars

"To Life," said Triton, "to the *Premonition* and to Life!"

Chapter Thirty-Eight

Finnie's Choice

"Finnie, that was delicious," burped Reggie, leaning back in his chair and wiping his snout.

Tibor shot him a disapproving glance from the far end of the table

"I made it myself, darling, just like the old days."

"Mom!" Lorelei exclaimed. "I didn't know you could cook."

"I suppose I wasn't very domestic when you were growing up."

"Domestic! Even the word sounds weird when you say it."

"Lorelei, let's not get into one of our dreary discussions about how I wasn't like everyone else's mother and how embarrassed you were as a child having to explain about me to everyone."

"Listen, Pookie," said Reggie, "your mother's example taught you a valuable lesson — to be yourself — much to her regret at times, I'm sure. What have you got to complain about? You know how to get what you want, and I've got the bank balance to prove it."

"Thank you, darling," said Finnie, blowing him a kiss.

"My pleasure," he said affectionately.

"You two are certainly very chummy," Lorelei said suspiciously, worried she might not be able to use her customary divide and conquer strategy with them.

A loud boom reverberated through the encampment, rattling the china on the table.

"What was that?" Reggie asked, alarmed.

"It sounded like a cannon," said Lorelei.

"Maybe something to do with the gypsy ceremony," said Finnie.

"I hear they do wild, pagan things," Lorelei said gleefully. "Maybe even virgin sacrifices."

Finnie laughed. "In that case, you have nothing to worry about."

"Mother, really," said Lorelei, pretending to be scandalized, "there's a child present."

Tibor glared at her.

"My boy," said Reggie, "they enjoy saying outrageous things. Don't take it seriously. It doesn't mean a thing."

"They never take anything seriously," Tibor said sourly.

"Oh Tibor, loosen up," Finnie scolded. "You're too young to be so serious."

"Mother, leave the child alone," said Lorelei, patting Tibor condescendingly. "Don't listen to her. You don't have to have a sense of humor if you don't want to."

Tibor pushed her hand away. "Some people think a sense of humor solves everything."

"Now, now, my boy," Reggie said paternally.

"Tibor," Finnie explained, "life is a wild, unpredictable thing. You've got to handle it with a light touch or it'll throw you."

"And trample you," Lorelei added cheerfully. "Come on, Tibor, give us a smile."

"Young man, don't let those two get under your skin," Reggie admonished. "It's just their way."

"Don't they ever take anything seriously?"

"Not if they can help it."

"Not to change the subject," said Lorelei, "but I for one can't wait to see what Felicity does when she finds out Amanda is marrying Duke's son."

"Who'd ever imagine Felicity had spunk enough to get involved with someone like Duke," said Finnie. "He's quite a hunk though."

"So, you find him attractive," Reggie said unhappily.

"Only superficially, dear."

"I met his wife, Lilli, at Cosmic Allure," said Lorelei, rubbing the spot on her forehead where her horn had been. "You wouldn't want to tangle with her. She's a real fighter."

"Duke's wife is Felicity's problem," said Finnie, settling herself in Reggie's lap. "Not mine."

Another loud boom resounded through the still night air.

"I wish they'd quit doing that," Reggie grumbled.

Evert J. Snidely burst in on them. He was beside himself with excitement, his shark-like jaws snapping open and shut as though chomping on prey.

"Calm down, Ev, you're drooling," said Lorelei, wiping his mouth with her napkin, her maternal instincts aroused.

"And to think I'm supporting this drooling idiot!" Reggie exclaimed.

"Oh, Daddiepoo, it's just the way he gets when he's excited."

"I've never seen anything like it," Evert shrieked. "A howling mob, fireworks, cannon, skywriting, the biggest yacht anyone's ever seen! Lorelei, quick, grab your camera. This is your BIG chance."

"Oh Ev, can't it wait?" Lorelei asked, pouting. "The conversation was just getting interesting."

"I knew it!" screamed Evert. "I knew you were too rich to take work seriously!"

"Seriously," Tibor said smugly.

"Lorelei working?" asked Reggie. "What is this lunatic talking about?"

"Really, Evert," Finnie said calmly, "get a grip on yourself. Why would Lorelei want to work? Give the job to someone who needs it."

"Exactly my sentiments," said Reggie. "Just like I'm always telling Beesely. Beesely, I say, I don't need your job but you do."

"Yes, and I'm sure he appreciates it, darling."

"I can't believe it!" Evert exclaimed. "This could be the biggest story ever and you're dithering about employment! Oh, Vern, Vern," he moaned, "my best photographer lost in a black hole."

"Oh, alright, Ev," Lorelei said sulkily, "but I don't see what the big deal is."

"Neither do I," said Finnie. "After all, oodles of people are coming to the wedding; what's special about this bunch?"

"Finnie, you of all people should ask?"

"What's Finnie got to do with it?" Reggie asked suspiciously.

"Go see for yourself," Evert said snidely.

Uh-oh, thought Finnie, slipping off Reggie's lap as he rose and stomped out of the tent.

"Just look at that," said Evert, pointing to the sky.

Fireworks blazed across the night sky spelling out WE WANT FINNIE! WE WANT FINNIE!

"Finnie, you promised," Reggie groaned, stricken. "How could you do this to me?"

"Darling, I had nothing to do with it."

"We agreed things were going to be different," he said, dejectedly. "No more mobs of suitors. I thought you meant it."

"But darling, I swear I had nothing to do with this. I don't know how they found me."

"I guess it was me," Lorelei said guiltily.

"Lorelei, how could you?" Reggie asked, exasperated.

"Why would you do such a thing?" asked Finnie.

"How was I to know you two were still in love?"

"Finnie, I shouldn't have accused you," said Reggie. "Forgive me?"

"After all the years you've put up with my escapades, I'm the one who needs to be forgiven."

"Lorelei," Reggie demanded, "what made you tell those fools where we were?"

"I thought it might make a good story for Ev."

"You did it for me?" Evert said, astonished.

"But stealing Triton's yacht was their idea. Honest."

"Lorelei!" Reggie said, alarmed. "You knew they were going to steal Triton's yacht and you did nothing about it?"

"I didn't think they'd really do it. I was just joking."

"What a story!" said Evert.

"Lorelei," Finnie said sharply, "what if Triton finds out?"

"That should be interesting," Tibor snickered.

"You're all taking this too seriously," Lorelei protested. "It's just a practical joke."

"Practical joke!" Reggie exploded. "It's piracy!"

"Oh daddiepoo."

"Ha, ha," Tibor laughed. "Bet you're sorry now."

"Oh shut up, you little sea pony," Reggie said distractedly. "Finnie, what are we going to do about those idiots on the yacht?" He looked at her intently. "You do really want to get rid of them, don't you?"

"Of course I do."

"No regrets? No looking back?"

"Lorelei, let's get going," Evert said impatiently.

"Wait. I want to hear mom's answer."

Finnie looked out at the magical ship crawling with buffoons firing cannon, setting off fireworks, bleating her name over loudspeakers. She felt so ashamed. The contrast between the poise and dignity of Triton's yacht and their behavior was mortifying. "Oh Reggie, don't ever let them near me again!"

Chapter Thirty-Nine

A Mysterious Interlude

In the bright moonlight Laura arranged herself on her favorite cliff overlooking the silvery sea and unsheathed Amanuensis from his protective cover, preparing to work on the Wedding Gazette. The vastness of the sea and the rhythm of the surf suited her mood and imagination. Sighing contentedly, she looked up at the moon, noticing that same strange cloud in its usual, unmoving position in the sky. The first time she'd seen it was after she'd interviewed Claribel and Dolly and realized what she really wanted to do was magical-ize life. Something had told her to look up, and there it was.

To her it was more than just a cloud. It was different, alive in some way. Instead of being puffy or having wispy edges, her cloud — she'd come to think of it as hers — was solid, more defined than other clouds. Another odd thing about it was most small clouds were vaporous, letting the moon shine through, but her cloud was dense, opaque, absorbing the moon. Rimmed by a halo of spilled moonlight, the cloud shimmered in the blackness. Then, like a king grown bored with a jewel, the cloud sent the silver orb spinning back into the sky.

Amanuensis hummed happily in Laura's hand, eager to record her thoughts, his aloofness gone now that they had become comrades in the quest for magic. With increasing frequency, ideas and images bubbled up in Laura like water from a deep spring, washing across the *Tablet* in torrents. At first these outpourings seemed random and meaningless, but the more she trusted the cascading stream, immersed herself in it, letting it flow over and through her, the more she realized it was neither random nor meaningless. The impulse to create her *doThings*, her play, the Locket of Dreams, the stories she gave to her father, the hummingbird thoughts, all rose from this same mysterious source. But there was something more, something important waiting to surface. "Soon," it whispered, "soon."

But what? What did it mean? The whisper was like the voice on the *Tablets* when it had asked, "When will he come? When will he come?" Since she was the only one who could hear the voice did this mean the question was meant for her? Her cloud and the voice were connected in some way. Looking up at the cloud, she sensed there was life in it, numinous, mysterious. Suddenly she found herself inside the cloud, mingled with the life in it. At first it was surprised. It had not expected her. It was intrigued. "Ask your questions, little one," it seemed to say. "In time the answers will come." Then she felt it withdraw.

Chapter Forty

Secrets Of The Heart

When Duke heard she'd arrived he went to find her, thinking he was prepared to see her again. But now, seeing her, even from the back, the way she stood, the way she tilted her head, he knew he would never be prepared. He had her too mixed up with the youthful dreams he'd kept enshrined in a sealed chamber of his heart.

"Felicity," he said simply.

Her back stiffened. She turned, her blue eyes opening wide.

"Duke," she exhaled.

Her eyes, her luminous eyes — they had stayed alive in his memory when other details had faded. No one had ever looked at him the way she had. Her manner had been cool when they first met, even disdainful, but the blue flame in her eyes had told him that she felt what he felt, a stunned recognition that each had met their other.

Seeing her now through a flood of memories, he searched for the blue flame, but her eyes were the dull icy blue of a winter pond. Duke's heart struggled with his mind, wanting to see what was no longer there.

"What are you doing here?" she asked stiffly.

Listening for the once familiar music in her voice, he heard only an instrument sadly out of tune. "That's not a very friendly question," he said more calmly than he felt.

"You took me by surprise," she said, self-consciously smoothing her dress.

"Beautiful as ever," Duke murmured, knowing that was what she wanted to hear, as well as what he wanted to believe. And on one level it was true. But there were other levels now.

He's still in love with me, she thought, relaxing a little; still thinks his Ice Princess can melt. She felt a twinge of regret but dismissed it. After all, he'd never been her social equal. "Norville will be here soon," she said formally.

"Your husband." Duke felt a stab of pain. "I'd like to meet him."

"Of course. Did you ever marry?" she blurted out. She hadn't meant to ask.

"Yes," he said blankly. The banality of their conversation was disappointing.

"How nice," Felicity said coolly, suppressing a pang of jealousy. "Any children?"

"A son," Duke said proudly.

"You have a son?"

Duke looked at her questioningly. "My son, Big Boy. He's marrying your daughter."

The look of shock and dismay on her face shattered the last of his illusions. "Amanda marrying your son? It can't be!"

Deeply hurt, Duke studied the face of the woman he'd enshrined in his heart. What he saw there set him free. Felicity, he thought, thank you for making me see. For her, their love had been only a brief intrigue, a frivolous escapade. Followed by a quick retreat back to the safety of her world.

Ashamed, she averted her eyes, her feelings for him churning around inside her, feelings she'd feared and run from long ago.

With a last quick shrug of the heart Duke was relieved of a great burden. "No matter what it meant to you, for me our love gave each day a radiance it wouldn't have had. I'm sorry it gave you so little."

"It seems to have given you rather a lot," she said hesitantly.

"Amanda and Big Boy are lucky," Duke said softly. "They can give to each other. He has a big heart and she has the courage to follow hers."

"And I didn't, I suppose."

"You had everything else."

The sympathy in his voice told her how far she'd fallen in his esteem. "Norville will never accept their marriage," she said defensively. "He's terribly aristocratic."

Duke smiled. "Norville will have to learn about aristocracy of the spirit. Big Boy has that."

"I'm sure he has."

"Felicity," Duke said gently. "Amanda has it too."

Chapter Forty-One

Making A Name For Himself

Spotting Triton's yacht, the *Premonition*, from their hovercraft, Officers Mason and Softlee throttled down, coming as close to the ship as they dared. Getting into their inflatable dinghy, they lowered it over the side, sending the hovercraft streaking back to OOPS. They approached the yacht stealthily, hitching a line to the stern.

Freshly imbued with the spirit of Officer's U, to be stoic in the line of duty — natural for Mason but less natural for Sharon who had a secret yearning for comfort — they hunkered down into the cold discomfort of their open dinghy, trailing behind the mighty ship as it plied the dark ocean of space.

"Maybe we should board her," said Officer Softlee, looking longingly at the warm glow of the portholes, wishing she were inside sipping a hot chocolate.

"There are many of them and only two of us," said Mason. "It would be safer to wait until we reach port."

He's so smart, thought Sharon, shivering in the cold.

"This dinghy wasn't meant for long voyages," said Mason, putting his jacket around her shoulders.

She looked at him gratefully. "Aren't you cold?" She knew he had to be. Thin people had no insulation.

"When I'm in pursuit of criminals my temperature goes up."

"I've never heard of anyone who could do that," Sharon said admiringly.

"It runs in my family."

"Isn't that wonderful," said Sharon, reaching out to pat down his stubborn cowlick. She'd always wanted to do that.

Mason blushed, glad it was too dark for anyone to see.

"Mason," said Sharon, all snug and warm in his jacket, "what's your first name?"

"I don't have one," he said uncomfortably.

"What?" She'd never heard of such a thing.

"My folks said I'd have to make a name for myself," he explained.

"Oh, Mason, that's terrible! Everyone's entitled to a first name."

"That's why I joined OOPS," he confessed. "I'm worried

maybe I'll be like some of my great aunts and uncles who still don't have first names."

Sharon looked at him thoughtfully. "Mason, I know your first name."

"You do?" he asked, astonished.

"Earnest. Your first name is Earnest."

Earnest, he thought, Earnest Mason. It felt right. "Are you sure?" he asked hopefully.

"Absolutely."

"Earnest Mason," he said, trying it out loud. It made him feel confident, more in command of things. "But what if I don't live up to it?"

"Oh, Earnest. That name has just been waiting for you. It is you."

Earnest Mason. Now when he met people he wouldn't have to feel embarrassed. He could say, straight out, *Hello, my name is Earnest Mason. What's yours?*

"What's more," Sharon said firmly, "you'll make it stand for something."

"Wow!" he exclaimed, feeling more manly already.

"Officer Earnest Mason," Sharon announced, saluting him. "I can already see the citation the Chief will give you for finding Triton's yacht."

> *To Officer Earnest Mason*
> *for meritorious service and bravery,*
> *this citation hereby entitles you*
> *to all rights and privileges*
> *of an officer with a first name.*

Mason stood there, letting the wonder of it all sink in.

Sharon thought he looked huskier, more broad shouldered. Even his jacket felt larger.

"I'm going to turn around now, Sharon."

"Why?" she asked, puzzled.

"So you can call my name."

Gosh, he's cute, thought Sharon. "Earnest," she called sweetly.

He turned to face her, newly aware of everything around him, the clean coldness of space, the rubberyness of the dinghy, the loveliness of Officer Softlee, how much taller he was than she.

"Earnest," she said shyly, an odd, quivery feeling in her stomach as the *Premonition* rode into port, "I think we're almost there."

Chapter Forty-Two

Laura The Dragon Slayer

Even from a distance she could tell what she'd heard about Gen's daughter was true — Tyrannosaurus Despotus, every inch of her. But Laura wasn't going to let anything like that interfere with her affection for Gen.

"Here she comes, Sheila," Gen said anxiously. "Be nice. I want you to be friends."

"I hate her," Sheila insisted. "I hate everybody!"

"I'm sick of hearin' you say that," Gen said wearily. "You don't mean it, so quit sayin' it. You don't hate me, do you?"

"Yes."

"Humpty," Laura squealed, rushing into his arms.

"Kid, you look terrific!" Gen exclaimed, grinning all over. "More grownup and everything."

"I missed you so much."

"Me too, kid."

Sheila sniffed scornfully.

"Look," said Laura, showing him the *I Love You* brace-let he'd given her. "I never take it off."

"I don't take mine off either," said Gen. "See?"

"Bracelets are so sappy," Sheila sneered.

"She's in a rotten mood," Gen said apologetically. "She doesn't mean all the bad things she says."

"I do so," said Sheila, glaring at Laura. "And I hate her most of all."

"Sheila, you're acting really stupid," Laura said impa-tiently.

"I hate you," she repeated, sticking out her tongue.

"Sheila," Gen ordered, "enough is enough. Put your tongue back in your mouth." He turned to Laura. "You sure got a lotta friends here. They tell me you're a writer now."

"Yes, I really am," she said happily.

"Who cares," Sheila snapped.

"I care," Laura said firmly.

"Sheila, why do you have to be so nasty?" Gen asked despairingly.

"Because I want to."

Gen looked helplessly at Laura. "It's just a phase she's goin' through. I hope."

"Don't feel bad, Humpty. It's not your fault."

"She's wearin' me down."

"I didn't ask to come," Sheila pointed out.

"I thought maybe I could keep her from bein' ruined by those Holier-Than-Thous, and their fake Holy Man," Gen explained.

"Finnie told me about him," Laura said sympathetically. "She said he tried to do something bad. A real Holy Man wouldn't do something bad, would he?"

"No, but a phony one might," said Gen.

"Wait till I tell him what you said," Sheila said smugly. "He'll put a spell on you. Then you'll be sorry."

"That guy's a lunatic with his spells and his look grim, feel grim, be grim stuff," Gen said, disgusted. "What kind of thing is that to teach kids?"

"I agree with everything the Holy Man says," Sheila said defiantly.

Gen groaned. "Sheila, you don't know what you're sayin'."

"I do too! I always hated everybody only I was afraid to say so."

"I don't like you," said Laura, turning away.

"You're so pleased with yourself," Sheila taunted spitefully, "getting my father to take your side and everything. What good's your writing and all your bracelets?

You don't have a father and I do!"

"Sheila!" Gen cried, shocked. Laura looked stricken. "Take that back. It's the worst thing I ever heard you say! You're hittin' below the belt."

"I may not be able to see my father or talk to him," said Laura, fighting back tears, "but I can feel his love. You can't feel anything except what's mean and nasty."

"Sheila, apologize," Gen demanded.

"I won't! I won't!"

"If you keep up this way, maybe you won't have a father," Gen said grimly. "Now, apologize."

"I don't want her apology," Laura said curtly. "People who are mean and nasty inside can't really apologize."

"I'm sorry if she hurt you, kid," said Gen, putting his arm around Laura's shoulder.

"I'm all right, Humpty." She turned to Sheila whose face was contorted with hatred and rage. "I hope you like being miserable, Sheila, because that's all you're ever going to be. At least I know how to be happy." Then it dawned on her. It was true! She really *did* know how to be happy! A fierce protective joy welled up in her. Of all the things her father had instilled in her, the ability to be happy was the most important of all. She saw that now. And nothing could take it away.

* * * *

Laura instinctively headed for her thinking place by the sea. She was glad to find Duke there, looking out over the water. There was no one she'd rather be with right now.

"Princess," Duke said, pleased to see her.

"I'm glad you're here," said Laura, sitting down next to him. "Guess what."

"Something good it looks like."

"I fought a fearsome dragon named Sheila and slew it."

"Oh, her. Want to talk about it?"

"Maybe later," she said, breathing deep of the moist, fragrant sea air. Side by side they watched a great orange moon as it rose, dripping, from the sea and vaulted exuberantly into the night sky.

"What a beautiful moon," Laura said dreamily.

"A happy moon, too, free in its own world."

"You're not sad anymore," said Laura, sensing the change in him.

"No, I'm not, Princess."

"Are you happy like the moon?"

"Like the wind, too. Listen to it sing."

"And the trees, they're dancing."

"And the stars, Princess, see how they twinkle."

"They sound like piccolos. My father said..." She stopped, overcome by a wave of sadness. Her father seemed so far away, even further than the stars. "Sheila made me feel bad."

"About your father."

Laura was silent for a while. "Sometimes loving someone really hurts."

"I know," Duke said quietly.

"But not being able to love anyone, that would be
worse," she said firmly, remembering Sheila's contorted
face.

"Some people are afraid to love," Duke said reflectively.

Something in his voice made Laura realize he was
thinking of someone in particular, someone in his own
life. "I'm glad we're not afraid."

Duke smiled at her. "Me too, Princess."

"But someone you loved was," she said, touching his
cheek.

"Yes, someone I loved," he said softly. "But I learned
something about love today, something very important.
The joy and sweetness of love belong to the one who loves.
No matter how much love they give, the joy and sweetness are always theirs."

"Even if the person you love dies?"

"Even then."

Laura looked out over the sea. "Then it's not wrong to
be happy just thinking about someone you love, even if
they died?"

Duke looked at her tenderly. "No one who's loved that
much ever really dies."

* * * *

After Duke had gone, Laura sat alone hugging her knees, gazing into the distance, letting her thoughts and feelings drift aimlessly.

Laura, a voice said quietly.

"Yes," she answered, looking up although she knew the voice came from within her.

Then you can hear me.

"Sure, you're the voice on the *Tablet*, the one no one else could hear."

So, you know about that.

"Why can't I see you?"

It is not yet time.

"Are you also the voice in my cloud?"

Your cloud? it said, amused. *Yes, I suppose I am.*

"Don't you know?"

I am the Emissary, it said, changing the subject.

"What's an Emissary?"

I bring word of The Elsewhere.

"The Elsewhere?"

Of the Rightness of Things.

The Rightness of Things. Laura liked that. "You were

the voice in my dreams, too. You were asking about someone."

So, you can hear us in your dreams, it said, surprised.

"Wasn't I supposed to? After all, they are my dreams."

We had no idea you were so far along. We were trying to reach someone close to you.

"My father?"

But the Emissary was gone.

Part Six

Chapter Forty-Three

Cameos And Caprices

The encampment was alive with activity — color, laughter, music. Final preparations were under way for the wedding and for the gypsy ceremony.

Mother Romany and Magdalena had gone into seclusion to prepare themselves for the Naming of the New Queen. Amanda and Big Boy were spending time alone together planning their future, relieved and surprised that Amanda's mother, Felicity, seemed to accept Big Boy as her son-in-law. Laura was busy putting the finishing touches on the Wedding Gazette.

The arrival of King Triton's yacht added to the already celebrative atmosphere. Hoping to meet the fabled King Triton, many of the wedding guests flocked to the *Premonition*. Among the first to board were Marcus Highwater and his wife Valerie. Marcus was eager to flaunt his relationship with Triton and take full credit for getting him to attend the wedding.

* * * *

"Marcus," Valerie wheezed, reaching the top of the gangplank. She'd always disdained exercise; it was too much like swimming upstream which only fools like salmon did. "Marcus, I want a yacht like this."

"Someday we may have this very one," said Marcus, possessively caressing a sleek handrail. Offended, the *Premonition* shot a sliver into his palm. "Ouch!" Marcus exclaimed, striking the handrail angrily, which only got him another splinter.

"What's wrong?" asked Valerie.

"Shoddy workmanship," Marcus grumbled, leaning over to inspect the handrail. It seemed malignantly alive. "Is that you, Triton?" he asked suspiciously.

"Marcus," Valerie snapped, "you're talking to a handrail, for God's sake! Your paranoia is getting out of control."

"Don't be so sure," he said, looking around warily. "You have to be suspicious of everyone and everything with Triton. He could be anywhere."

"Get a grip on yourself. If Triton wanted to hurt you he wouldn't have to become a handrail. He could just be himself."

She did have a point there. Not that he was willing to admit it.

* * * *

What a dumb move, thought Vern Light, scion of the

infamous Ma Light and ace photographer for Evert J. Snidely's gossip empire. Till now he'd gotten away with taking risks. It was part of his job, a part he liked.

He'd been dancing around the rim of a black hole, agile as a photon ballerina, whistling while he worked, his wild, golden filaments bristling with excitement. He'd been angling for the best shots, chunking whatever was handy into the Maw of Darkness, camera dangling from his neck, seeing how close he could get without being sucked in. Not thinking, he'd leaned over just far enough for the voracious maw to suck in his camera and with it his neck on which sat his idiot head and then all the rest of him, into the abyss — which is where he was now, how many hours, days or aeons later, he couldn't be sure. One thing he was sure of, he was missing the chance to photograph the biggest story of his career. Ev must be going crazy without him.

As a creature of light, Vern wondered how long he could hold out against so much darkness. The place was giving him the willies, threatening to suffocate his lifelight. "Okay, Black Belly, enough's enough!" he shouted into the blackness with more bravado than he felt. "Here's the deal. I'll stop shooting off flash bulbs if you'll quit sucking me into your gut." Black Belly only burped.

Berating himself for the umpteenth time, Vern turned his personal radiance up to max, eliciting only a faint mewling sound of indigestion from Black Belly. If he didn't get a recharge pretty soon his lifelight would go out, an especially dark thought for a creature of light. Cameraman to the end, he aimed at the center of darkness and blasted it with light.

* * * *

Evert J. Snidely was so intent on getting to Triton's

yacht he didn't notice the shooting star headed straight for him.

"Ev, watch out!" screeched Lorelei.

He danced out of the way as the star plowed into the sandy beach before them. It was Vern! "Vern!" Evert exclaimed. "Where did you come from?"

"Ev, that greedy 'so and so' kept my camera!"

* * * *

My dear, you are fanciful as a field of flowers," said Oliver to the colorfully bedecked Myrtle.

She beamed happily at his compliment. She wanted him to be proud of her when he introduced her to his sister, Valerie, and her husband, Marcus Highwater. Myrtle was wearing her most treasured dress. She'd been saving it for the wedding. It was a fantastical array of many-colored, real, imitation rhinestones that lit up when she pressed her belt buckle. She'd never owned anything so beautiful.

When she'd seen the dress shimmering on the sale rack in Monkey Ward's basement, she was sure they'd made a mistake. It was in an obscure corner, next to discontinued wallpaper and remnants of linoleum. But the salesperson assured her there had been no mistake.

Even marked down, it was too expensive, but every time she decided to leave without it, the department manager lowered the price. The next thing she knew, she owned it, taking possession amidst cheers from onlookers who'd been rooting for her to get it. Now, seeing Oliver's admiring look, she was doubly pleased with her purchase.

Oliver, on the other hand, was discontent with his newly repaired suit. It reminded him of the rigidity and narrow-mindedness of his former self. "I feel more like me dressed as a gypsy."

"But Oliver, you look so distinguished." He was dapper as could be. "Anyway," she reminded him, "we agreed your family will need time to get used to the new you."

"As usual, my dear, you are both correct and delightful." With Myrtle on his arm, Oliver headed jauntily for Triton's yacht, ready to face his formidable sister Valerie and her intimidating mate.

* * * *

Seated in Finnie's dressing room, Reggie watched unhappily as she discarded the frilly, domestic, calico pinafore she was wearing, slinking into her sexiest gown instead, determined to end her liaison with the suitors on a celebrative note.

"What's wrong with the pinafore?" Reggie asked plaintively, afraid her change of costume indicated a change of mind about giving up the suitors.

"Oh, Reggiepoo," she cajoled, checking herself in the mirror, "I'm going to break their hearts. I want to do it in style."

"I don't get it," he said glumly.

"Darling, for aeons I've been a beautiful fantasy to them. I wouldn't want them to feel their lives have been wasted. That would be cruel," she said, giving him a kiss and undulating out the door, headed for Triton's yacht.

* * * *

Ev, I will not give Vern my camera," pouted Lorelei. "First you rush me away from momsie and daddy. Then you accuse me of not wanting to work. And now you want to take my camera away from me so I can't work."

"Lorelei," Ev pleaded, "think of what Vern's been through."

"Well, what about me? I'm the one who got the yacht here. What do I get out of this?"

"I'm gonna marry you, remember?"

"Is that a threat?"

"Lorelei, this is no time for a tantrum. Vern's the best. This story is too important for an amateur."

"I see," Lorelei said icily, swinging her camera by its strap. "In that case, I won't be needing this." She smashed the camera on a rock and threw the pieces into the sea.

"Oh my God, Lorelei," Evert wailed. "You're ruining my life."

"Gee, that's too bad," she said, fiddling with her bracelets.

"Forget it, Ev," said Vern. "I'll find a camera. I can do better with a toy than she could with that expensive pile of junk anyway."

"A toy camera for a toy brain," quipped Lorelei, discovering she liked sparring with Vern.

"Some crack, coming from a toy talent," countered

Vern. "Maybe we could auction you off for enough to buy a cheap camera."

"Children, children," admonished Evert.

"Shut up, Ev," said Lorelei. "This is fun."

Vern cocked an eyebrow. "Hard finding somebody in your league to fight with, is that it, kiddo?"

"Kiddo. You called me kiddo, just like daddy," she cooed, batting her eyes at him.

"Don't get carried away," Vern grunted.

"Lorelei, what are you up to?" Evert asked suspiciously.

"Up to?" she asked innocently. "You told me Vern was the best there was. Maybe I can learn something."

"Maybe," said Vern, looking at her from a new angle. "Okay, you can tag along while I look for a camera. Just don't get any ideas."

"I can't promise."

"Then keep them to yourself."

"I can't promise that either."

"Listen," Vern said gruffly. "As far as I'm concerned, having you around is better than being in a black hole, but you're no substitute for a camera."

"I'm never a substitute for anything," she said cockily.

* * * *

"Earnest?"

"Yes, Sharon?" he asked briskly.

"It's very quiet on the yacht now. Why don't we climb on board?"

"I'll go first and check it out," he said, exercising the new found authority that had come with having a first name. He climbed up the ladder to the main deck, careful not to scuff the polished surfaces. Impressed with the quality of craftsmanship he saw everywhere around him, he peered into the huge porthole of the main lounge, feeling a beckoning warmth. It was almost as if someone were calling to him, inviting him to enter.

"Earnest," Sharon called from the dinghy. "I'd like to come up. I'm cold."

"Gee, I'm sorry," he said, helping her up the ladder.

"Oh," she exclaimed as she reached the deck, "this is beautiful."

"Let's go in here," said Earnest, indicating the main lounge.

* * * *

Triton assumed his kingly form, hoary beard, golden crown, glittering trident and all, a fatherly image which had been created millennia ago by an itinerant Greek poet in order to make his awesome powers seem less terrifying. The illusion suited him and he'd adopted it. The ultimate truth was not affected.

* * * *

What's with you, Lorelei?" Vern complained. "I almost had the kid's camera."

"What's with me? I saved your life."

"Don't exaggerate. Nobody dies for trying to swipe a kid's camera."

"Tell that to the kid's big bull of a father. He was about to charge."

"No kidding," said Vern, not having noticed the angry bull who'd been pawing the sand and glaring at him. "I guess I owe ya," he said gruffly.

"Getting sentimental, are we?" she said archly.

"There's nothing sentimental about owing you."

"Forget it, forget it," Lorelei said airily. "You don't have a thing I want."

"Except talent. Now, let's find a camera."

"Will this do?" she asked sweetly, pulling a very professional looking camera out of her purse.

"Lorelei, I could strangle you."

"Temper, temper."

* * * *

Without Oliver, who'd gone off to find his sister, Valerie, the main lounge of the *Premonition* was intimidating to Myrtle. It wasn't just the sheer size of it but the sense of powerful forces there. "Hello, is anybody here?" she called out, nervously fiddling with her belt buckle. Suddenly a blinding light exploded in the chamber. "Yipes!"

"Do not be afraid," said the presence, kindly dimming its radiance for her comfort. A commanding, luminescent figure stood before her.

"King Triton," Myrtle whispered, awestruck.

"Yes," he said, smiling engagingly.

"My name is Myrtle," she said, feeling encouraged by his manner.

"Yes, I know. Sebastian told me."

"You know Sebastian?" she asked, astonished.

"Your former husband and I are very close, in a way."

"Imagine, you knowing Sebastian," marveled Myrtle. "That makes it almost like we're all related to each other or something."

"I imagine it does."

"You have a beautiful ship."

"Would you like me to show you around?"

"I don't want to be any trouble."

"Friends are never trouble. We are friends, aren't we?"

"Oh yes," Myrtle said happily.

"I may need a favor from you."

"A favor from me?" she asked, surprised.

"Would you mind?"

"Oh no, of course not. Only, could we hug on it?"

His warm, comforting light embraced her.

* * * *

Oliver, what are you doing here?" Valerie demanded to know.

Oliver flinched. "I was looking for you," he said nervously, backing up against the rail.

"Don't touch that rail!" snapped Marcus.

Oliver jumped back, trembling and demoralized. Oh, how he wished for a nip from his black bottle, but he'd promised Myrtle and he was determined to keep his promise. "I want you to meet my, my..."

"Your what? Spit it out!" Valerie said impatiently.

"...friend," he said quietly, deciding not to tell her more.

"Oliver, I have no time for you and your pathetic friends." She waved him away. "We have important business with Triton."

"We?" said Marcus, instantly on guard. Valerie was always trying to worm her way into his relationship with Triton. "Triton is my business, Valerie, not yours."

"You promised me that night in your room."

"But we were alone. You have no witnesses."

"*Au contraire*," said Valerie, brazenly pulling a tape cassette out of her *décolletage*.

"Valerie, I am shocked!" Marcus exclaimed. "Tape recording our night of love. Shocked and hurt!"

"But Marcus, you're always telling me not to trust anyone."

"Yes, so I am. Well, I forgive you, dear," he said generously, congratulating himself on having had the presence of mind to switch tapes while she slept.

"Humph," Valerie snorted. Marcus had given in far too quickly, leaving her with a rather large supply of bad temper to dispose of. Of course, there was always Oliver. She decided to vent it on him. But Oliver was gone.

* * * *

Noticing Myrtle seated just inside the main lounge, Earnest and Sharon approached her. "Ma'am," said Earnest, trying to sound professional, "I'd like to ask you some questions."

"That would be nice," chirped Myrtle, still glowing from her encounter with Triton. "I'm just waiting for a friend."

"We're investigating a crime," Sharon Softlee said enthusiastically.

"Well, isn't that interesting," Myrtle declared. "Tell me about it, dearie." She rummaged around in her purse for her *Tablet*. "Maybe my friend Laura could put it in the

Wedding Gazette."

"Ma'am, would you mind telling us your name?" Earnest asked politely, pulling out an official OOPS note pad.

"My name's Myrtle, dearie. What's yours?"

He took a deep breath. "Earnest Mason," he said proudly, feeling euphoric at using his name with a stranger for the first time.

"I like the way you say that," said Myrtle.

"Me too," Sharon said admiringly. Earnest blushed.

"Isn't he sweet? And what's your name, dearie?"

"Officer Sharon Softlee at your service, ma'am," Sharon said crisply.

"Call me Myrtle. It's friendlier, don't you think?"

"Myrtle," Earnest said, buoyed by the happiness bubbling up inside him. "Your friend, the one you're waiting for, could you tell me his name?"

"You really like names, don't you, Earnest?" Myrtle asked, curious. "Do you collect them?"

"This is my first one," he confessed. But he liked the idea.

"My friend, Laura, collects words and phrases," said Myrtle, "and I have another friend who collects pear shaped moonbeams. They're mighty pretty but they do take up such a lot of room."

"That's nice," said Sharon, trying to get the conversation back on track. "We're trying to find out who stole this ship."

"But dearie," said Myrtle, "how could it be stolen? It's right here."

"Yes, it is here," agreed Earnest, "but the question is how did it get here?"

"That's a very good question, Earnest," said Myrtle, wishing she had an answer.

"It's a wonderful question," said Sharon.

"Maybe it sailed here," Myrtle said hesitantly, fiddling with her belt buckle — accidentally lighting up her dress. "Ooops!"

"Oh Myrtle," Sharon sighed admiringly, "I've never seen a dress like that."

"It's a one of a kind," Myrtle said proudly.

"I've never had a dress," Sharon said wistfully. "Just trousers. My parents made us wear uniforms all the time. They were glad when I joined OOPS because they loved the uniform."

"You can make it light up if you want," Myrtle offered kindly.

"Could I?" Sharon pressed the buckle gingerly. "Oh my!" she exclaimed, dazzled.

* * * *

No longer interested in being their *fantasy trivial*, Finnie boarded the *Premonition* to say farewell to her suitors. Their frenzied pursuit, and her encouragement of it, had lost its appeal.

Impressed by the quiet dignity and grace of the yacht, she felt hideously overdressed. What she had intended as a grand gesture of farewell seemed a little tawdry now, compared to the grandeur and nobility of the *Premonition*. Just the thought of it being overrun by her frivolous suitors was repugnant. She turned away, realizing that in her heart she had already said goodbye.

* * * *

Valerie was in a foul mood. The exertion of wandering around the enormous yacht made her feel hot, rumpled and fat, especially compared to Marcus with his lithe frame and gliding gait, never a green lock out of place. And why hadn't Triton come to greet them if he and Marcus were so close? "Marcus," she said grumpily, "I'm sick and tired of wandering around this tub. Where's Triton?"

"I hope you're in a better mood when you're introduced."

"Don't lecture me about manners. I'm the aristocrat in this family, remember?"

"Then act like one," he said curtly, secretly pleased that she'd had to invoke her social status. Admiring himself in a porthole, Marcus spotted Oliver in the main lounge. He was holding hands with a short, hairy, bow-legged creature who was wearing a dress that looked like a cheap Christmas tree. Standing over them were two uniformed officers. Were they under arrest? "Valerie, come look!"

"It better be worth the trouble," she warned. "Oh, would you look at that dress. It's ridiculous. Maybe she's Oliver's new friend. Let's go see," she said wickedly.

"If they're being arrested, pretend we don't know them."

"That dress must violate some law. Probably a sign ordinance."

"Now, now, Valerie, don't be catty." Marcus entered the lounge, calibrating his smile just so. "Greetings," he called out.

"It's Marcus and Valerie," Oliver whispered to Myrtle as his sister and brother-in-law approached. "She doesn't look well at all."

"Dearie, you look terrible," Myrtle said sympathetically. Marcus flinched, thinking she meant him.

"Park it here," Myrtle said considerately, patting the seat next to her.

"Don't tell me what to do!" Valerie snarled.

"Valerie," Oliver protested, coming to Myrtle's defense, "why are you being nasty? She was only trying to help."

"How dare you speak to me that way!"

"Ma'am," said Officer Mason, "you look overheated. Would you like a glass of water?"

"Maybe she's having a fit," muttered Officer Softlee.

"Oliver, I'm warning you."

"But Valerie," Myrtle explained, "Oliver didn't mean no harm."

"And don't call me Valerie!"

"What should she call you? Toots?" joked Marcus,

trying to appear amiable.

"Toots, why what a nice name," Myrtle said friendlily.

"Marcus, I am going to kill you," Valerie hissed under her breath.

"I have an aunt named Toots," said Myrtle.

"My name is not Toots!" screeched Valerie.

"Ma'am," Earnest said cautiously, "what is your name?"

"Who the heck are you?"

"Officer Earnest Mason of OOPS," he said, taken aback.

"So?" she said, giving him a withering look.

"It's a very important job," Marcus said ingratiatingly.

"Sir," said Earnest, turning to Marcus with relief. "Do you know anything about the theft of this ship?"

Marcus gave a guilty start. Coming so quickly on the heels of his remark to Valerie about owning the yacht someday, the question seemed like an accusation. A quick glance into Officer Mason's guileless eyes assured him the kid knew nothing. "Is someone planning to steal the ship?" he asked casually, leading the conversation away from himself.

"It's already stolen," said Officer Softlee. "You're on a stolen ship."

What was she talking about? Marcus wondered if she was trying to confuse him at Triton's behest. That was it. Triton was behind this.

"Pardon me, dearie," Myrtle piped up, "but wouldn't my friend, Mr. Triton, know if his ship was stolen?"

"That's right," said Oliver, giving her hand a squeeze.

"*Your* friend, Mr. Triton?" scoffed Valerie.

What does she mean her friend Mr. Triton? A million thoughts rushed through Marcus' brain. Was Triton toying with him? First the handrail, then this jabber about stealing yachts, and now these characters — where had they come from anyway? Any one of them might be Triton. He looked around desperately, fixing his glance on Earnest. "Are you Triton?"

"I'm Earnest Mason," Earnest explained. Were they trying to take his name away? "My name is Earnest Mason," he repeated forcefully.

"But is that your real name?" Marcus asked, pressing the point. "You act very strange when you say it."

"He's just trying to get used to it," Sharon said protectively.

"I thought so," Marcus said triumphantly. "It's an alias. Okay, Triton, you've had your fun," he said, laughing shrilly. "We're on to you now."

Earnest looked at him blankly.

"Marcus," Valerie snapped, "pull yourself together."

"Mr. Marcus, no one here is King Triton," Myrtle assured him.

"How would she know," Valerie said dismissively.

"Myrtle, is King Triton on board?" asked Sharon.

"He was a minute ago."

"He's here, he's there, he's everywhere," Marcus said giddily.

"Then he was kidnapped after all!" exclaimed Earnest. "Wait till OOPS hears about this!"

"And you found him, Officer Earnest Mason," Sharon said admiringly.

"Of course, it could have been one of the kidnappers in disguise," Earnest said thoughtfully.

"Oh, Earnest, you're so smart." Sharon gave him a peck on the cheek, replacing his thoughts with a cluster of effervescent bubbles.

"Myrtle, how can we be sure it was King Triton?" asked Sharon. "What did he look like?"

Marcus couldn't stop himself. "A handrail."

"Well," said Myrtle, "he was very bright, and real friendly. He gave me a big hug."

"She's making this up," Valerie declared. "Why would King Triton have her for a friend? It's absurd."

"I won't allow you to talk about Myrtle that way," Oliver said angrily. "She's a wonderful person. She's changed my whole life."

Myrtle's eyes filled with tears. "Thank you, Oliver," she said, gratefully.

"Oliver," Valerie said sharply, "take some of your black liquid and calm down. If Triton is anyone's friend, it would be Marcus."

"Myrtle, my friend," boomed a voice that seemed to come from everywhere. King Triton phosphoresced before them, blinding them with his brilliance.

"Oh, Mr. Triton," said Myrtle, shading her eyes with her hand. "This is my friend, Oliver."

"Marcus, is it really him?" Valerie asked excitedly.

Ignoring her, Marcus turned on Officer Mason. "Why did you pretend to be Triton?"

"I didn't! I pretended — I mean I *am* Earnest Mason!"

"Not sure, are you?" taunted Marcus.

"Earnest, pay no attention to him," said Sharon. "Of course you're sure."

But Earnest wasn't sure. "I have no proof, not one document with my name on it, not even a birth certificate."

"But Earnest," Sharon implored.

Something swirled out of the luminescence that was Triton, coming to rest in Myrtle's hand. "Earnest," Myrtle said excitedly, "look at this! She handed him a parchment scroll embossed with the Triton Family Crest:

EARNEST MASON
In name and deed
official citizen of Paradise and the universe beyond.

"Wow!" shouted Earnest, overjoyed. "Wow!"

"Marcus, I can't make out a thing in this blinding light," Valerie complained. "Is it really King Triton?"

"You never can tell," Marcus said warily.

"If you're so close to Triton, why is he paying attention to everyone else?" Valerie asked irritably, galled by Triton's attention to Myrtle.

Before Marcus could answer, Evert J. Snidely burst into the lounge. "Quick, which one of you is King Triton? I'm Mr. Cosmic Communications, here to give you fantastic coverage."

Hmm, thought Valerie, sidling up to Evert. If she could work herself into Triton's interview everyone would think she knew him.

"You're not Triton," Evert said brusquely.

"Of course not," Valerie said sweetly, playing up to him. "I'm Valerie Highwater by marriage, a member of the Oceanus family by birth, if you please. My husband is Triton's closest associate."

"Yeah, maybe later, Toots," said Evert, dismissing her. "Hey, you," he shouted at the blinding light that was King Triton, "turn down that light. Vern, get over here and start shooting."

"Watch me, kiddo, and learn," Vern said confidently, pushing Lorelei aside. This time there'd be no slip ups. Scanning the room with a professional eye, he zoomed in on the shimmering, elusive image, enigmatic smile and all. Something about the smile bothered him but he was too focused to think about that. His hands hot and sweaty, his shutter finger on the button, licking his lips in anticipation, he tasted something peculiar. Chocolate? Melting chocolate! There, in front of everybody, especially Lorelei, he felt his camera melting down his chin and running down the front of his shirt as he stood helpless before Triton's shimmering, ironic smile.

"Marcus," Valerie demanded, "what is going on?"

"It's a plot, Valerie, a plot. Triton's trying to humiliate me."

"It's not a plot, Marcus. It's a farce."

Chapter Forty-Four

Deeper Understandings

"Rubies are the Eyes of Eternity," said Mother Romany, handing the enormous Ruby to Laura. It was so big she needed both hands just to hold it.

The Ruby cast an incarnadine light, scattering blood-red flecks that broke free and hid in the shadows of the ceremonial tent, occasionally sparking like live coals in black ash.

"The Ruby will be yours to hold during the ceremony, little Indra," Mother Romany explained. Her voice was like a golden mist enfolding Laura. "At the proper moment you will give the Ruby to Magdalena."

As each new detail of the ceremony to come was revealed, the beauty of it made Laura feel both melancholy and joyful, for along with the sadness of parting came an inexplicable joy. She was surprised at how readily she accepted such contradictory feelings now. How free this made her feel. How large it made the world feel.

"As the *Unifier*, " Mother Romany continued, explaining Laura's part to her, "you have the gift of making people recognize their own goodness, however much of it they may have. And when they do, they become good."

"But?"

Mother Romany smiled. "You need not understand, child. It happens because of who you are." At the same time, she knew Laura wanted to know more. "You are thinking about the *Mirror*, little gypsy, aren't you?"

"Yes." Of all the mysteries of the ceremony, the *Mirror of Miracles* was at the core, waiting behind a veil not yet lifted.

Mother Romany's voice seemed to come from faraway, like the voices in her dreams.

*"When you are ready to know,
you will already know."*

* * * *

Duke seated himself on Laura's rock overlooking the sea and read Lilli's letter once again.

My darling,

I'm taking the coward's way and sending this letter before I join you. I want to give you time to think about what I say. And, I admit, I'm terrified that you will leave me now that you've seen Felicity again.

Yes, I know about her. I've always known she was enshrined in a sealed chamber of your heart. How I envied her, an ever-luminous memory, a perfect flower in a secret garden, never exposed to the commonizing weeds of daily life. Sometimes I raged at the unfair advantage this gave her. How I wanted to destroy her shrine in your heart. But how could I without also destroying you?

Because of my fear I imposed a condition on my love, extracting your promise that you would give up your dream of exploration. For this I am profoundly ashamed and sorry.

I tried to compensate by loving you tenfold and fluttering lightly around your heart, like a humming-bird around a blossom, taking my nourishment without burdening the flower. Your heart was so full, this hummingbird never went hungry.

Sometimes guilt overwhelmed me, guilt and shame, and I would fly into a rage, beating my wings against her shrine, wanting to rip out what I could not have, the wild dreaming heart of the flower, to suck it dry and leave nothing for her to feed on.

Asking you to set aside your dream was a shameful and unworthy thing. It was also impossible. For it is your secret, dreaming heart with all its mysteries intact that makes you who you are, the person I have always loved and will continue to love, until even time runs out.

Our favorite poet, Augustus, described so well how rich I feel my life has been because of you.

Our lives have been
lisle-threaded,
spun of moonbeams
and mistakes,
a tapestry of daily riches,
its fibers somewhat frayed,
but the basic fabric sound,
and oh-so-worthy of repair
because the beauty is still there.

Lilli.

Lilli, Duke sighed, folding her letter and putting it in the pocket closest to his heart.

Chapter Forty-Five

Palmyra Pushes On

Walking at a brisk clip toward the gypsy encampment, Palmyra Loveseat felt pretty frisky, even if she was out of shape, as Dr. Bogus was always quick to remind her. She hoped her husband would be okay handling their betting parlor by himself. EeeZee was a one-thing-at-a-time kind of person. He always marveled at how she could watch the fights, answer the phones, take bets, figure odds, tally the day's receipts and eat dinner all at the same time. Of course, she chuckled to herself, she could always eat dinner, no matter what. It was a good thing EeeZee liked her well upholstered.

Somewhat out of breath, Palmyra slowed her pace. Apparently, all the time she'd spent watching the fight between the Sun and the Moon on TV and sending out for junk food had taken its toll. Not that she was going to give that fraud, Dr. Bogus, the satisfaction of knowing he was right. She could just picture him shaking an accusatory finger at her, his irritating voice berating her. "Ya sit on ya duff and watch TV. Ya eat junk food, ya fatso. Ya never exercise. It's gonna kill ya!" Who did he think he was anyway, Chief of the Calorie Police? He was a Bogus, after all. The whole family were frauds. She preferred to think of herself as taking on substance, not weight, becoming more of what she was.

> *'In food we've been given*
> *a slice of heaven.*
>
> *Life without flavor*
> *gives little to savor.'*

She had memorized this inspiring poem from the *Witches' Book of Culinary Comforts* and what a comfort it was, an antidote to Dr. Bogus' bitter pills. "Ya gotta exercise," he admonished. "Ya don't get something for nothing." Her sentiments exactly. That's why she'd gone to him in the first place. He charged nothing, which made his advice worthless, leaving her free to ignore it.

Needing to rest, Palmyra entered the woods and found a cool spot by the river. Arranging her broad mahogany legs under her like abutments, shoring up her corpulent posterior, she stretched her frond-covered frock to its limits and wiggled into a comfortable position, extracting a candy bar from her capacious purse. Mentally thumbing her nose at Dr. Bogus, she took a defiant bite.

The upcoming banquet was so close she could almost taste it. At last she would partake of the witches' culinary magic, far from the scrutiny of that fractious fraud, Bogus. For too long she'd lived downwind from the witches and the Universal Dump, her imagination stirred by their cooking smells. Mingled with the piquant odors from the Dump, they created a longing in her that had to be satisfied. Everyone had a dream and this was hers.

Spurred on by her thoughts, Palmyra rose with a heave and a sigh. Ignoring her complaining joints, she headed for one of the hospitality cupolas that ringed the gypsy encampment. A garrulous Greeting Guard, bedecked in rainbow streamers, scurried out, did a clumsy pirouette, sang a few bars of "I feel pretty," and ground to a halt in front of her. "Invitation, please," it said with mechanical politeness.

"I left it at home," said Palmyra, expecting an argument.

"Oh, how terrible!" gushed the Greeting Guard, manufacturing a metal tear to prove it.

"Step aside," ordered Palmyra, unimpressed with it's manufactured sympathy.

"I have a lovely gift for you," it prattled rapturously, handing her a cleverly ornamented box.

"In exchange for what?" asked Palmyra, suspecting there were strings attached.

"I'm just trying to be nice," it said, irked that people didn't trust Greeting Guards bearing gifts.

"Then get out of my way."

"Well, if that's the way you're going to be," snapped the Greeting Guard, snatching back the gift, "I'll just have to sing a different tune." It did a couple of pirouettes as it rang forth with wicked glee, "I don't want her; you can have her; she's too fat for me. Hee, hee, hee."

That laugh! It was Dr. Bogus! "It's you!" shrieked Palmyra, giving the Greeting Guard a whack with her purse.

"Thank you. Thank you," wheezed the Greeting Guard, staggering backwards. "I don't know what came over me."

"Bogus, it's not going to work. You are not going to keep me from the banquet!"

"Nah, nah," said the Greeting Guard, sticking out its metal tongue, "you don't have an invitation. You've got to go home."

"Not on your rivets!" shouted Palmyra, gathering her heft. "Out of my way!" she bellowed, hitting the robot with such calamitous force she buckled its plates. Propelled by her own momentum, Palmyra trampled over the Greeting Guard, barreling onward toward her dream.

Chapter Forty-Six

Father Of The Bride

Amanda's father, Norville, was so immersed in the latest earnings reports from Oceana Investments he almost missed his stop on the shuttle from Starport to the wedding site. Jamming his papers into his attaché case, he made it through the doors just before they could close their metal jaws on him. He was always getting stuck in automatic doors. They never noticed him until it was too late. Something about his bland, colorless demeanor rendered him unnoticeable to doors and people alike. He was usually so absorbed in matters of finance and business gossip he failed to notice that no one noticed him anymore than he noticed them. Knowing this, he'd even wondered briefly if anyone would notice if he didn't show up for his daughter's wedding. But an urgent note from Felicity put an end to that idea — something about Amanda and a gorilla.

Their only child had always been a trial — talkative, full of high spirits, invading his peace like an army of tax collectors, always distracting him. Felicity, on the other hand, was an ideal mate, a soothing whisper, a pleasant hum, barely noticeable at all. He seldom actually had to listen to her words. Sometimes the cadence of her voice was all he needed to guide him to an appropriate understanding and response. He expected life to be comfortably placid from now on. Amanda was getting married, and that waiter, Maurice, had vanished from the household.

He plugged into CosmicLink, getting through to his broker on her direct line. The pleasure he got from hearing her seductive, monied voice felt vaguely sinful. "Misty, buy a trillion shares of Frank 'n Stein," he commanded, feeling unusually masterful.

"Oh, Norville, not that dog. Talk about reviving the dead."

"Misty," he repeated firmly, "buy a trillion."

"But Norvie," she cooed, wondering if he knew something she didn't. "It's so risky. Are you sure we should go that far?"

Titillated by the way she put things, he wanted to string out their conversation. "I heard a rumor."

"A rumor? Tell me," she said, suddenly all business. If it was an inside tip she could make lots and lots of money.

Her avarice was an aphrodisiac to him. "I don't know if I should."

"Norville, we're talking about money," she said breathily, her voice inviting as the sheen on a stack of gold bars.

"Okay, Misty, are you ready for this? It's a takeover!"

"Ooooooo," she squealed, "tell me more."

"Buy it now!" he ordered, breaking off the connection. He felt a certain satisfaction in leaving her wanting more.

Chapter Forty-Seven

Old Friends And New

The Night swept in with brio, wearing a diadem of stars. The Moon in his cloak of clouds, looked down, unseen. Far below, the gypsy fires and lanterns burned like fallen stars.

The first of several banquets that would culminate in the Grand Ceremonial Feast, was about to begin. Claribel and Dolly flew around their kitchen chuckling over the culinary surprises they were preparing.

It was a time for closeness, for love and celebration, but also a time for goodbyes. Laura had come to realize not all goodbyes were terrible. Her participatioin in rehearsals for the beautiful and serene ceremony — Naming the New Queen — had given her comfort. Goodbyes could still be sad, but not terrible.

She went to visit her *doThings* who were humming contentedly in their gazebo, admired and cared for by the musicians. They had become so much more beautiful in their freedom, their brash initial exuberance changing to a serene, mellow, inner harmony and a sweeter flow of musical peace. She felt proud of them, proud of herself. She'd been right to let them go. There could be a kind of happiness in letting go, letting go with love.

* * * *

Laura wandered over to see what Claribel and Dolly had cooked up. She hoped it wasn't food. "Hi, what's not cooking?" she teased, sticking her head in the door. A hand reached out and pulled her inside. The door latched behind her.

"Shhhh," whispered Dolly, "Claribel's putting the finishing touches on the feast."

There was no food in sight but there were funny smells and sounds coming from the cupboards and ovens. Claribel was stuffing empty boxes into a roaring fire. Judging from what Laura could see of the labels, they had contained some of the best designer foods in the cosmos. She'd been hoping the witches would do something magical. "Are you going to pretend you made the stuff from those boxes?" she asked, disappointed.

"You should know us better than that," Claribel chided, tossing the last telltale box into the fire.

"Anyway, what fun would it be using someone else's food," said Dolly, just bursting to tell Laura more. "Besides..." But a warning look from Claribel stopped her in her tracks. "Anyway, what we've got in mind will be a masterpiece."

"It's so brilliant," Claribel chortled. "I wish we could brag about it to everyone in advance, but then it wouldn't work."

"Me too! I'm dying to tell," squealed Dolly.

"You can tell me," said Laura.

"No she can't," Claribel said firmly. "It's a secret."

"I won't tell," Laura promised.

"We want it to be a surprise," Claribel insisted. "Our interview with you has inspired us to outdo ourselves. You wouldn't want to spoil that, would you?"

"As long as the surprise isn't your stew," said Laura, making a face.

"You're not going to get anymore out of us," said Claribel, shooing her out the door.

* * * *

Strolling past the garlanded main banquet table, Laura was pleased to see they had done as she'd asked. Her name was on place cards here and there down the length of the table so she could visit with her friends more conveniently during the banquet.

She heard a joyous outpouring of music from the *doThings*. Together with the Musicians they were creating a symphony for *doThings* and orchestra. Its infectious euphoria swept her away.

"You must be a Cloud Maiden," a lively mezzo voice said playfully.

"Because of my white dress?" Laura asked, turning.

"That, and your faraway look, as though you were

floating on a cloud."

"I guess I was."

"It might be fun to live on a cloud. You could rain on people you don't like," the stranger said mischievously.

"If my cloud wants to," Laura said playfully.

"Can anyone come aboard?"

"Anyone who believes in magic clouds."

"That's wonderful."

"Who are you?"

"My name is Lilli."

"You're Lilli?" said Laura, taken by surprise. "I mean I didn't expect you ...to be so nice," she said lamely.

"Thank you, I think," Lilli said jokingly. "But you haven't told me your name."

"Laura."

"Why didn't you expect me to be nice? Did someone tell you I was a monster?" she asked playfully.

"It's just that... I didn't know you'd be so nice," Laura said uncomfortably.

"Would you rather I was mean?" she teased. "I don't think I'd like that."

"I can see why Duke loves you."

"Did he tell you that?" Lilli asked, surprised, her heart beating faster.

There was an urgency to her question that made Laura want to reassure her. "Duke thinks you're wonderful."

"I think he's wonderful too."

"So do I," said Laura, blushing.

Lilli looked at her curiously. "I'm so glad Duke has a friend who loves him."

"Why do you say that?"

"We women can sense such things."

"Then you're not angry?" asked Laura. "It's okay?"

"It's very okay."

"I don't see how Duke could ever have loved anyone else," Laura said earnestly, her earnestness turning to dismay as she saw Lilli's distress. "I'm sorry. I mean, I didn't think." She stopped, realizing Lilli might be the only one who didn't know about Felicity.

"It's okay, dear," Lilli said reassuringly. "It was a lovely thing to say."

"I really like you," said Laura, relieved.

"It's all right. Tell me, is she pretty?" Lilli couldn't bring herself to say Felicity's name.

"Not like you."

Lilli gave her a hug. "You're prejudiced."

Laura hugged her back. "Maybe I am. But it's true."

Lilli smiled. "Let's go find our guy."

Chapter Forty-Eight

Things Beautiful And Brave

Sprinting barefoot through the forest, intoxicated by the damp, green-scented air, Magdalena plunged head-long into the deep indigo night, full of joy and expectation, her black hair flying from her like the beating wings of a raven.

Since she'd had the Dream of Confirmation and seen the ecstatic faces of the three boys, she was no longer in rebellion against her destiny and all it implied. She'd begun experiencing life as a succession of moments, each to be savored and then let go to dissolve in the inexorable River of Time. Being truly alive meant surrendering her-self to the River, trusting it to bear her safely to the source from which all things spring.

Coming to the deepest part of the river, Magdalena dove in, cleaving the water joyfully.

Casting off his human form, King Triton rose above the lace of leaves that dappled her, joining his brother, the

Moon. Seeing her immersed in the dark water, her radiant face a luminous blossom uplifted to the light, he was moved to pity for all things beautiful, ephemeral and brave.

On this, her last night of freedom, Guitano came to her, his heart overflowing with love. Seeing the rapturous look she gave him, the Moon cried out in thunderclaps of anguish.

* * * *

Duke put Lilli's letter in his breast pocket, grateful that she'd swept away the guilt he'd felt about having loved Felicity, and the frustration of wanting to pursue his dream. Line by line her letter conveyed her warmth, her sensitivity, her unfailing humor. It reminded him how much he'd relied on these qualities, how much they'd actually helped him sustain his dream.

With the sediment of illusion washed away, Duke saw everything with refreshing clarity. From Laura's high bluff he could see the stars in the sky, the trees in the forest and the reflections on the sea, with a freshness and keenness of feeling he hadn't felt since he'd been a child filled with wonder. Like Laura, he too was poised on a threshold of change. Thinking about her, he realized how much she and Lilli had in common. They each had a certain inner dignity.

With a profound sense of peace Duke watched the Moon gazing with its cratered eyes on the forest below as a great light rose up to join it, forming a halo around the Moon. Then, shaken by a series of thunderclaps, it rained down a mist of light on the forest where the River ran.

Chapter Forty-Nine

Palmyra Manages Things

Determined to crash the gypsy wedding and ceremony, neither of which she'd been invited to, an oversight she was determined to correct, Ma Light concentrated all her voltage on the effort. Sizzling her way down through the stratosphere like a bolt of lightning, she incinerated two trays of hors d'oeuvre and startled Palmyra Loveseat into dropping a large sugared cream puff. Already annoyed by her encounter with the Greeting Guard, Palmyra had settled herself in at the first snack booth she'd come to and now she was being attacked! Taking a swing at the incendiary intruder with her purse while snatching up a couple of tempting petit fours, she knocked something into the punch bowl.

"You've ruined my hat, you peon! Do you have any idea whom you are assaulting?"

Palmyra recognized the hoity-toity act of her gambling house rival, Ma Light. "Ma, you old pigeon plucker!"

"Oh, it's you," sniffed Ma Light. "Madam-Stuff-Herself."

"Trying to sneak in, aren't you," Palmyra chortled, knowing if Ma had had an invitation she would have shown up with it gold plated and glued to her forehead. "On top of which you have no finesse," said Palmyra with a wave of her hand, indicating the charred hors d'oeuvre and tablecloth, confident Ma hadn't seen her flatten the Greeting Guard while making her own entrance. "All this just because you didn't get an invitation?"

"I've simply misplaced it, what with all the redecorating going on at the Club Galaxy."

"Redecorating?" scoffed Palmyra. "Cleaning up the wreckage left by the Benefit of the Doubt, you mean. Everybody knows what a mess it was."

"I wouldn't talk about messes if I were you," Ma Light said primly. "I'm not the one who's 75 pounds over-weight."

"Well, you always were a lightweight."

"At least my establishment isn't next to the Universal Dump."

"You're out of touch, Lightsie-poo. Living next to the Dump is considered Eco-Chic."

Hating to be called poo anything, Ma splattered a phony smile across her face. "Palmie," she wheedled, "I don't quite know how to say this, but after all, we're old friends."

"Since when?"

"Well, if not exactly friends," said Ma, continuing to ooze solicitude, "perhaps comrades in arms."

"Do tell," said Palmyra, waiting to see what the old phony was up to.

"This wedding is very high society. I'd hate to see you embarrass yourself by committing some social gaffe like using the wrong fork."

"Don't worry, I'll use my hands," Palmyra said airily. "Sometimes the right one, sometimes the left. I always know which is which."

"Palmyra, you force me to be blunt."

"Spit it out, Lightsie, before you choke on it."

"It's obvious your invitation was meant for me.'"

"They probably got us mixed up because we look so much alike," Palmyra said innocently.

"Don't be ridiculous," Ma Light said scornfully. "It's just that we're in related ... occupations." She grimaced, hating to admit it. "An understandable mistake. What would robots know of the difference in our social standing?"

"What indeed?" said Palmyra, yawning. "Now, go be social somewhere else."

"You mean you're not going to let me take your place?"

Palmyra looked her straight in the eye. "You couldn't take my place if your life depended on it. Now run along. I have some serious snacking to do."

"If you want a canapé that bad," Ma Light shrieked, arcing out of control, "here, have a whole tray full!" Beside herself with rage, she dumped a mountain of hot cheese canapés onto Palmyra's plush lap.

"Ooooo," Palmyra squealed delightedly, "a food fight."

She licked a cheese-coated finger. "Garlic and herb, my favorite." With a kick she disabled a nosey cleanup robot that was hovering a little too closely.

"Palmyra Loveseat, you are disgusting. You haven't the breeding of a Snerd."

"Go fish your bonnet out of the punchbowl."

"That invitation was meant for me and you know it!" Ma Light hissed, taking off like a streak of light to avoid being thrown out by an onrushing squad of Greeting Guards. "You'll pay for this, Palmyra!"

Chuckling, Palmyra cheerfully submitted to the ministrations of cleanup robot #2. Having secreted away a stash of canapés in the food compartment of her redoubtable purse, she was, for the moment, content.

* * * *

Finnie much preferred silk but for Reggie's and Lorelei's sake she was wearing gingham to be more domestic, hoping that by dressing the part she could absorb domesticity through her skin. Lorelei had always wanted a gingham kind of mother, probably because that would have been opposite of the one she'd had. Prompted by contrition, Finnie had given in to her daughter's whim, even allowing Lorelei to braid her hair with gingham bows which made her look like a child's doll. All she lacked was red polka dots on her cheeks and the ability to stop blinking.

Thus attired and feeling absurd, Finnie headed for the banquet area to check on her contribution to the décor, a vast, gauzy canopy flecked with bits of silver, which covered the entire banquet area, adding intimacy and elegance to the outdoor setting.

Wandering along the banquet table, Finnie was amused to see how frequently Laura's name appeared on the place cards. When she saw Tibor's card next to hers she plucked it from its spot and mischievously put it at the far end of the table, next to that brat, Sheila's. It tickled her to think of those two trying to make light conversation.

Lost in thought, she wandered on, not noticing twilight was descending. Looking around, she could just make out an unmanned hospitality outpost and a lumpy, abandoned looking loveseat with a large lumpy bag on it and a mop head dangling over the back. It looked like the clean up crew had forgotten a few things.

Despite the sofa's well-worn look, it positively radiated comfort, inviting her to sit a while. Reaching over to move the bag and make room for herself she was startled as a thick, frond covered arm came seemingly out of nowhere and snatched it away. "It's not nice to steal, little girl," grumbled a sleepy voice from deep within the cushions. Finnie realized what she'd taken for a mop head was the hair of someone who'd been lolling in sleep.

"I wasn't trying to steal anything," said Finnie, flustered.

"It's not nice to lie, either, little girl."

"I was trying to sit down."

"What do you think I am, a sofa? Didn't anyone teach you manners?"

"I must confess, I did think you were a sofa," Finnie said, puzzled.

"I am a Loveseat," Palmyra said firmly. "We're a special branch of the Seating family."

"I'm sorry," said Finnie. "I didn't know."

"Most people make the same mistake," Palmyra said, softening. "Sofas are different. You don't have to ask their permission to sit down."

"I promise I'll never make that mistake again," Finnie said sincerely.

"Good," said Palmyra, satisfied. "So, why are you dressed like a child? Trying to get into something for half-price?"

Finnie laughed ruefully. "I dressed this way to please my family."

"Do they collect dolls?" Palmyra asked, laughing.

"I look pretty silly, I suppose."

"You don't look comfortable."

"I don't feel comfortable. Gingham is scratchy."

"Silk's the thing," said Palmyra, thrusting out a hefty arm. "Here, feel this. Never catch me in gingham."

"I'm sure I wouldn't," said Finnie, trying to picture her abundant curves upholstered in calico country scenes, her udder-like purse nestled in the meadows of her lap. "I've always preferred silk myself."

"Why let your family push you around? You're not the gingham type."

"I'm trying to reform," Finnie said with a sigh.

"I don't believe in reforming," Palmyra said emphatically. "Mostly it means trying to be something you're not.

It's not healthy."

"I suppose you're right. It's such a dilemma."

"Have a seat, honey. We need to talk," said Palmyra, patting her cushiony lap.

"You don't mind?"

"I wouldn't invite you if I did." Finnie sank gratefully into her lap. "Tell me," said Palmyra, "what makes you think you need reforming?"

"I've led a useless, frivolous life."

"Ever harm anyone?"

"Not intentionally."

"So, what needs reforming?"

Finnie was silent for a moment. "I guess it's just not fun anymore."

"Ah, that's a different matter. What you want has nothing to do with reforming," Palmyra said confidently. "You're just tired of being silly. You need to find some way to be an adult and still have fun."

"I think you're right," Finnie said thoughtfully. "I'm just not sure how to proceed."

"Let's start with these pigtails," said Palmyra, reaching up to undo them. "Grownups in pigtails never have any grownup fun."

"Probably because no one knows they're grownups."

"You got it. It's not so much growing up as growing out. Once you're as tall as you're going to get, that's it for growing up." She chuckled, patting her ample girth. "After that you have to grow out. I don't mean grow out wide, necessarily," Palmyra laughed. "Though that's okay too. I mean out from the inside."

"Are all loveseats as wise as you are?" Finnie asked appreciatively.

"Are all mermaids as beautiful as you are?" Palmyra teased.

Finnie laughed. "You know more about me than I do and I don't even know your name."

"I'm Palmyra Loveseat."

"Really! *The* Palmyra Loveseat?" Finnie asked, delighted.

"The one and only."

"I'm honored," said Finnie.

"Thank you," said Palmyra, pleased. "Just remember, it's a chancy thing, this growing up business. Even for an adult."

"You're an expert on the odds," said Finnie, "tell me, what do you think my chances are?"

Palmyra's eyes twinkled. "Honey, back in your racing silks, you're the odds-on favorite."

Chapter Fifty

Healing Hearts

Laura felt Lilli tense as they spotted Duke on the high bluff, facing out to sea.

"Don't be afraid," Laura said reassuringly.

"I'm not usually such a coward."

"You're not a coward."

"It's just that I love him so much," Lilli said anxiously.

Laura tried to think of something to say. "I know I'm not a grownup, but when I'm afraid of something when I shouldn't be, I try to make myself do it."

Lilli looked at her admiringly, this child with so much wisdom. "Laura, you are the most grown up person I know. And you're absolutely right. Living in fear is barely living at all."

Laura was silent for a moment, remembering the Little Princess, how she had overcome her fear of the evil demons and freed her father. "I know," she said sadly, thinking of her own father.

Lilli sensed that Laura was speaking from a deep inner aloneness, as though wrapped in her own arms, perhaps because there were no other arms to hold her. Her heart went out to the child, and as it did, Lilli's own fear vanished. "You know what helps at times like these?" she asked brightly.

Laura looked at her questioningly.

"A friend you can talk to. Someone you can count on," said Lilli, opening her arms.

* * * *

As she and Laura reached the top of the bluff, Lilli called out, "Hi, handsome, is this rock reserved?"

Duke whipped around, surprised. "Lilli!" he exclaimed jubilantly, scooping her up and covering her face with kisses.

"Wow!" Lilli laughed breathlessly.

"Princess," Duke said, reaching out to Laura. She put her small hand in his. "Come, let's sit. There's a lot I want to tell you two."

"I'm so happy," said Lilli, looking at him lovingly.

Duke smiled. "I'm not sure where to begin," he said shyly. "It feels funny talking about it."

Lilli squeezed his hand. "It's okay. We love you."

Laura kissed his cheek.

"I'm a lucky guy," said Duke, taking a deep breath. "Okay, here goes, but if I get goofy,"

"Goofy is fine," said Lilli.

Duke smiled gratefully. "I suppose, like most kids, I dreamed of finding a place where I could be whatever I wanted to be, a magic place where bad things couldn't get me, where I could be free."

"Grownups want that too," said Laura, thinking of her father and the Books With the Golden Edges, and the distant music and laughter from the place beyond time.

"Some of us do," said Duke, "but life can tear some awful big holes in our dreams. We're so busy patching things together we forget about the magic world or we lose heart. But some of us never forget. We grieve for our lost world until the longing for it becomes a soul ache. Without knowing it we're always trying to find some way back to it. If we don't keep trying something in us dies."

"Everyone feels that way, deep down," Lilli said quietly.

Duke was surprised. "Everyone? You feel that way too?"

"Yes," she said softly.

"You never told me."

Lilli sighed. "I couldn't."

"But... Why?" Then, seeing the pain and love in her eyes, he understood. "Oh. Felicity."

Lilli nodded. "I felt part of you was already taken."

"If I hadn't been such a sap I would have known," said Duke, putting his arms around her. "I thought you thought my dreams were silly, even irresponsible, somehow."

"I never thought that, my darling. They're part of the wild, dreaming you that I love."

"What an idiot I've been!"

"What idiots we've both been."

* * * *

Love and understanding deepened between the three of them as they quietly watched the night make its grand entrance on the vast proscenium of the sky accompanied by the rustling sound of stars taking their places, all a-glitter.

In the loving peacefulness Laura felt safe to ask something she'd been wondering about. "Where's The Elsewhere?"

"You know about The Elsewhere?" Duke asked, startled.

"The Emissary told me."

Duke struggled with his disbelief. "You've met the Emissary?"

"He talks to me. He lives in my cloud," she said pointing to an odd looking cloud wedged into a corner of the sky.

"What else did he tell you?" asked Duke.

"About the Rightness of Things."

"He did?"

"Rightness of Things?" Lilli asked, puzzled.

"He wouldn't explain," said Laura, equally puzzled. "He was surprised I could hear him in my dreams too."

"I bet he was," said Duke.

"I think he was lost. He was looking for someone in them."

"Did he say who?" asked Lilli.

"I think he was looking for me," Duke said quietly.

"You?" Lilli and Laura chorused.

"Could be."

Lilli gave him a kiss. "You're always in my dreams. He should have looked for you there."

Duke sensed there was a connection between the Emissary, Laura, The Elsewhere and the magic he wanted to recapture, and he was determined to find out what it was. "Laura, did you ever hear about the Books With the Golden Edges?"

Laura's eyes opened wide. "Oh yes. My father and I read them together every night!"

"Your father," Duke murmured. "Tell me, Princess, do you remember a poem called The Elsewhere? Near the end of one of the books?"

"I guess we didn't get that far," Laura said wistfully.

Lilli brushed back Laura's mass of red hair and kissed her on the forehead.

"I think your father would want you to keep reading the books," Duke said softly. "If you like we could read them together."

"I'd like that," she said. Then her face grew troubled. If she read them with someone else would her father feel she didn't love him anymore?

"Would you like to hear the poem?"

She nodded.

> *I will go*
> *where you don't know.*
> *I will be*
> *where you can't see.*
> *I will play*
> *so far away*
> *no one will find*
> *what's on my mind.*
> *The Elsewhere.*
>
> *...I will be free*
> *and all that is me*
>
> *and no one will know*
> *where I go...*

Laura let the words go deep inside her, winding and twining around her heart, stirring memories of her father and the laughter that came from far away.

Chapter Fifty-One

The Rightness Of Things

Still under the spell of the poem, Laura, Duke and Lilli sat side by side watching the moon's gaze glide over the sea, feeling closer to each other and themselves.

"Duke," Lilli began. She was interrupted by a loud racket overhead as Laura's cloud clattered clumsily down from the sky, dissolving as it descended. Soon there was nothing left but a few wisps clinging to its odd occupant, a squat, cross-eyed, gnome-like creature of transparent pink jade, his large domed head crowned with a mass of leafy green curls, his webbed hand holding a rainbow which streamed from it like a kite.

"Great mongooses and moonbeams!" he chittered like a scolding squirrel, "I can't stand it, can't listen to another word! Talk, talk, talk. Blather, blather, blather!" His arms churned like windmills in a gale. "Action! We need action!"

"Are you the E-e-missary?" Laura asked, not knowing

what to think. She'd imagined someone more dignified.

The creature's eyes crossed and uncrossed while his malleable mouth chewed on an answer. "Sure," he said finally, his eyes coming to a stop, crossed. "Sure, I'm the Emissary."

"You seem so different," Laura said, puzzled. "I mean from when you were in my cloud and I talked to you."

"That wasn't me, little seeker, that was Apodictic, my mentor. He's an Ancient," he said reverently, his voice now like the deep gong of a ship's bell in a fog. "Allow me to introduce myself." Tipping his leafy green curls like a hat, he bowed with such exuberance he fell on his face. "Sometimes I get carried away," he giggled, his giggles sounding like sleigh bells. Eyes dancing mischievously, he brushed off his shiny red pantaloons and scooped up his thick vegetation of curls, firmly replanting them on the jade-smooth dome of his head. "I am the Gnome of the Tome," he announced, striking an attitude. "The Gnome of the Tome?" he repeated to himself with a quizzical frown. "So, whaddaya think, folks? Is it me?" he asked, his pliable mouth taking the form of a question mark.

"It sounds very catchy," Duke said agreeably.

"Dignified," Lilli added.

"You think so?" the Gnome trilled merrily. "I was trying for a little dignity for a change, a counterbalance you might say. One should always strive for balance," he said pedantically.

"So you won't keep falling down," Laura said gleefully.

"Balance, falling down, very clever," the Gnome chortled appreciatively, as though she'd given him a delightful gift. "Did you hear what she said?" he asked himself, his voice a lively glissando. "Balance, falling down," he warbled, dancing a jig. "The child said the right thing at just the right time to keep me in balance."

Then, calm as the eye of a storm, he reached out to stroke Laura's hair with his delicately webbed fingers. His touch was surprisingly gentle, not at all what she'd expected. Suddenly, he was back in motion. Puffing up his fat, pink cheeks, he plucked a monocle out of nowhere and popped it in his right eye. "One must strive for balance," he said owlishly. "Ahem, blah, blah and all that ROT." At the word ROT his cheeks deflated with a whoosh and his monocle popped out. Poof, it vanished in mid air. "Gone back to the Never Was," he said with a wave of his hand.

The Never Was? Laura wondered where that could be.

"One must strive for balance, equilibrium. Oh my, oh my," the Gnome chided himself, "such heavy words. Heavy talk weighs you down. Lightness is balance," he fluted. "Buoyancy! Action!" Exploding into motion, he somersaulted in the air, got tangled up in his rainbow and crashed head-over-heels to the ground. "I may not be good at somersaulting," he said sheepishly, "but I'm very good at getting up."

Rising with the grace of a dancer, slowly, elaborately, his rainbow fluttering from him like an outstretched wing, he faced the three companions. The moment for something of importance had come round. "Nothing is just as it seems," he intoned, his voice warm as a cello. "It is always more." His words lingered in the air.

> *"Life is a playground*
> *for the childhood of the soul."*

"Oh!" Laura exclaimed, catching her breath.

The Gnome did a little shimmy as though to shake free

of something. "Speaking of ROT, which we were not," he giggled, pleased by his unintended rhyme. "It's time I told you about the Rightness of Things, or ROT, as I call it.

> *Ready or not*
> *we're going to ROT.*
>
> *(A ROTten pun*
> *is better than none.)*

"Get it? ROTten pun is better than none," he twittered, sprinkling himself with glitter while spinning like a top. "As you can see," he giggled, coming to a full stop, his eyes still spinning in their sockets, "wisdom can come from some surprising places, like a gold ring in a box of cracker jacks. Never judge your wisdom by your wise-cracker," he quipped. "Got it? Wisecracker, Cracker-Jacker?" Overcome with glee he leaped off the cliff, land-ing securely in mid air, still rattling on. "Come on folks, this is my first solo performance. Gimme some encour-agement. I feel like I'm spinning my wheels out here."

"You're like a merry-go-round spinning real fast," Laura said delightedly, imagining a blur of colors, calliope mu-sic, painted horses bobbing up and down.

With a smile wider than his face, the Gnome flung out his arms to the moon. "Okay, moon, gimme a kiss. Shine your spot on me. This is my big scene!" There came the ratatatatatat of a drum roll. "Ladies and gents, I'm gonna give ya some immortal thoughts, some elixir for yer souls."

Adopting the style of a carnival huckster, his rainbow billowing out behind him like a sail, he smiled craftily. "So. Ya wanna know about the Rightness of Things. Well, it's the flip side of the Wrongness!" he declared, doing a back flip. "El Wrongo is easy to spot. He's a gloomy Gus with dead eyes. Grimmo is his middle name. Sneaks around the dark alleys of the soul trying to sell bitter snake oil — hatred, self-pity, blame, you name it. Sometimes he takes you by surprise. Knocks you down. When you're down he can really pitch that snake oil, folks, but only if you let him. So," the Gnome said, snapping his fingers, "you gotta brush off your backside, knock that snake oil outta his hand, and flip that bully. And, presto-change-o, who'll ya find on the flip side? None other than Mister...?"

"Rightness!" Laura squealed, clapping her hands.

"You got it, kid!" The Gnome did another little shimmy and suddenly there were two of him, each one astride the opposite end of a seesaw rainbow. "Rightness is balance," the two Gnomes said in unison. "Anyone want to ride the rainbow?" A shimmering skybridge with golden handrails appeared, spanning the distance between seesaw and cliff.

"Oh, yes!" cried Laura, rushing across it to join them before Duke and Lilli could stop her. One of the Gnomes lifted her onto his end of the seesaw. Her added weight flipped the other Gnome high into the air where he vanished with a whoosh.

Laughing, Laura scrambled back to Duke and Lilli before the sky bridge vanished too, promising them she wouldn't do such a thing again for a while. "Did the other Gnome go back to the Never Was?"

"If that's where he came from," the Gnome said cheerfully. "As you can plainly see," he chuckled, "when it comes to balance, the smallest thing can make a difference."

"Very good," said Lilli, applauding.

"Thank you. Thank you," said the Gnome, wrapping his rainbow around himself like a cape. "What more can I say? Rightness is how you live your life. Of course," he added, shinnying up his rainbow which was now a rainbow rope, "a sense of humor goes a long way. El Wrongo hates humor like negatrons hate positrons."

Reaching the top of his rope, which had been vanishing from under him as he climbed, the Gnome hung there, suspended in nothingness. "See ya ...Elsewhere..." he said with a wink.

And he was gone.

They could hear him in the distance, his words looping back to them.

> *I will be*
> *behind a tree*
> *and in the sky*
> *or in your eye,*
> *in the ground*
> *and all around,*
> *in the air*
> *and everywhere...*

* * * *

Despite his antics, much of what the Gnome had said reverberated in them, turning their thoughts inward. A silvery fog rose from the sea, misting them with a shimmering blanket of quietness, making the world seem far away. Within the quiet, they felt a sense of timelessness, of time suspended.

They gradually became aware of someone floating above them, someone both like and unlike the Gnome. He was cloaked in serenity and seemed very, very old, with silver curls and alabaster skin touched by a hint of pink so subtle you felt, rather than saw it. "I am Apodictic," he said, settling himself on a cushion of mist. "I am an Elder." He cocked his head as if listening to someone. "Correction, I am an Ancient," he said good naturedly. "At my age memory can be selective."

"You're the one in my cloud!" Laura said excitedly. "The one I talk to."

"Yes, I am, child," he said fondly.

"You're like I imagined."

"Imagination is a third eye," said Apodictic, touching the center of Laura's forehead with his finger, the fragile webs between his fingers rustling.

His touch was pleasantly disorienting, like when you lay on the beach looking up at the sky and float with the clouds.

"The Gnome and I," Apodictic explained, "are part of a loosely connected organization or organism or whatever it is," he said, with a flick of his hand as though brushing away trivial distinctions. "It is a group comprised of those who have found The Elsewhere, each in their own way, of course. We are its caretakers, dedicated to preserving the ...Rightness of Things, is the only way to describe it."

"Oh," Duke said hesitantly, "Rightness of Things, ROT, the Gnome called it."

Apodictic chuckled. "The Gnome has a unique way of expressing himself."

"I like him a lot," said Laura. "He makes me laugh."

"His enthusiasm is a tonic," said Apodictic.

"I'll say," Lilli giggled.

Apodictic smiled. "In time, perhaps a millennium or so, not long for such as we, he will achieve personal equanimity. Is the word equanimity familiar to you, child?"

"No, but I feel what it means."

"Delightful answer," said Apodictic, pleased with her. "I shall leave you to the sweetness of discovering things your own way, which is as it should be."

Taking a deep breath, he fixed his eyes on something beyond seeing. The air around him began to vibrate. A third eye opened in the center of his forehead, startling Laura and her companions. "You three have embarked on a quest," he said, his three eyes searching theirs, seeing, in combination, what could not otherwise be seen. "And three you shall be for a time, for three may sometimes see what one alone cannot."

"Then we can go to The Elsewhere together?" asked Laura.

"The ways are infinite," said Apodictic. "There are many hearts, but only one Heart."

"But we are three hearts," said Lilli, concerned.

"For now your three hearts are one."

"Do you mean we have to go by ourselves?" Laura asked, disappointed.

Apodictic looked at her compassionately, feeling her sense of loss. "In a way, all of us are orphaned from birth, even orphaned from ourselves. But not ultimately." He turned to Duke and Lilli. "In your quest you will enter a universe filled with the essence of yourselves, although, at times it may not seem so."

"But what about love?" Lilli objected. "Loving is a journey with those you love."

"Ah, but first you must become your own companion."

"I'm going to The Elsewhere!" Laura declared, jumping to her feet. "No matter what!"

"Yes, child, yes," Apodictic assured her. "I'm sure you will." His third eye closed.

I will, Laura thought fiercely.

As Apodictic faded into the mist, he reached out to her and Laura felt the gentlest touch of something at the center of her forehead.

Chapter Fifty-Two

The Banquet

It was a perfect night for the banquet. The fall air was unusually mild. The full Moon was in attendance with his retinue of stars. Guests kicked off their shoes and frolicked like children on a lush carpet of grass and flower petals, singing, dancing, tossing handfuls of autumn leaves into the air. Enticing, exotic spices scented the air.

The *doThings* contributed to the occasion by composing a music teased from the sounds and silences of the encampment — laughter, the ebb and flow of voices, the tinkle of utensils, the rustle of leaves, wind in the trees, sounds of the night — meandering between notes, inventing new tonalities, vanishing and reappearing, creating a delicate, sinuous, fantasia of joy and life.

Guests were milling about, laughing, talking, renewing old acquaintances, making new ones. Laura was delighted to see so many of the elegantly dressed guests were going barefoot. Eager to be with her many friends,

she searched the crowd, spotting Loki, Gen and
Pinocchio talking to Sheila and Tibor. Kicking off her own
shoes, she ran to meet them.

"Guess what, Laura," Pinocchio said gleefully, throwing
his arms around her neck. "Gen is coming to visit us on
Contentment for a while, and we're going by gypsy wagon,
thank goodness! No more light beams for me!"

"The gypsy wagon, that's wonderful," said Laura, remembering the pleasure of her own magical journey with
Magdalena, Amanda and Big Boy — the fiery red horses
galloping across the starry sky.

Glancing at the *I love you* bracelet Laura had given
him, Gen also remembered that night and their tearful
goodbye. Reaching out, he took Laura's hand in his. "I'm
takin' Sheila with me. Loki thinks Contentment might
mellow her some," he said, knowing Sheila was listening
to every word.

"I'm not going," Sheila declared, clinging possessively to
Tibor. "I'm going to Misery and I'm taking Tibor with me.
So there!"

"You're makin' me miserable right here," Gen
grumbled.

Sheila's possessiveness made Tibor feel rushed. Being
pouty and humorless was one thing, but Misery? Was he
really ready for that?

"Why not bring the young man to Contentment?" Loki
suggested.

"Good thinkin', pal," said Gen. "Whaddaya say, Tibor?
Contentment would do us all some good. Make you think
twice about Misery."

"Tibor is going to learn to be miserable with me!" Sheila

insisted. That didn't sound right.

"I can always go to Misery if I don't like Contentment," said Tibor, taking advantage of Sheila's confusion.

"Contentment is a waste of time. Don't listen to them," Sheila said determinedly.

"Laura," Gen asked, concealing a smile, "want to come with us?"

"I'm going to The Elsewhere."

"The Elsewhere," Gen said thoughtfully. "Well, kid, if anyone can get there, it's you."

"But, but, that's in the Unexplored!" Pinocchio protested. "Anything might happen. What if you got lost?"

"Not a chance," Loki said, smiling.

"There is no such place," Sheila grumbled.

"Is there?" Tibor asked hopefully.

The Mystery of the Missing Shoes

When the guests went to retrieve their shoes they discovered they were gone.

Seated at a table with Reggie, Lorelei, Evert, Vern and her new found friend, Palmyra, Finnie was dealing with a family matter. "Reggie, darling, I'm afraid I can't promise you a gingham me. I'm too fond of silk." Palmyra nodded approvingly. "But I can promise all of me. No looking back. No regrets."

"My love, that's all I ever wanted," said Reggie, giving

her a kiss. "You can go around dressed in rags if you want to," he said fondly.

"That's not exactly what I had in mind, dear."

Basking in a glow of self-content, Palmyra felt something trying to pull off her shoe. She kicked hard, connecting with whatever it was.

"Laura," Finnie called to her, motioning Laura over. "Everyone, this is my very wise friend, Laura. She asks the most remarkable questions. It was Laura who asked why I never married you," she told Reggie.

"What did you tell her?" Reggie asked cautiously.

"That I would."

Overjoyed, Reggie jumped up, knocking over his chair. "You will?"

"Mother," Lorelei said excitedly, "will you really?"

"Of course I will," Finnie trilled merrily. "We are getting married."

"Wow, what a scoop!" Evert exclaimed, beside himself. "Finnie, the Fabled Femme Fatale, gets married! Who's the lucky guy?"

"Nincompoop," Reggie snorted.

"Lorelei, quick, where's your camera?" asked Vern.

"You left it in my suite, I guess."

"Oh no," groaned Vern. "I must be jinxed."

"I've got a camera right here," said Palmyra, reaching into her bottomless purse.

"Sure," Vern said cynically, "my best camera falls into a black hole, then Lorelei smashes one, then one melts on my shirt. What's yours made of, licorice?"

"If it was I'd have eaten it," Palmyra chuckled.

"Laura," Reggie said gratefully, "if it hadn't been for you, I'd have been a bachelor forever. How can I ever repay you?"

"How about a trip around the galaxy in your yacht," Finnie suggested. "Would you like that, Laura?"

"Could I go to The Elsewhere instead?"

The Elsewhere! Everyone looked at her, each in their own way. Vern captured it all — surprise, fear, doubt, amusement, suspicion, hope, happiness, despair.

> *Sharon and Earnest were toasting their engagement aboard the Premonition when they heard about the missing shoes. They realized it was their duty to investigate.*

Camera in hand, Vern was eager for Lorelei to see him in action, catching people in unguarded moments, shorn of their customary disguises. But before he could get started he felt an unpleasantly familiar tickle in his ear. Nuts.

"Vern!" Lorelei exclaimed. "There's a beam of light stuck in your ear!"

"Vernon," it said, vibrating impatiently, "this is your mother speaking."

"It's Ma," Vern said wearily, knowing it was hopeless to try and ignore her.

"That beam of light is your mother?" Lorelei asked incredulously.

"Vernon, pay attention!" Ma Light demanded.

"I thought I had a problem because my mother was different! At least she's a person."

"Vernon, who is that creature?" Ma Light asked suspiciously, turning a beam on Lorelei.

With a sigh Vern introduced them. "Ma, this is Lorelei. Lorelei, this is Ma."

Reluctantly, Lorelei offered Ma her hand.

"Lorelei, don't!" Vern shouted. "Don't touch her!"

"I'm just trying to be nice," Lorelei complained.

"Vernon," said Ma, "where are your shoes?"

"Gee, Ma," said Vern, feeling like a guilty kid, "on the beach somewhere, I guess."

"I suppose she's responsible for that," Ma sniffed haughtily, turning a high beam on Lorelei to give her the once over. How interested was Vern in this irritating person?

"Hey, quit that," Lorelei snapped.

"Vernon, what is this creature to you?" Ma demanded to know, increasing the wattage on Lorelei.

"Oh, go plug it in a socket," said Lorelei, marching off.

What a gal, thought Vern, traipsing after her, leaving Ma to sizzle. All the more so when she heard Palmyra's familiar chuckle.

The gypsies usually went barefoot so they were the last to notice the disappearance of the shoes.

Novelty, in the form of two Sebastian Sea Lions arrived, surprising one another and everyone else. Instantly recognizable from their publicity holograms which blanketed the cosmos, the two Sebastians were equally handsome and had equally perfect teeth framed by equally winning smiles. Marcus Highwater was greatly unnerved, knowing, as the others did not, that Sebastian Sea Lion, the Great Gypsy Impersonator, was one of King Triton's favorite disguises.

Aware that Myrtle had been married to Sebastian, Oliver felt threatened, thinking he was no match for even one Sebastian. "Oh my, oh my," he moaned, watching them vie for Myrtle's attention. They seemed to be smirking, making fun of him, diminishing him in Myrtle's esteem. "Oh my, oh my," he sighed, releasing a puff of black smoke.

"Oliver," Myrtle cried in alarm. "What's wrong?"

"Nothing," he mumbled, looking dejectedly at his rivals.

"Oh," said Myrtle, following his glance, "I was just telling the Sebastians that you're my gentleman. They're both very happy for me."

"They weren't laughing at me?"

"Of course not. They're smiling at you, trying to be friendly."

"Myrtle, I'm an old fool."

"Oh, Oliver," she said, giving him a hug.

Looking on from down the table, Valerie Highwater was amazed. "Marcus, what's all the fuss over that absurd Myrtle creature?"

Paying no attention to his wife, Marcus' eyes were riveted on the two Sebastians who seemed to be as taken with each other as if they were twins who'd been separated at birth and reunited on this spot. His mind was in a panic. Even if it was only one Triton pretending to be two Sebastians, it would still be one too many. Trembling, he watched the two Sebastians gambol off together, marching in step, their arms swinging in unison, their identical heads bobbing up and down in conversation.

"Laura, honey," asked Myrtle, making room beside her, "how's the Wedding Gazette coming?"

"Oh, it's almost finished."

"I bet it's awful good."

"I hope so," Laura said thoughtfully. "I think everything fits together but I don't know for sure."

"What do you plan to do next, dear child?" asked Oliver. "A book, perhaps?"

"First, I'm going to The Elsewhere."

"Dearie, I hear it's a lovely place," said Myrtle, "so friendly. Everybody must hug everybody there."

"I've always wanted to go there," Oliver said wistfully. "But I never dared."

"It would be fun to go there, don't you think?" asked Myrtle.

"It would be fun to go with you," Oliver said fondly.

Valerie looked on disdainfully. "Marcus, they're crazy. They're talking about something out of a children's poem, a myth. I don't know what's come over my brother Oliver."

"Myths can be tricky, Valerie," Marcus whispered furtively. "Especially when they come in pairs."

"Two Elsewheres?" Valerie asked, baffled.

"Elsewheres?"

"What are you talking about?" Valerie asked, exasperated.

"Two Tritons, of course. What else?"

"Two Tritons? Good Heavens, that's all you need!"

> *Here and there in the forest, Sharon and Earnest found parts of shoes — buckles, bows, sequins, jewels, heels. "I wonder where this is leading," said Sharon as they followed the footprints. "It's like waiting for the other shoe to drop."*

> *"We're hot on their heels," Earnest said earnestly.*

> *Deep in his secret workshop, Maurice, the mad perpetrator, proceeded with his plan. "I wouldn't want to be in their shoes," he cackled.*

Guests started seating themselves according to the place cards, eager for the feast to begin. They were surprised to find their missing shoes under their chairs. Except for a few mix-ups, like heavy hoofwear where dainty bird sandals should have been, everyone's shoes were back where they were supposed to be.

"There's more afoot then meets the eye,"
said Earnest, upon learning of the mystifying
reappearance of the shoes.

Duke and Lilli arrived, hand in hand. Felicity felt a pang of jealousy. How happy they were. "You would think they were the ones getting married," she said enviously. Her husband, Norville, nodded, deeply immersed in the latest issue of *Real Life Investment Thrillers* and the cheerfully venal world of financial buckaroos & buccaneers. With staggering lack of self insight, Norville fancied himself one of their number.

Used to being ignored, Felicity put on a social smile and looked around, startled to find Lilli looking at her.

So that's Felicity, thought Lilli. Pretty, but oh so cold. A cold fish. She smiled sympathetically without intending to, sensing something sad and lost behind Felicity's cold exterior. Taken by surprise, Felicity allowed Lilli a moment's glimpse into the chasm of neediness and desperation within her before her blue eyes iced over, becoming opaque as a winter pond.

Smoldering with fury at having his genius
ignored, the villainous shoe-napper linked the
last of the complex incendiary cable together,
dreaming of conflagration.

FANFARE!

Resplendent in a long golden robe, Mother Romany took the place of highest honor, everyone standing in deference to her as the *doThings* broke the bounds of music, their joyous cadences cascading down like a waterfall, then rippling out in a long, whispering diminuendo till the night was drenched in silence.

With a graceful sweep of her arm Mother Romany invited everyone to be seated. The Great Poet took his place on her right, Magdalena and Guitano on her left. A murmur of polite conversation arose as everyone waited for the feast to begin.

Laura went to sit between Amanda and the Great Poet. "I'm going to miss you a lot, Amanda."

"Me too," said Amanda. "If you ever decide to leave the gypsies our little atoll has everything you could ask for, sea breezes, lush tropical forests, white beaches and a perfect climate."

"You're always welcome at Casa Amanda," said Big Boy, putting his arm around his bride-to-be.

"I love it when you call it Casa Amanda," Amanda cooed, snuggling against him.

"You'll always be home to me," Big Boy murmured shyly.

"Oh, Big Boy," said Amanda, giving him a kiss.

"Casa Amanda," Laura repeated. "It sounds wonderful. Maybe I could come and see you after I go to The Elsewhere."

Amanda chuckled. "I should've known you wouldn't stay in one place very long. Remember when we met and I asked if you'd like to go traveling with me? Who'd have thought?"

"I love new places."

"And a good thing too," Amanda said playfully, "otherwise I wouldn't have met the groom."

"And I wouldn't have met Humpty or Magdalena or the

Great Poet or Loki or Aunt Myrtle or Mother Romany ...or
anyone ..." Laura's voice trailed off as she realized how
much she would be leaving behind.

"Or us," Lilli chimed in from across the table.

"Or Maurice," Duke said, laughing.

"We never found out if dragons can swim," said Laura.

"Is it safe for her to go off alone?" Big Boy asked, concerned.

"Oh, she's not going alone," said Duke, putting an arm
around Lilli. "We're going too."

"I'm glad you're starting your journey with such loving
companions," the Great Poet said fondly."

"Trust yourself and your companions and the goodness
of the Universe," Laura said teasingly, quoting his own
words back to him.

Laughing, the Great Poet opened his arms. Laura
climbed into his lap and kissed him on the tip of his nose,
as she had done so many adventures ago, but now it was
out of love instead of need.

> *Maurice felt the heat rise in him, threatening*
> *to incinerate him if not released. His inflamed*
> *eyes boiling, he all but swooned with rage —*
> *pent-up, irrational, all-consuming rage!*

"When she reaches The Elsewhere," Mother Romany
said quietly, "she will find indescribable beauty and the
source of unending dreams."

* * * *

Palmyra could hardly contain herself. For years the witches with their bubbling cauldrons had been down-wind from her betting parlor, endlessly tantalizing her with their pungent concoctions. From time to time she would arrange to run into them at the Universal Dump, hoping they would invite her to dinner. But no matter how broad her hints, she was always politely but firmly rebuffed. If she tried to peek in their shopping bags to see what kind of culinary refuse they were collecting one or the other of them would contrive a fainting spell and collapse upon the bags. But now, this very night, in this very place, after years of unsatisfied longings, seductive aromas and overwrought imaginings, her ravenous hunger would at last be satisfied! Or else!

The banquet tables were arranged in an arc before a raised stage. Peeking out from behind a curtain of mist created by blocks of dry ice, Claribel and Dolly sized up their audience. Except for that nosey Palmyra Loveseat, for whom they had made special preparations, everything looked O.K.

Over the years, starting from when they'd met at Kitchen World, the witches had built their reputation as the greatest chefs in the universe mostly by accident, then by deliberate design, without ever having to deliver the goodies. And now, for this occasion, with the eyes of the universe upon them, illusion would be heaped upon illusion like custard trifle, layer upon layer, bewitching what the eyes would see, the nose smell, the tongue taste, and, most important of all, what the mind would believe. This was to be their moment of truth, the truth of illusion.

> *At the business end of his incendiary fuse,*
> *Maurice huffed and puffed, choking on the*
> *ashes of revenge. He managed only a feeble*
> *puff of smoke which curled up from under the*
> *stage, unnoticed among the vapors of dry ice.*

Carping and complaining in their irritating, metallic voices, a crew of snooty Able Bodies (Willing and Able Bodies being more expensive and harder to find) who'd been hired from *Tools of the Trade,* looked on disdainfully. They found the ritual consumption of organic substances, as compared to a quick jolt from a fresh battery, just plain silly.

Despite hours of rehearsing them, the witches had not been able to get the Able Bodies to perform the simplest tasks correctly, not even when bribed with their favorite delicacy, deep fat fried electrical cable dipped in melted insulation. The twits couldn't distinguish pies from pickles, nor did they want to. As a result, Claribel had nightmares of the guests being offended and dismayed by what was placed before them.

> "Hey, buddy, that lava on the rocks is mine."...
> "Be my guest, steel tooth."... "Pass the grey matter, please." ...
> "So that's what those lumps are." ... "This is a bloody mess!"
> ..."If it's orange it's carrot blood, and it's mine." ...
> "Watch out for that hemlock pudding, it's bad for you." ...
> "Once a year won't kill me." ... "No tubers for me, thank you.
> I hear they eat their young."

At Dolly's suggestion, the Able Bodies were given cue cards depicting the various dishes and their logical recipients, though Claribel found the use of cue cards beneath contempt and hostile to the spirit of illusion.

The noise of glasses being raised and set down, silverware being shuffled, plates being lifted and lowered with a polite thump, was music to the witches' ears — everyone was impatient for the feast to begin.

Speeding up an array of oscillating fans, the witches wafted tantalizing fragrances of food over the hungry crowd, making tongues tingle in anticipation, noses sniff greedily, tummies twitch shamelessly.

A RESOUNDING FANFARE OF TRUMPETS AND DRUMS

Claribel and Dolly prance out, chanting their spell.

*We can feed
your every need,
cast a spell
so you'll eat well.*

*You who eat beef
or nibble on reef,
you who eat tree
or berry or brie,
chimp or fish,
we've got your dish.
Man or fowl
or picky owl,
even prickly porcupine,
anyone who wants can dine.*

*Fang or trunk,
you won't get junk.
Good things to chew
are waiting for you.
Tooth or beak,
the tastes you seek
are oven hot,
made on the spot.*

*Every confection,
made to perfection.
Try not to waste
a single taste.*

*Cook with the mind
and you will find
nothing you eat
tastes quite as sweet
as what you've wrought
with food of thought.*

A blood-curdling shriek of indignation shattered the spell as Palmyra Loveseat lurched to her feet, certain the witches were up to no good. Cushions heaving, she made for the stage, determined that nothing was going to come between her and her culinary dreams. For once the Able Bodies were on cue, scooping her up like so much delicate soufflé and whisking her away to the witches' kitchen — which was stocked with every imaginable epicurean delight.

Finding herself in what could only be the Kitchen of Paradise, Palmyra's protests became gurgles of pleasure. Everywhere she looked were tables groaning with delectable goodies, cupboards redolent with consummate consumables, shelves overflowing with buttery fancies, ovens sizzling with roasted dreams. Overcome, she swooned onto a frothy bed of meringue.

With Palmyra out of the way, the witches regained their hold on the guests' imaginations, spraying the air with the intoxicating aroma of Eau de Cuisine.

The Kingdom of the tongue
grants many pleasures
but the Kingdom of the mind
grants unsurpassable delight.

Yes, my friends,
you can have it all,
every delicacy, every morsel,
every voluptuous bite.
No fear, no remorse,
no secret snacking in the night.
But boldly, openly,
with aching pleasure and wanton delight,
with fanfare and revelry.
You can have it all — tonight!

There was a rapt, collective, catching of breath at the prospect, followed by the uplifting anthem, *Food, Glorious Food.* It was the fight song of Universal Rights to Gustatory Enrichment (or URGE), an organization dedicated to fending off the unwholesome tyranny of weight loss fanatics who were forever plaguing joyful, carefree, multitudes of overeaters.

Looking out at all the hungry, spellbound faces, Claribel felt a sudden sense of mission. She had to help them understand that life was a battle between the forces of Gusto and the forces of Self-Denial, a battle older than time, older even than the struggle between Good and Evil. For in the beginning there was FOOD!

> *Take your pleasure in big wedges.*
> *Don't just nibble at the edges.*
> *Guilt is such a bitter thing,*
> *Starves the soul, clips the wing.*

"Now," Claribel said firmly, "close your eyes and imagine all those luscious, forbidden foods, the ones you most desire, rich, pungent and delectable. Taste them, smell them, feel them in your mouth, imagine platters and platters of them set before you. Now, with your eyes closed tight, let the feast you are creating marinate in your mind."

The stirring Hymn to Abundance drowned out the whir of the Able Bodies who were surreptitiously bringing trays of food to the tables. They were, as usual, indifferent to the cue cards and the sensibilities of the guests, placing pickle pate where pie was supposed to go, hobnail pudding before guests without teeth, steamed effluvia before those with queasy stomachs, fricassee of Phoenix before birds of a feather — with gobs of axle grease slathered over everything.

*Maurice saw red. All the singing, talking and
merriment going on overhead was about to go
up in smoke. The fools who'd always ignored him
would never know it was because of the shoes.
The shoes were the key to his magnificent revenge,
the greatest, most painful, most fiery hot foot of
all time! All those tender feet shod in fiery misery!
Never again would they grind his genius under
their heels. They would have no heels! Hee, hee,
Heel-less!*

*Taking deeper and deeper breaths, his tortured
fire ducts wheezing, his flame sputtering and
dying, sputtering and dying, his imprisoned rage
threatening to backfire on him, Maurice took one
last, huge, reckless breath, and*

IMPLODED!

*A maw of nothingness opened, sucking in voices,
smells, napkins, leaves, pulling petals from
flowers, dust from the earth, matter from anti-
matter, whirling and swirling and furling inward,
ending in the silent spiral scream of vacuum.*

Brushed by the breath of nothingness, the guests
opened their eyes, stunned to see the wreckage before
them, a miasma of noxious substances, designer foods,
brown sludge, broken glass, decaying vegetation, a
dragon's toe nail and things unrecognizable.

Without missing a beat, Claribel turned reality into just
another prop. "I know you are all disappointed with yourselves." The guests stared at her, baffled. "But you
mustn't be too hard on yourselves. You've done very well
for first time ...Manifesters!" she cried triumphantly.

First time Manifesters? Impressed with themselves,
some of the guests sat up straighter and began paying
closer attention.

"Of course, in the beginning there are bound to be mistakes," Claribel assured them. "Transforming thought into food, the impossible into the possible, dreams into reality can be tricky business. Nod your heads if you agree." Heads nodded. "At the same time some of you are confused, asking yourselves how you could possibly make *palatable* food so imperfectly manifested." That was for sure. "But remember, as children how you hated certain foods yet came to appreciate them years later because someone prepared them in a special, more attractive way? Voila!" she exclaimed, indicating the wreckage piled up before them. "You have created a mass of imperfections, not just a paltry, piddling few. So, believe in yourselves! You can do it! "

It was true. They had created a mass of imperfections. They should be proud, not disappointed.

"After all," Claribel said cheerfully, "the road to perfection is paved with mistakes."

"Imperfection is a force of, of nature!" Dolly declared. "Perfection? Pooh on perfection!" With a sweep of her arm, she brushed it away.

There was a stir of excitement. Some of the guests looked at each other, tentatively proud.

"Strike up the band!" Claribel commanded, calling for the Song of Imperfection.

> *Stand proud atop a mountain of mistakes,*
> *ta-rah, ta-rah.*
> *Stand proud and keep on climbing,*
> *ta-rah, ta-rah.*
> *Nothing perfect is as good*
> *ta-rah, ta-rah,*
> *As imperfection understood,*
> *ta-rah!*

And now, ta-rah, ta-roo,
We have a surprise for you!

You have passed the entrance exam to our
Academy of Metaphysical Cooking!
Ta-rah, ta-roo!

"Don't forget about the franchises," Dolly reminded.

Ah yes, thought Claribel, what franchises? "Those who show promise will qualify for a franchise."

Franchise, a word dear to Norville's heart! He put down *Confessions of a Consummate Charlatan*, determined to be first in line for one.

"Wait," said Dolly, pulling out a cosmogram. "It's from Hollywood, Inc.!" she squealed.

"What are you talking about?" Claribel hissed.

"They want to buy the rights to our life story," Dolly whispered. "They want us to star!"

"Let me see that cosmogram." Claribel examined it suspiciously. "I thought so."

"Thought what? What?" Dolly asked anxiously.

"They want to pay us with Thought Money."

"But that's only good at amusement parks," Dolly said, crestfallen.

"So much for Hollywood, Inc." Claribel turned to the audience. "It's true. Hollywood, Inc. wants to do the story of our lives!" she announced triumphantly, waving the cosmogram for all to see.

"I already said that," Dolly said, puzzled.

"Here, wave the cosmogram," Claribel ordered. She turned to the audience, arms outstretched. "Hollywood, Inc., take us! We are yours!"

A thunder of cheers, whistles and stomping feet shook the stage.

"Thank you. Thank you," Claribel said loftily. "We appreciate the support of all the little people who made us what we are today. Speaking of which, Madam Dolly will take your tuition checks."

Joining hands, they launched into the rousing finale.

> *Who knows what's real?*
> *It's how you feel.*
> *What's on your platter*
> *Is mind over matter.*
>
> *Even sludge*
> *can taste like fudge*
> *if you add a pinch of dream and awe*
> *before you stick it in your craw.*

As the last wisps of dry ice evaporated, the guests stood around, uncertain of what to do next. Some stole away in search of something to eat. Some joined Norville in the line for franchises. Others stared blankly into space, utterly bewildered.

Part Seven

Chapter Fifty-Three

Epiphany

The Mirror abides, its dimensions shrouded in mystery. It radiates subtle light in the dark chamber. It's iridescent skin crackles with energy. Laura is drawn to it, sensing a presence so vast one gulp of the eye cannot consume it. She feels its prickling current on her skin. She tries to see into the iridescence, to what lies within, but a shimmering light deflects her vision. The Mirror is forcing her to see by other means. She hears it breathe, the sound of crystal chimes in a faraway wind.

Impulsively, she plunges her hand into the crackling veil. Her hand vanishes. It touches something glacial. Startled, she pulls it back. It tingles synchronously with the pulsing energy of the veil. Its rhythm dances through her. She shivers. It stops. She looks at her hand. It seems to be made of the substance that sheathes the Mirror.

She senses she is not the same.

Nothing is the same. She finds herself in a space between the Mirror and its iridescent veil. It is a place familiar to her from dreams.

But she is not dreaming.

She turns away from the Mirror to the veil. She sees herself on the other side of it, looking in. She feels no surprise, only wonder.

Turning back to the Mirror's reflecting surface, she sees herself. But everything behind her is white, white. She cannot see the shimmering veil. She cannot see her other self. They do not exist in the Mirror. Only she exists. She looks back over her shoulder. The veil is still there. Her other self is still there. She turns back to the Mirror, knowing she must go deeper to know more.

She examines her face in the Mirror. It is almost the same. Something has been added. Or taken away. She exhales. Her breath ripples the Mirror's surface like eddies on a pond, shattering her image, scattering it outward. A white mist rises.

She hears a flapping sound of images spinning away from her like a reel of film rapidly rewinding. The Mirror clears.

She sees her face again. She sees her features blur. Her face becomes a flower. A stone. A star. She is an oriental Emperor. A fish with iridescent scales. A golden lizard in a golden desert. A black raven against the moon.

The air swirls around her, enclosing her in a shell of darkness. Nothing exists. Nothing but herself. She exists. A spear of light pierces the dark shell. It shatters, flies apart. Its fragments form stars in the blackness. She hears a sigh that comes from everywhere. No where. She hears the beat of a heart. It is not her heart. She knows her heart from every other heart. From the heart of a flower, the heart of a stone, the heart of a star. It is the heart of the Mirror she hears.

The Mirror calls her to its dark theater. Its light illumes her face. Her eyes are enormous. Another face, transparent, indistinct, begins to impose itself upon her own. Her pulse quickens. It is her father's face, calm and smiling. But she sees his weariness, what the journey back has cost him. He has made it because he knows she needs to say goodbye. She never got to say goodbye. His lips form the word.

She sees the strain of staying etched on his face, his good face. Her lips form the word. A gust of wind blows the fine sand of grief into her eyes, into her father's eyes. Their tears wash it away ...goodbye.

There is no such thing as goodbye.

Chapter Fifty-Four

The Weddings

The Autumnal Equinox is a time of truce between the Sun and Moon. They share the sky equally. It is the time the gypsies choose for weddings.

The guests were meandering toward the natural amphitheater of surrounding hills from which they would view the wedding ceremony.

* * * *

"Marcus," Valerie Highwater whined, "I'll never live this down. It's bad enough my niece, Amanda, is marrying a tree species, but from the looks of it, Oliver is about to do the same thing, only worse. I don't know what's come over everybody." She shot him a barbed look. "Marcus, are you listening?"

"Wish I had binoculars," Marcus said impatiently.

"Valerie, look over there, on that hillside. Can you tell if that's Triton or the other guy?"

"Marcus, you didn't hear a word I said. All you ever think about is Triton, Triton, Triton. Maybe you should've married him instead of me."

"Maybe," Marcus said distractedly.

"Marcus!"

"What?"

"You know," she said insinuatingly. "Triton could be right under your nose and you wouldn't even know it."

"What's that supposed to mean?"

"How do you know I'm not Triton?"

"You," he scoffed.

"How better to keep an eye on you?" she said slyly.

He stared at her wordlessly. Could it be?

* * * *

Finnie, my love," said Reggie, taking it all in, "do you want a big wedding like this or shall we just elope?"

"If we elope we'll have to take Lorelei with us, otherwise she'll never believe we got married."

"Lorelei, on our honeymoon?"

"Unless you've got a better idea."

"We could give her a new space yacht and send her off to interesting places with that young man she's so smitten with, that Vern Light."

"Don't let on you like him or she'll do just the opposite."

"I didn't say I liked him."

"You wouldn't send your daughter off with someone you didn't like. Of course you like him. I like him too."

"He's a big improvement over that Evert Snidely she's been running around with," Reggie admitted. "The guy hasn't asked me for a dime."

"That's a refreshing change."

"Then, it's settled."

* * * *

Oliver," said Myrtle. "Did you remember the rings?"

"My dear, I have them all," Oliver said confidently. "I even have an extra one."

"An extra one?"

"For you," he said formally, presenting her with a velvet box. It contained an emerald as big as a fig.

"Oh, Oliver," Myrtle gasped, "it looks just like a real emerald."

"It is, my dear. Do you like it?"

"An emerald! But ...are you sure?"

"It means we're engaged. Will you accept it?" he asked anxiously. "Will you accept me?"

"Of course I accept you. I love you."

His many arms embraced her. Myrtle never had a better hug.

* * * *

What do you mean no gifts!" Norville said indignantly. That was the part of a wedding he looked forward to most. People always gave presents, hopefully money or stock. He felt cheated.

"Norville," Felicity whispered, embarrassed, "do you realize you're shouting?"

"It's bad enough our daughter is marrying a tree species!"

"Norville, please," Felicity pleaded, indicating Duke and Lilli seated nearby.

"Who ever heard of a wedding without gifts?" he grumbled. "I'll be the laughing stock of the Stock Exchange." It violated the law of supply and demand — supply a bride, demand gifts.

"Norville, control yourself," Felicity begged, looking at Lilli apologetically, grateful to receive a sympathetic look in reply.

"You don't understand," he explained. "It's not good business."

"But Norville, it's your daughter's wedding, not a business deal."

"Felicity," he said sternly. "Everything is a business deal. Negotiation, proposal, counter proposal. Marriage is no different, except there's more monkey business."

"May I say something?" Lilli asked tactfully.

"Please do," Felicity said gratefully.

"About gifts," Lilli said to Norville, "the gypsies have a wonderful tradition. As wandering people they have found the best gifts are those that can be carried in the heart — poetry, music, good wishes, love."

"Poetry! Music! Love!" Norville exclaimed, astounded. "You can't be serious. You can't take those to the bank."

"True," Lilli said understandingly, "but they never tarnish or wear out or diminish in value."

"Very clever, I suppose," said Norville, "but it's not only my daughter who won't be getting any gifts. It's your son, too. Don't you want them to have a good start in life?"

"What makes a better start than love?" asked Felicity, giving Lilli a look of thanks.

"Love?" Norville said startled. "Well, um, I suppose there is something to be said for love."

* * * *

Feeling lucky to love and be loved, Lilli put her arms around Duke's neck. "I'm so lucky," she sighed.

"You're very pleased with yourself," Duke said, smiling.

"I'm pleased with you too."

"How come?"

"Because I love you," she said, kissing him.

THE CEREMONY

On this, the night of autumnal truce, the Moon waits just over the horizon as the sun slowly descends, sculpting shadows on the hills while the guests in their bright clothes stream onto them, setting them aflower. They take their seats as the last rays of the sun linger on the golden wedding altar.

Mother Romany makes her entrance, moving to the altar in graceful strides, her robes burnished by the oranges and mauves and golds of the setting sun. The wedding guests rise as does the Moon, ascending to bless the occasion, despite the sorrow of his unrequited love for Magdalena. Mother Romany opens her arms to embrace the setting sun, the rising moon, the sky, the earth, the hills, the gathered throng.

The wedding party follows in procession toward the altar, led by Laura in white tulle, holding four white roses. Uncle Oliver comes next, looking very regal in his sea green garments with fringes worked in gold. He bears before him in four gathered hands four gleaming wedding bands. The radiant brides are dressed in crimson, their proud grooms in royal blue. The Moon releases a sparkling mist of tiny silver stars.

"Big Boy, I'm going to sneeze," Amanda whispers, "all this silver dust." Big Boy whips off the satin scarf from his neck and offers it to her with a flourish. She sneezes into it softly, thanking him with her eyes.

Amused, Mother Romany waits till she is through.

Guitano can feel Magdalena's tension, knowing it comes from her awareness that someday they will part — a lifetime too soon. Looking at her now, so beautiful and good, he is grateful to have even one second of her love. Putting his arms around her, he draws the tension out of her. She nestles against him.

* * * *

Mother Romany raises her hand for silence. There is silence. In a voice commanding reverence, she begins, "Love is the Heart of Eternity giving itself in marriage to Life and all living things." Extending her hands, she opens them, palms up. "Put your hands on mine." The brides put their right hands on her right hand. The grooms put their left hands on her left hand.

"Your love is strong. Feel its power. Feel it flowing freely, back and forth, forth and back, giving and receiving."

She lets their hands fall. They turn to face their partners. Uncle Oliver presents the rings which they place on one another's fingers. Laura gives them each a white rose. They speak their vows in unison:

> *I love you*
> > *because*
> *I am able*
> > *to love,*
> *because*
> > *loving*
> *makes me kind,*
> > *because*
> *I am generous*
> > *when I love*
> *and beautiful.*

I am
expansive,
          tender,
open,
          free
when I love.

My heart
          creates wonder
when it loves,
          richness,
comfort;
          it embraces
the splendor
          of life
when it loves.

I love you
          above
all others
          because
when you are near
          I am closer to
the great
          good soul
of life,
          closer to
the sweet
          celebration
of being complete,
          of being
more than one,
          being two
who are more than two
          when we are together.

I love you
          above
all others
          because

I am free
> *to be*
extravagant
> *with my love,*
unjudged,
> *unjudging;*
because
> *above all others,*
> > *you*
are not afraid
> *to be loved,*
and
> *because*
you
> *are able*
to love me too.

And so they are wed.

Chapter Fifty-Five

A Different Kind Of Knowing

Pre-dawn quiet. Soon the stars will drift off to sleep in the soft mauve blanket of sky and the moon will sink indolently into its dark bed as the sun stretches its bright arms around the horizon to rim the world with gold.

Except for a few stragglers the wedding guests have gone, taking with them many uplifting memories. Laura, Duke, Lilli and the Great Poet remain with the gypsies to witness the Naming of the New Queen. Triton remains. And the *Premonition*. Mother Romany and the Great Poet smile to one another when Laura receives an invitation to visit the great ship.

Exhilarated, Laura runs along the beach through wisps of mist toward the *Premonition*. Since her moments in the Mirror she has been experiencing things differently, just as she now feels herself running on many beaches on many worlds, each world only a thought apart, each requiring only a slight shift of perspective to be experienced. Each beach, each world, once identical except perhaps for a single grain of sand now, because of accumulated differences, transformed into something almost unrecognizable while remaining in essence, the same.

She can still see things as she always has but now she can sense what is there but not seen, like hummingbird thoughts on the *Tablets* — all things are suffused with mystery — nothing is just what it seems, but infinitely more — the world accepted by everyone as real, true and final is but the rumor of a greater world of greater truth. Sometimes when a person speaks she hears many voices speaking, hears layers of voices, a churning sea of voices telling her things beyond words.

*The deep-hearted engines of the Premonition
quicken as she feels the child coming.*

Alone in his quarters reflecting on Magdalena and his brother the Moon's infatuation with her, Triton smiles ruefully. Magdalena and Guitano and their perishable, sweet dreams awaken memories in him of a time when the possibilities of life, not life itself, seemed endless, a time when as a luminous child playing in the Oceans of Eternity he had not known that possibilities could shrivel like the roots of a dying tree, leaving only a hollow sense of endlessness.

* * * *

Guided by the *Premonition's* welcoming presence, Laura enters the great ballroom bringing light, youth, and the scent of rain freshened grass. A blossom of light opens before her, revealing a vision of an eerily beautiful child asleep on the surface of the sea, his golden hair radiating from his peaceful face like strands of sunlight, an unearthly being made of sea foam, light and air. When he opens his eyes she gasps, startled by the joy in them. The blossom contracts into a seed of light and vanishes.

A majestic figure enters the great room. Ghosts of light cling to him in tatters. Though still vigorous he seems old beyond age, his soul possessed of a weariness profound and undisguised. As he approaches, Laura feels the purity of his sadness, a sadness that is unconsoled, unself-pitying ...and somehow familiar.

"Welcome." His voice resonates with echoes of music faintly sad. His eyes are smoke and dying embers.

"Why are you so sad?" she asks softly.

He smiles, charmed by her directness.

"Sometimes when I'm sad it helps if I talk to friends."

"Friends can be a comfort," he agrees.

"We could be friends."

"Yes," he says, a lift in his voice. "I'd like that. Let us be friends." He feels drawn to her, to the life that leaps from her eyes and sparkles in the bright flame of her hair.

"See, you're feeling better already. What were you sad about?"

At her words Triton feels the familiar tug of the Old Gameplayer's net. "My sadness comes of having lived so long," he says, opening himself to her, allowing her to see within him as stars, planets, oceans are born, live and die while he endures but little changed, increasingly alone.

"Oh," she whispers. "Alone."

Looking into her sympathetic eyes he feels her aloneness, feels her grief, her courage, her enthusiasm and her sadness, so like his own. He sees her in the Mirror, lonely for her father, sees her father, sees his face melding with hers, hears their whispered goodbye, sees them discover there is no such thing as goodbye. He is moved, remembering that whether mortal or immortal, all are caught inexorably in Life's luminous net. For her he sees this is a comfort, not a reason for despair. Once it had been so for him. He feels a tug of hope. "I thought I'd used life up," he says, bemused.

"Use up life?" Laura giggles. "You can't use up life. It just keeps making more."

Just keeps making more! The shameless Old Trickster. Triton feels Laura's infectious laughter bubbling up in him. He hasn't felt this good in a long, long time.

* * * *

Standing on the bridge with Triton, Laura hears the *Premonition's* contented hum. "Have you ever been to The Elsewhere?"

"Not for a very long time," says Triton.

"Didn't you like it?"

"I liked it very much."

"My friends and I are going there right after the Naming of the New Queen. Maybe it would cheer you up to come with us."

"You cheer me up," Triton says, laughing.

"It tickles when you laugh all over."

"Then I'll do it more often. Which friends are you going

with?"

"Duke and Lilli."

"After the gypsy ceremony."

"Yes." She frowns slightly.

"What are you worried about?"

"It's a very important ceremony. What if I make a mistake?"

Triton smiles. "I'm sure Mother Romany will cherish any you make. Even mistakes can be precious, if you love someone."

"Really?" She'd have to find out more about this.

The imp in her delights him. "Laura," he asks, eyes twinkling, "how would you like to take the *Premonition* to The Elsewhere?"

"Oh!" she exclaims. "Could we?" She couldn't imagine anything more wonderful.

* * * *

Laura did a pirouette for Duke and Lilli, showing off her ceremonial finery.

"How lovely," Lilli said, very impressed.

"Splendiferous," said Duke.

"Now, don't laugh. This is very ceremonial. I'm going to make you honorary gypsies."

"Anything you say, Princess," Duke said, smiling.

"I think your Princess has become a Queen," Lilli observed.

"I will anoint you with my ancient essences," Laura explained. "Kneel, please." She took a small silver vial from a pouch at her waist. "Don't get any in your eyes." She shook the vial so hard the cap flew off and in a trice everyone was enveloped in aromatic essences. "Oh dear."

"I guess we're anointed now," Duke said, laughing.

"Well," said Laura, trying to recover her composure. "Just the same, this is serious."

"Yes, Your Majesty."

"Mother Romany and I wrote these vows together."

"Which makes them even more serious," said Lilli.

"Yes. Now, pay attention. And repeat what I say."

"We are at your command."

Laura began. "As a gypsy ..."

"As a gypsy," they repeated.

"I will follow my heart ..."

Duke put his arm around Lilli. "I will follow my heart."

"And as a gypsy ..."

"As a gypsy,"

"I will always respect ..."

"I will always respect,"

"The hearts of others."

"The hearts of others."

"How lovely," Lilli said.

"How lovely," everyone repeated, laughing.

* * * *

Triton holds the ancient chalice in his hands. It has been a long time since he looked at it with pleasure. Once he had sipped immortality from it. Turning it in his hands, he smiles, looking forward to seeing things with Laura's freshness and wonder. He presses the goblet to his lips before setting it aside. Sinking back, his hand on the *Pastviewer,* he drifts slowly into the realm of dreams.

Chapter Fifty-Six

Draining The Cup

In the predawn light the gypsy queen and her companions sit under a glittering canopy set with precious stones.

"Miracles happen at dawn," she says, her voice young and strong. She looks at Augustus with love. The Great Poet's eyes are sad. She takes his hand. "I am Veronica again, your Veronica. We are so fortunate to have this newborn time." He kisses her hand. The Locket of Dreams rests at the pulse point of her throat, moving with every beat of her heart. "May I share your poem with our friends?"

"Of course," he says softly.

> *The iridescent veil*
> *parts.*
> *Life's mirrored surface*
> *divides,*

revealing
          the words
that have always
          been there
for those
          who return
and those
          who depart,
words
          at the twice-crossed juncture
that say:
Care for Life;
Death cares for its own.

There are visions
          in the Mirror
that reel backward
          peeling away
the layers
          of life and time
so all may see
          The Beginning,
the Mythic Core
          of our essential selves,
that nothing is
          just what it seems.
It is always more.

There is part of us
          that is perfect
and speaks
          the pure language
of the Cosmos.

To be a living thing
          is to be a Myth
for in our essentials

> *we are Mythic,*
> *the stuff of Life,*
> > *the stuff of Death:*
> *we are each a miracle.*

> *And at the last*
> *we are homesick*
> > *for the endless future,*
> > *for the endless past,*
> *for the place where they meet*
> *and all things will be known.*

Magdalena fills the ancient, fluted goblet with the sacred elixir, holding it for a moment, adding the warmth of her body to it before passing it to Laura who needs both hands to hold it. "To each in proportion to their years remaining," says Magdalena, steadying the cup for Laura. "Drink, little gypsy. For you the Cup of Life is nearly full." Laura drinks and passes the goblet to Guitano who drinks his portion of what remains, handing the nearly empty goblet to Augustus. The Great Poet hesitates then drinks all but the last few drops. Helpless before fate he hands the goblet to Veronica. She takes the goblet from him and drinks the last drops.

Chapter Fifty-Seven

The Naming Of The New Queen

The glowing Mirror, the sound of muted guitars, one lone voice singing faraway, the gypsy people seated on the ground in semi-circular rows before a dying campfire — the ritual of Unburdening has begun.

Wearing her golden veil, the gypsy queen appears at the other side of the fire. A murmur runs through her assembled people. In her outstretched hand throbs a great Ruby, the Eye of Eternity. She moves it twice in a circle over the campfire. The dying embers flare up with renewed purpose, as all things do when the Eye of Eternity is upon them. She gives the blood-red stone to Laura as the lost gypsy child, Indra.

The queen holds out her hands, palms up, to Magdalena who places her hands on them, palms up. There is a hush.

"When you accept the Ruby," intones the gypsy queen.

"When I accept the Ruby."

"You accept the knowledge of eternity."

"I accept the knowledge of eternity."

"And with it, your duty to life and to your people."

"And with it, my duty to life and to our people."

"You will reign a thousand years. You will suffer the deaths of many loved ones, of people yet unborn. When you accept the Ruby, you accept this."

"I accept this."

"To see life through the Eye of Eternity is to see that life is our dominion. Death takes care of its own."

Withdrawing her hands, the gypsy queen reaches for the ancient, fluted goblet. Arms extended, she holds it out before her. "When we are born we carry within us our portion of the Great Ocean of Life, and when we return to it, our portion returns. Not one drop of life is lost." She turns the goblet upside down. Empty.

The sounds of ancient instruments vibrate the air

Magdalena kneels, hands cupped to receive the Ruby.

"Do you accept your destiny?" the queen asks gently.

"I accept my destiny."

Laura places the Ruby in Magdalena's hands.

The new queen rises to face her people, the Ruby burning in her hands. She holds it high for all to see. The red of the sun and the sky and the Ruby are one.

* * * *

The Mirror is warm and red in the rising sun, casting a ruby light before it. The air is saturated with the mellow richness of autumn.

Music comes from everywhere — the pulse of drums, the shake of tambourines, the click of castanets, laughter and song and the wine-dark sound of strummed guitars.

Her formal robes now in Magdalena's arms, still warm from the heat of her body, Veronica dances to the pulse of the drums, fresh as the rain-rinsed dawn. Her eyes are quick and gay, mischievous even. In her crimson garments she is the sun itself, come to earth to dance with mortals.

"Augustus, Laura, Magda, Guitano! Come dance with me in the newborn light!"

The four dance in a circle around her, dance to the beating heart of the drums. As the heartbeat quickens, the gypsies dance in concentric circles about the departing queen, their feet lustily pounding the earth, their faces reflecting the joy they see on her face.

"Faster!" she cries, dancing ever closer to the Mirror. Dawn rushes toward her. She is the color of dawn, the color of the Mirror.

"Run, little gypsy! Run!" she cries as the Mirror parts.

Laura breaks from the circle in alarm.

"Run to The Elsewhere and to life, little gypsy! Run to the day that begins!"

Laura runs and runs along the beach toward the *Premonition*, her cheeks bathed in tears. Although she hears the laughter Mother Romany had promised, she cannot stop her tears.

Epilogue

Palmyra was awakened by an unnatural quiet. Everyone was gone. She looked around in a mellow daze, feeling something soft and magical in the air, not the sort of
thing she would usually notice.

Her tummy gurgled, reminding her how full it was. She
patted it affectionately, noticing another seam of her frock
had burst. Oh well, she thought dreamily.

Rising slowly, she meandered over to the banquet
tables. They were littered with leftover food. She plucked
a few goodies from the assortment and slipped them into
her insatiable purse. For later, she thought, just in case.

She wandered through the woods to the expanse of
white beach. The sea had washed it clean, leaving not
even a footprint behind. She sat herself down at the edge
of the water and looked out at a sea the color of raspberry
cream. She kicked off her shoes, enjoying the feel of the

sand between her toes, warm and comforting as a glass of milk at bedtime.

The sea air stimulated her appetite.

Taking a lemon lollipop from her purse, she licked it meditatively to the soft plop, plop of the waves on the beach.

Gazing out at the far horizon, she saw the *Premonition* riding the rosy waves like a mirage. A wink of light and it was gone.

Sometimes, when your tummy is very, very full and your mind is very, very empty.... Palmyra drifted off to sleep, her lollipop dangling from her hand. The waves rose up to lick it before breaking gently at her feet.